DRIVEN TO MURDER

By Alan Dennis Burke

FIRE WATCH
GETTING AWAY WITH MURDER
DRIVEN TO MURDER

Alan Dennis Burke

DRIVEN TO MURDER

The Atlantic Monthly Press
BOSTON / NEW YORK

COPYRIGHT © 1986 BY ALAN DENNIS BURKE
ALL RIGHTS RESERVED. NO PART OF THIS BOOK MAY BE REPRODUCED IN ANY FORM OR BY ANY ELECTRONIC OR MECHANICAL MEANS INCLUDING INFORMATION STORAGE AND RETRIEVAL SYSTEMS WITHOUT PERMISSION IN WRITING FROM THE PUBLISHER, EXCEPT BY A REVIEWER WHO MAY QUOTE BRIEF PASSAGES IN A REVIEW.

FIRST EDITION

Driven to Murder is a work of fiction. The characters, incidents, and circumstances are products of the author's imagination, and any resemblance to actual characters, incidents, or circumstances is purely coincidental.

LIBRARY OF CONGRESS CATALOGING IN PUBLICATION DATA
Burke, Alan Dennis.
  Driven to murder.

  I. Title.
PS3552.U7213D75   1986   813'.54   85-22897
ISBN 0-87113-033-5

MV

Published simultaneously in Canada

PRINTED IN THE UNITED STATES OF AMERICA

To my father,
Albert Patrick Burke

DRIVEN TO MURDER

1

GROVER DURHAM was born to it. Slim and short, he seemed able to shrink, to wriggle through the narrowest opening. Like an Indian (and he claimed some Cherokee blood) he could move soundlessly. Surprisingly strong, he could carry the heaviest object, from a television to a small safe, without strain.

Grover was a thief in the way other men are bankers or truck drivers. It was simply a job, though a bit more exciting than most. He had no interest in violence, dumb-dumb muscle tactics. A true professional, he believed, gained his edge with concentration and stealth.

The look of a house would give him clues to the location of bedrooms, doorways, and valuables. His educated guesses were nearly always right. Thus, he could plot an efficient search pattern to get in and out within minutes.

At 3:00 A.M. there was no traffic, nor a hint of life in an upper-middle-class neighborhood. The darkened Dutch colonial was almost certainly empty. Grover decided the attached garage would allow the easiest access. Moving to it, he looked for a dish or chain or scratches on the door, any sign of a watchdog. He was pleased to see none.

And he was lucky in other ways. The garage window was unlocked. Climbing inside, he was amused to see an expensive burglar alarm rigged to the door. As he touched the floor gingerly, his heart began to race. He was alert to every sound, his body tingling.

This was another important talent. After breaking into thousands of homes, after stealing over a million dollars' worth of property, he still knew enough to be scared. Fear kept a man safe.

No car was in the garage, further evidence of an empty house. But Grover still did not relax. He waited, motionless, until his eyes adjusted to the dark. Then, he stepped carefully over a garden hose.

He'd stolen more than a million dollars' worth of goods in his time! Where had all that money gone? On good times mostly. On Claire. And Mary. Liz. And others. Some, he couldn't remember the names. But you don't look back. The money isn't wasted if you have a good time.

He worked the door with a small, crowbarlike tool, easily, quietly, popping it open. The home within was silent, empty. In the spacious kitchen he passed walnut cabinets and brickwork around the oven. Plants hung here and there. A shelf of cereal included Cap'n Crunch, Sugar Pops, and Apple Jacks.

Grover carried a small flashlight, but mostly he moved without it in the shadows. His night vision was remarkable.

The first thing he checked was the refrigerator freezer. Once, he'd found several thousand dollars' worth of silver in a freezer. Here he found only ice cubes and Eskimo Pies.

In the dining room, he was pleased to see the hutch crammed with crystal and fine china. He had an increasingly optimistic feeling about this job, a rich man's house. Swiftly, eagerly, he went through the downstairs rooms, taking the most expensive-looking items he could find.

Maybe he could take Liz to Florida this winter. He pictured himself on the beach with Liz, her regal face turning heads. Sure, they called him "Little Grover." But come see what's hanging on my arm, assholes. Just look and drool.

He found the silver, hidden beneath the trapdoor on the fireplace floor, and tucked it into a canvas bag. He placed the canvas bundle on the kitchen table with, among other things, a video recorder, a watch, and a stamp collection. Then he decided to go upstairs, obeying an instinct that told him he would find a fantastic payout, probably jewelry.

He was positive now that this was an unoccupied home. Grover could smell people. Even from the first floor he could hear them breathing on the second.

The carpeted stairs did not creak. Halfway up, he paused, peering into the dark above. He saw movement. Wondered . . . Then, he saw it again.

Pointing his flashlight, he began slowly to comprehend something unexpected and quite improbable.

A figure loomed in the shadows. A naked man, muscled and motionless, like a statue or a bodybuilder. His face was stern and unblinking.

Grover's impulse was to holler or run. But before he could do either, he was dead.

The single shot, an ear-shattering *crack,* exploded in his heart, sending him back and down. Limp, his head hit the wallboard at the bottom of the stairs, breaking his neck and cracking the wood.

The killer flipped on the light and came downstairs. For a moment he studied the intruder's face, the pop-eyed look of surprise accented by an unnatural tilt of the head.

The gunman searched for a pulse and, finding none, laid his pistol on the hall table. He was excited, of course. But it was a cool thrill. For the past month he'd been reading of housebreaks in the area. The truth, however, was that he'd been waiting years for a night like this, the gun always within reach of his bed.

Still naked, he slid his hand into the burglar's warm pockets, pulling out a little money and the keys to a Lincoln. No weapon.

He was pleased. *Clean.* That was the only word to describe this. The burglar hadn't suffered, nor had he caused any trouble. Moreover, he hadn't bled all over the place. If they all came home from vacation tomorrow they would see no sign of what had happened.

The killer went back upstairs and dressed. Then he went out

for a walk. It was a warm, bright night. Among the perfectly groomed lawns and hedges of his neighbors, he calmed. He found the dead burglar's gleaming car only a few doors away.

Taking the wheel gave him a strange lift. The car had a different feel, a different scent. It was like making love with another man's wife. He drove the Lincoln back to the garage, which he'd left open.

Next, he fetched a trash bag from the kitchen. He took this to where the burglar lay in the dark. Getting the plastic bag over his body, with much pulling and tugging, left the killer breathless. He had to stop and rest.

Grasping the feet, he dragged the body through the dining room into the kitchen — where the bag snagged on the aluminum molding at the threshold, tearing slightly — and finally to the Lincoln waiting in the garage. Here, the dead man had to be lifted from the concrete onto the front seat, passenger side. The killer managed this by wrapping his arms around the plastic-covered torso, giving it a bear hug. He lifted without thinking.

Finally, he locked his home and got behind the wheel. He tore away the plastic bag, exposing dead eyes, the gruesome bend of the neck. He briskly slapped the bag into a ball and stuffed it under the seat. Before driving away, he fastened his passenger's seat belt.

The roads were virtually deserted. Once, however, at a red light, a police car came up behind him. It slowed, then pulled alongside. Run, he thought. Give it gas. Off into the night.

But the patrol car roared through the red light, taking no notice of the black Lincoln with the corpse in the front seat.

Killing an intruder was perfectly legal. And that was only right. A man has to protect himself, his family, and property. Especially these days. God knows, the authorities are useless. Even when they catch these bastards, which is seldom, they soon let them loose.

As for policemen, he had only contempt for their questions. He'd seen enough of police in his life, didn't trust them, didn't like them.

He drove to a beachfront parking lot. Even at this hour two

cars faced the bay, couples within entangled, thoughtless. He felt superior, knowing how shocked and frightened they'd be if they discovered what he was about.

He left the Lincoln and walked along the beach. He enjoyed the smell of salt air and the light breeze on his face. Above all, he was amazed at his own composure and confidence. Eventually, he headed home on foot.

In the morning, the body was found. Newspapers reported that Grover Durham, a known felon, had probably been the victim of an underworld execution. "A real professional job," said one policeman.

The killer read that with pride.

2

Assistant District Attorney Jack Meehan was in the first assistant's office, stretched out in a padded chair. For some reason, it was a scene Jack would always remember, Frank Mullins smiling and the flip way he began.

"Oh, shit. Another day, another homicide."

"Who's dead now?"

"Goodfellow. James. Shot five times with his own pistol. Died in the driveway next to his Porsche. Last night. You didn't see the papers?"

"Yeah, I wish I was like you, Mullins. I wish I had time to read the papers."

"The wife seems to be responsible." The first assistant tossed over the tabloid.

MOM OF YEAR
PLUGS HUBBY
FIVE TIMES

"Mom of the year?" Jack shook his head. "Must've been a bad year."

"I was considering asking your friend Stern to prosecute."

"You could do worse."

"I have a question about Stern. And I'm not saying this necessarily affects his work. But I have the feeling sometimes that he's just not on the team around here. You ever get that feeling?"

"Oh, that feeling." Jack slid back and gazed at the ceiling. "That feeling usually means he hasn't kicked in his ten percent."

"This is an election year." Mullins carefully unwrapped a Milky Way. "It's been in the papers and everything. But. Your friend Stern. I get the idea he hasn't heard."

"So, go tell him, Frank."

"A friend. I was thinking a friend should do that. Should take him to one side. Explain the facts of life."

"Don't look at me. If I wanted to be a bill collector I'd still be in private practice."

Mullins leaned forward. "I'll let you in on a little secret, Jack. Because we're friends a long time. I'll tell you why this election is so important. How come Mr. Flaherty wants to make such a big score. See, it's not just an ego thing like everyone's been saying. He's looking down the road to next year. Congressional elections. In a few months there's going to be an announcement. A seat opening up. A seat in the United States House of Representatives. Now. How does that sound?"

"It sounds." Jack sat up abruptly. "It sounds like my job is running for Congress."

"No, no, no." Mullins swallowed his candy. "This is good news."

"Maybe for you."

"For both of us. You're the number-two guy in this office. You've given more time, done more in the campaign, given money. And Rich Flaherty is not the sort of guy who forgets."

Jack smiled doubtfully. He'd just heard the first promise of the next campaign.

Jack Meehan could not understand men who cheated on their wives. In the first place, you had to lie to your own family. Go look in the mirror after that. Second, it's dangerous. Jack had seen the extremes. In private practice he'd handled bitter divorce suits. As an assistant district attorney he'd known even worse, including a grisly double murder and suicide.

"When I was married," Steve Stern wore a half-smile, "we had a lot of . . . problems. But I'll say this. We never came close to shooting each other. Actually, Susan didn't approve of physical violence. Emotional violence is neater and the pain lasts longer."

"Too bad," Jack replied. "Too bad Georgine Goodfellow didn't have that enlightened attitude."

Heading for the nearby muffin shop, Stern was nearly bouncing with enthusiasm at his new assignment. While murder is generally simple to prosecute (in this case, for example, the accused had already confessed), trying a homicide carries some prestige. This would be Stern's first.

"We can't be sure she shot him over another woman," he said. "But the local guy down there. Sergeant Silva. Knew both of them. Figures it's got to be some sort of triangle thing. Because these people were Mr. and Mrs. America. Affluent. Churchgoers. Three cute kids. Faces you see on cornflakes boxes."

"Did Mrs. America explain why she blew her old man away?"

"Interesting. Because, you know, she told us what she did in step-by-step detail. But she didn't really tell us why she did it."

In the muffin house, Jack waited until his friend was chewing on a roast beef sandwich before saying, "I was talking with Frank Mullins the other day."

"Please . . ." Steve swallowed. "Not while I'm eating."

"I was talking to Frank about this case, your being given this case. I recommended you, in fact. But Frank, he mentioned another thing. A . . . well, you know, the campaign."

A look of distaste crossed young Stern's face. He put his food down. "You know, Jack, you're about the fifth guy they've sent poking around, asking for money."

"Well, every office has its little collections."

Steve touched the sandwich and then looked away, exhaling. "Why should I, Jack? Huh? I earn my lousy fifteen thousand a year. I work hard. Why should I kick back a penny to Flaherty?"

"It's not kickbacks. Come on. Kickbacks are illegal. What I'm talking about are legitimate campaign contributions. Like they have in every D.A.'s office." Jack lowered his voice. "Nobody likes this business, Steve. When I first came here they asked me for money. Well, we had the new baby on the way and Rose wasn't working. So, I didn't have a dime to spare. And I'm thinking, what's this shit? But I paid. With borrowed money I paid. And, in a way, it makes sense to pay."

Stern rolled his eyes.

"No, really. When you look at it a certain way. We serve here at the pleasure of the district attorney. If he loses his election. If he goes. We go. So, it's in our own self-interest to contribute."

"Oh, come off it, Jack."

"Listen, Steve. I'm going to educate you. Because in case you haven't noticed. It's damned hard to make a living out there. That is, if you want to get some use out of that law degree. Of course, there are plenty of lawyers working as teachers and real-estate salesmen. My cousin. He's got a practice. But you can't call him except in the day. At night he's managing a Burger King. Yeah."

"It doesn't worry me."

"Well, it should. All I'm saying. You're just starting out. So the idea is to keep your head above water until you get established. The idea is. When something comes along that floats. You hold on tight. Put into Flaherty's campaign. Buy yourself a seat on the lifeboat. There's nothing wrong with that. And later on. You'll have more options."

"What about you, Jack? You're still here. After how many years?"

"I like it here. I don't mind giving Flaherty money. I —" Jack shrugged. "I've even voted for him."

After a protracted silence, Jack began to whisper to his friend. "If it's a money problem. If you're short or anything. Well. I can probably scrape a few bucks together. A little loan?"

"Thanks, Jack. But. You know, it's not the money. With me it's, you know, principle."

"Jesus, Counselor, grow up. What sort of an office would this be if all the decent people quit? Do you want to leave the field to the guys who have no principles?"

Steve Stern went back to his roast beef. After a long while, he said glumly, "Susan could tell you. There doesn't have to be a motive."

"What?"

"The Goodfellow homicide. With some people, marriage is motive enough."

That evening, Jack stood for an hour on an expressway overpass with a large "Flaherty!" sign. Thousands passed on their way home from the city. Sometimes they tooted, whether in support or derision Jack could not say.

His nose ran in the cold and he hunched over, back to the wind, hands in his pockets, the sign post propped under his arm. In the next life, he vowed, he would be a corporation lawyer.

At home, Jack met Mrs. Kiely, the baby-sitter. Lukewarm chicken pot pie sat on the stove.

"Your wife says there's frozen turnovers you can cook for dessert. She wanted to make a bread pudding but she fell asleep on the couch instead. I don't know how she managed to crawl out of here to her class tonight."

Mrs. Kiely reached for her coat, her face pinched in disapproval as she eyed Jack.

"She wants to do it," the prosecutor blurted. "She wants to get her master's degree. The school will give her a big raise once she's got it. And I can't stop her from trying."

"None of my business," the woman sniffed.

Once she'd gone, Jack read Dr. Seuss to Karen and John.

"That's a pretty short story," complained five-year-old Karen.

"When you get a little older," Jack muttered, "we'll read *War and Peace.*"

"Read it now," urged three-year-old John.

It was a familiar problem, finding time for the children. In fact, there was never enough time for anything. Supposedly, the situation was temporary, caused by Rose's class load and

11

Jack's politicking. Eventually they would both be making bigger salaries, and life would get back to normal.

But what was normal? He couldn't remember.

When Rose returned home, they went directly to bed.

"I can't sleep," Rose said. "I'm too tense or something."

In the dark, Jack replied, "Mrs. Kiely thinks you work too hard."

"She's right."

"She thinks I should make you stop."

Rolling over, Rose asked, "You and what army?"

"Mrs. Kiely thinks you and I don't see enough of each other."

"She actually told you that?"

"No," Jack admitted. "But I could tell. I could tell that's what she was thinking."

Jack concentrated on the ivory crucifix on the opposite wall, the brightest object in the room. "Sometimes I wonder. What's the point of all this work we do? We're going to make more money? What for? You want to buy a cottage on the Cape. When will we get time to use it?"

Stroking his hair, Rose climbed partway on top of him. "It's not going to be too much longer. And if you feel neglected or something. Well, why didn't you say so?"

He began feeling her back, working his fingers along the smooth curves of her shoulders. After a while, he reached down to squeeze her soft, bare bottom. "Rose," he whispered, kissing her lips, discovering that she'd fallen asleep.

3

I<small>N</small> the morning, the office buzzed with the news that Steve Stern had resigned. Jack Meehan was assigned to prosecute Georgine Goodfellow for the murder of her husband, James.

* * *

"When can I see them?"

The voice of Georgine Goodfellow grew hoarse. The tape was marred by background noise: crumpling paper; a chair scraping the floor; a male voice, far-off and indistinct.

"Why don't we finish up these questions, Georgine? Then, we'll look into that."

"I know what you want," she said. "And I'm telling you. I killed him. I admit it. Okay?"

"We have to know more than that."

"More?"

"What led up to it?"

"Tell us, Georgine, how did it happen?"

"Oh, well." She cleared her throat and coughed. "Excuse me. It's . . . it's a long story."

Jack Meehan listened to the tape in his office at home. Dressed for a rare night out, he expected Rose to summon him at any moment. In the meantime, he followed the tape with a transcript prepared by his secretary. Once, he compared the voice with a police photo taken several hours after the crime.

Mrs. Goodfellow looked haggard, her eyes puffy, her hair straggly, her lower lip drooping in shock. She'd made a very big mistake. Face to face with the camera, she seemed to realize this.

"I followed him out the door. I can see him, see him walking, across the lawn, to the driveway. Getting the keys. Fishing them out, out of his pocket. And he's halfway across and he looks back and sees . . . sees me. And he walks a little faster. He looks annoyed, I think. But not worried especially. And when it goes off. The gun . . . He falls right away. He's stumbling off to one side. Down. Kind of sitting on his leg. And now he's getting up. Right back up. But it keeps going off. And he's like pitching forward. On his face. And just lying there. Never saying a thing."

"And then what?" asked Harwood Police Sergeant Anthony Silva.

"And then nothing. He didn't move again."

"So you stopped firing?" asked the state-police investigator, Detective Lieutenant Lyle Sullivan.

13

"I remember smoke. Coming from him. Like his jacket had caught fire. Jim, he's weight conscious. That's like the main thing he cares about. That he doesn't gain weight. And I saw him on the ground. He looked . . . thin. Funny, I should notice that."

"Where did the gun come from, Georgine?"

"Jim. Jim's gun."

"Was it registered?"

"I don't know. I don't think so."

"Where'd he get it?"

"I don't know."

"How long had he had the gun?"

"A year or so, I guess."

"Where did he keep it?"

"In our bedroom closet. In the back. Jim's afraid. Of housebreaks."

"At what point did you go to the bedroom for the gun?"

"I don't remember getting the gun at all. It was just there."

"Just there?"

"Some things I can't remember so well. Like something turned off my brain and I just did it. Blank spots . . . Blackout, you call it . . . I don't know."

"Tell us what led up to the shooting," Silva suggested. "Tell us step by step how it started and maybe things will come back to you. You know, were you arguing?"

"Where are my children?"

"Where are the children?" Silva asked.

A man mumbled unintelligibly.

"They slept through it all," she said. "Thank God for that. I . . . Can I see them tonight?"

"Georgine, I really think they're better off with their grandparents. Don't you?"

Her voice quavered. "His family, they never liked me. I can imagine the lies. The lies they'll tell my babies. Turn them, turn them against me."

"I'm sure the kids are in bed. Asleep by now."

"I want to explain, you know? Tell them what happened."

"Tell us what happened," Sullivan suggested.

"I told you already. I killed him."
"Did you have an argument?"
"No. No, there was no argument."
"Well, did you have words? Did he say something to upset you?"
"Lady, you killed this man. Give us a reason."
"I can't give you one specific reason. Just. I'm sorry it happened."

Jack shook his head. Mrs. Goodfellow's statement read better than it sounded. Her voice was tremulous, inconsistent. A defense lawyer, playing this tape, could raise questions as to her state of mind.

Further muddying the waters, Sergeant Silva had given Georgine Valium prior to the interrogation.

"We had to give her something," Detective Sullivan had explained. "She was bouncing off the goddamn walls."

SULLIVAN: Did you and your husband fight a lot?
GOODFELLOW: Oh, sure. That's mostly what we do. We fight.
SULLIVAN: Did he ever strike you?
GOODFELLOW: No.
SULLIVAN: Ever threaten you? Physically?
GOODFELLOW: It isn't a problem, that stuff, abuse, beatings.
SULLIVAN: Well, what? Did he squeeze the toothpaste in the middle?
GOODFELLOW: I don't understand the question.
SILVA: What we're trying to get at, Georgine. We're trying to get at the reasons you fought. And why, how come this happened.
GOODFELLOW: It's not . . . not easy to explain.
SILVA: Do the best —
GOODFELLOW: I want to be exact.
SULLIVAN: Do you know the reason yourself?
GOODFELLOW: Of course I do.
SULLIVAN: Well, is it a secret?

GOODFELLOW: It wasn't any one thing that made this happen. It wasn't any big thing. It was little things. Things even I didn't notice. Building, you know. Building up over time.

SULLIVAN: Give us an example. Of something.

GOODFELLOW: (Long pause) The night before it happened, right? (Long pause) He was supposed to pick me up at the market. After work. But he didn't. I waited over an hour. And I had the kids with me. (Long pause) Eventually, I had to call him to come get me.

SULLIVAN: And you shot him for that?

GOODFELLOW: You asked for an example.

SILVA: Georgine. Georgine, how long had you been planning to do this?

GOODFELLOW: Do what?

SILVA: The shooting. Killing your husband.

GOODFELLOW: I didn't — It wasn't planned.

SILVA: But you must have thought it out beforehand.

GOODFELLOW: No.

SILVA: Didn't you even daydream about killing him? I mean, at some point, you must have imagined how much easier your life would be if he was dead.

GOODFELLOW: No.

SILVA: Well, did you ever — Maybe you didn't think about killing him. But did you ever wish him dead?

GOODFELLOW: No. It never occurred to me to wish him dead.

SULLIVAN: What about divorce?

GOODFELLOW: What about it?

SULLIVAN: For Christ's sake, if you didn't like the guy, why not just divorce him?

GOODFELLOW: Yes. I suppose that would have been better.

Steve Stern had left behind a brief résumé of James Goodfellow's thirty-one years on earth. Born of a Harwood family, the victim lived in the town all his life.

At Harwood-Howe Regional High School he had been a B student and a member of the track team.

A graduate of Boston University's School of Business Administration, he became a CPA and went to work at Chevy City. After five years, he opened a small office in Harwood Center, specializing in accounting and tax preparation.

He had married Georgine, his high-school sweetheart, shortly after leaving college. They had three children, ages three, five, and seven. Recently, he had moved his family to a $225,000 home in the new Apple Acres development.

A clipping from the *Harwood Observer Weekly* showed a photo of Goodfellow, among others, at a Rotary Club function. Stern had circled him with red pencil. With his round face and receding hair he looked older than thirty-one.

Goodfellow was remarkable only in the sense that no one interviewed could remember anything remarkable about him. He had many business acquaintances, but no known enemies and no close friends. In the Harwood Center office, his own employees seldom saw him before noon. He preferred to spend the morning working in a small office at home.

Though James Goodfellow had been shot five times, only one wound was mortal. A single bullet had smashed his kneecap. Another had lodged in his side. A third had broken his index finger. And a fourth had sailed through his jacket and shirt, grazing his underarm.

The final shot, to the back of the head at extremely close range, was literally the coup de grace.

In Sergeant Silva's photo, not much of the damage was apparent. A pity, Jack thought, because a gory photo can put jurors in a hanging mood.

Later in the tape, Georgine began to sniff and whimper. "I'm tired."

"We're almost finished," Sergeant Silva said.

"When can I see my children?"

"Soon."

"When? Because, you know, Nicole. She's afraid of the dark. She needs her night-light. Her Mickey Mouse night-light. And it's got to be in a place where she can see it. See it from the bed."

"Her grandparents must know all that," Silva said.

"No, they don't." The woman grew excited. "They don't know . . . oh, God, those poor kids. Everything's been so easy for them. I tried so hard to make them happy. And . . . all this . . . what's it going to do to them?" When no one answered, she asked, "Do you think they'll hate me?"

Sergeant Silva replied softly, "I'm sure they won't."

"I want to see them. They'll be worried. They'll want to know where I am."

"You'll be seeing them soon."

"They can't take them away from me. Can they? No. They never take children from their mothers. I never heard of that."

"We still need some answers here," Sullivan said.

Someone coughed. No one spoke.

Finally she said, "Ask your questions, Detective."

"Did your husband have a girlfriend?"

"Ha!"

"Didn't you find out he was seeing another woman? Isn't that why you shot him?"

"My husband seeing another woman? Well, I'd be very much surprised."

"Why is that?" Sullivan asked.

"Well . . . Because sex doesn't interest Jim very much. He's interested in business . . . was interested . . . in . . ."

"That must have been tough on you, Mrs. Goodfellow."

"I survived."

"Well, tell me. Where did you go when you wanted to get it on?"

"Jesus," she sniffled. "I didn't go anywhere, Detective Sullivan. In my opinion, the most overrated thing in the world is sex. Believe it or not, people can live without sex. There's priests and nuns who never have sex at all and they don't go around . . . go around . . ."

"Shooting people?"

"Georgine," Silva interjected, "are you involved with a man?"

"Oh. Now I'm the one fooling around. Well, sorry. Wrong again. Why don't you people listen? I told you what happened. I shouldn't have done it. I'm sorry I did it. I'd do anything to

18

go back. . . . But it wasn't — I didn't do it because of affairs. Or anything of the kind. I did it because, because after ten years, I couldn't live anymore with his . . . indifference. I couldn't live anymore with my husband showing more interest for his accounts and his contracts than he showed for me. . . . I . . ." She began to sob.

For a few moments they let her cry. Then, Silva said softly, "Georgine?"

"It's not fair . . ."

"What? What's not fair?"

"All my life I did the right thing. I was careful. I never even got a moving violation. And just once I do wrong, and everything's wrecked forever."

"Sad." Rose stood at the door. Dressed for an evening out, tall and slim in a bright skirt, she was lovely.

Jack switched off the tape.

"She sounds so beaten . . . beaten down."

"It's her husband that's beaten down. And he's not getting back up."

"Still. She must have suffered. She must have been really miserable to do it."

"Remind me never to put you on a jury."

"We have to go. And your daughter wants her good-night kiss."

"In a minute."

"In a minute she'll be asleep."

"Okay, okay."

Jack put away his papers and tape recorder. He'd heard the confession on several occasions now, and grew more disturbed each time, realizing that pieces of the story seemed to be missing. Jack wanted to understand why this woman had killed her husband, the father of her children. He still hadn't found an explanation.

4

"WE haven't had a homicide here since 1924. This was a hell of a shock to the town." Sergeant Anthony Silva, a coffee-colored man with short, graying hair, was out of uniform. "Everybody knew Jim Goodfellow. And I suppose they liked him well enough. But her. She's a real popular lady in this town. Did all sorts of good works. Just like the paper said."

"You knew them well, Tony?" Jack started his car.

"I knew them to say hello. Certainly not socially. They were young people. With money. Not exactly in my social set."

"How about professionally?"

"A thing like this, you'd think there'd be a history of domestic disturbances. But no. As far as I remember, we never sent a car to the house."

It was cold, the sky solid with clouds. Jack drove along a route without sidewalks or sewers. The streets were lined with pines and apple orchards. Homes were set far from the road. Occasionally, at intersections, there would be a convenience store or gas station.

Harwood was rural. For many living in its several developments, it was a bedroom community serving the city more than fifteen miles away.

"Anyone talked with neighbors?"

"Me," Tony said.

"What kind of questions did you ask?"

"Just, you know. Anyone see anything? And no one did. In fact, aside from the guy directly across the street — Garritt, the one who called us — I couldn't find anyone who'd even admit hearing the shots."

"How do you figure that?" Jack questioned.

"I figure some people heard. But they don't care to get involved. This isn't a real neighborhood, you see. These houses have been occupied less than a year. Most of the people are from out of town. The place doesn't have any history, if you know what I mean."

The policeman produced his notebook. "I also talked with relatives and friends. Some of her friends. They weren't very cooperative. They all seemed shocked. Nobody could even guess why it happened. Couldn't or wouldn't."

"Maybe you're asking the wrong people, Sergeant. Try Goodfellow's office. His employees. These are the people he saw everyday, and sometimes a guy'll say things in front of his secretary he won't say in front of his wife or his family or his friends."

The road wound past picturesque farms, stone walls, and cranberry bogs. And yet Jack didn't envy the people who lived down here, tending their cesspools and electrocuting mosquitoes in the midst of all this beauty. The prosecutor was a confirmed city boy.

"What did you think of the confession?" Tony asked. "The interrogation."

"What about it?"

"Do you think we did a good job, or what?"

"Sure," Jack said. "You covered everything. Very professional."

"I couldn't figure that Sullivan there."

"Sullivan?"

"Here he is from the state police. Supposed to be so experienced at all this. And I'm talking to the woman, trying to get her to say she planned this thing. Planned it out ahead of time. Which I'm smart enough to know makes an important difference. And all of a sudden. Out of the blue. Sullivan asks how come she didn't just get a divorce. And I'm saying to myself, Why did he ask that? Because until he interrupted I had her going, kind of. And I look at him. In his face. And I can see. The stupid bastard only asks because he wants to know. For his own information. I can see that."

Jack smiled.

"He's not a friend of yours? Sullivan?"

"Not especially," Jack replied.

"Well." The sergeant lit a cigarette. "In a way it was a good question. Why didn't she just divorce him?"

"It would have made things a lot easier."

"Some people. They got a talent for screwing up their lives."

The developers of Apple Acres had preserved as many trees as possible, so that each yard had its little grove of evergreens and a stand of birches. Even a few apple trees grew here and there. The lots were large, and Jack could see how such distant neighbors might have missed the excitement.

The Goodfellow's ranch-style home was at the bottom of a cul-de-sac.

"When did you interview the neighbors?" Jack stopped his car in front of the victim's home.

"The morning after. Went to every house on this street."

"You might try a second visit, Sergeant. I'd appreciate it. In the evening. You'll have a better chance of finding people who were at home on the night of the incident. And don't just ask about the shooting. Find out whatever you can about the Goodfellows. I know you say this isn't a very friendly neighborhood, but there's always somebody. On any street. Somebody who knows all the gossip."

"Right . . . only, when I'm collecting this gossip, what am I looking for?"

"Whatever. Did the Goodfellows fight in public? How'd they treat their kids? Visitors? Who came to the house? You know, find out anything you can. You never know what odd piece of information is going to be important."

"I thought we had the confession," Tony said. "I didn't think we needed anything else."

"Well, I'll tell you, Tony. First thing a good defense attorney's going to try. He's going to try to get that confession thrown out. I don't think it'll be thrown out. But, just to be on the safe side. We want to be able to prove our case without it."

"I see."

"Besides. Confession or not. The jury wants to know why

she killed him. My case will be that much easier to prove if I can give them something, some bit of evidence or some theory to explain her motive."

Jack pointed to the end of the road where a footpath disappeared into the woods. "Where does that go?"

"Leads to another street."

Jack turned to the Goodfellow's one-story home. "What's behind the house?"

"Another house."

"And did you talk to the occupants?"

"They didn't see or hear a thing."

Jack stared for a moment at a child's yellow and red plastic pedal-car on the Goodfellow's brown lawn. Stained with December mud, it might have been there since the crime. Jack's little girl, Karen, had one just like it.

"He fell near the driveway." Tony pointed. Jack stared, but there was nothing there to indicate violent, sudden death.

"What gets me," the sergeant said. "I wish we'd had the medical examiner's report when we questioned her. Because according to that, she fired four times. And he was still alive. And she walks up to him. Puts the gun to his head. And pulls the trigger . . . Well, I can see how she might go berserk and start firing. But to calmly walk up to him. When he's lying there helpless. And blow his brains out. Shit. I thought I knew this lady. I thought she was like all the others up the Star Market with their kids and their carts full of food." He gave a slight shudder. "Just leaves you wondering what's ticking away inside people."

Jack was beginning to back up the dead-end street when a green station wagon came barreling toward them. "Whoa!" He had to pull over and let it pass.

"That's her," Tony said.

The big vehicle rocked into the driveway. Quickly, she bounced out. No more than ten yards away, Jack got a good look.

Her hair was jet black, cut in bangs. Clear, smooth cheeks of bright pink brought color to an overcast day. She walked with a kind of dignity, pretending not to notice the two men who were watching her. "She's beautiful," Jack said. In fact, he had the eerie sensation that he'd seen her before. "And she murdered her husband."

"Yeah. What a pitiful waste, locking her up with all them dykes."

"I first heard on the radio. The names. Georgine's name. And I couldn't believe it. I thought I'd heard wrong. And I started turning the dial until I heard it again." Mary Antonino winced. "I still didn't believe it. In fact, I don't believe it yet."

"You don't believe what?" Jack Meehan asked.

"That Georgine killed Jim. Oh, I'm sure it happened. You say it happened. Georgine admits to it. So, it happened. But. Inside, you know. I can't accept it. Like tomorrow someone's going to come out and say how it's all a big mistake."

Over coffee, Mary glumly picked at a stain on her tablecloth. Georgine Goodfellow's closest friend, she was one of those Sergeant Silva had labeled uncooperative. At first, she'd refused to let Jack in. "You might have information that'll help Georgine," he said, adding that her friend's situation was so bad already, nothing Mary said could make it worse.

"My Matthew played with Georgine's Nicole. I haven't told him yet. . . . Well, I don't know what . . . exactly what to tell him."

"Georgine. She's a good mother?"

"Oh, God, yes. Are you kidding? She lived for those kids. I'll tell you what kind of mother Georgine's been. When the middle one was born. Vicki. You never saw such a cranky, unpleasant baby. Cried nonstop. And they didn't discover why until she was two years old. A malformation. Birth defect of some kind. Something to do with her hip. To straighten it out, she had to have an operation and hours and hours of very painful therapy. And who do you think was the therapist? Georgine quit her job. She spent all her time with that kid. Helping her. Encouraging. Coping with all the tantrums, with Vicki screaming all the time. I don't know where she got the patience. I don't think I could have done it. But Georgine. She was like that with all her kids."

Mary stopped abruptly, aware that she'd been talking about Georgine as if this life with her children was a thing of the past.

"She's a good friend. Dependable. A sweet, gentle person. I never saw her do . . . violence. A violent act. Or show animosity toward anyone."

"If that's true. How do you explain what happened?"

Mary seemed to deflate. "The last year or so. I've been very busy. I got my real-estate license. Georgine and I . . . We haven't seen as much of each other as we should have. So I can't . . . I don't know. I just don't know how to explain it."

"Tell me this. Was Georgine the type to leave a gun lying around? A loaded gun? With three kids?"

"I don't know anything about guns," Mary replied. "I was under the impression, I read that the gun belonged to him. And I suppose he kept it wherever he wanted."

"He was a bit of a tyrant then?"

"I didn't say that."

"Well, what *would* you say, Mary? What sort of marriage did the Goodfellows have?"

"Well." She pushed back her hair. "They weren't in love or anything. But, how many married people are?"

"Georgine told you that? About not being in love?"

"She didn't have to. You could see they weren't in love. You could get them together in the same room and they'd hardly even look at each other."

"Do you think, Mary. Do you think maybe one of the Goodfellows. Just maybe there was somebody else? A third party?"

"Not Georgine. I don't know about him. But Georgine. She had too much respect for herself to be sneaking around."

"And yet . . ."

"I know." Mary stared at the tablecloth. "It doesn't fit with what's happened, does it? I . . . don't ask me to explain. You depend on someone to be a certain way. Your best friend. You depend on her. Maybe she'll change a little over time. Maybe she'll have some crisis. But you don't expect this. Not from Georgine.''

"Where can I find Jill Roche?" Jack Meehan approached a gym teacher at Harwood-Howe Regional High School.

"Miss Roche is with her class and can't be bothered."

Across the huge gym, young girls were leaping, shrieking, playing volleyball.

"It really is important." Jack gave her his card. "Official business."

The teacher hurried off toward the volleyball game, where she showed the assistant district attorney's card to a second teacher. The game stopped. All eyes turned to the stranger across the gym.

Jack scooped up a loose volleyball and gently launched it toward a nearby basket. Though he was restricted by his heavy coat, his shot seemed to float into the hoop. He glowed.

"Mr. Meehan? I'm Jill Roche."

The prosecutor offered his hand, but she pretended not to see it. Jill was small, even delicate. That was surprising because she sounded tough on the phone.

"As I explained, Mr. Meehan, I'm afraid I can't see you now." She fingered the whistle that hung around her neck. "I've got a class. Classes all day. And appointments in the afternoon."

"I've taken care of that."

"Excuse me?"

"I've been to see your principal, Miss Roche. And, of course, he told me that his teachers would gladly cooperate with the district attorney's office. He expects that. In fact, he's sending down a substitute to cover your class."

Jill's face fell.

In the teacher's room, Jill Roche nervously puffed on a cigarette.

"No good for your wind," Jack smiled.

She gave him a sharp look. She was wearing a gray jogging outfit, and her face was moist with perspiration. Jack opened his briefcase and retrieved his notepad. Plainly visible were newspaper clippings referring to the murder of James Goodfellow.

"It's a shame what they're doing to Georgine." Jill stared at the headlines. "An ugly shame. I mean, she worked hard around this town. If you ever needed help. Getting something done. Like the Youth Soccer. You called Georgine. That 'Mom of the Year' award. We did that to thank her. For the work she'd done running the Toddler's Carnival. And now they twist it into a sick joke. Use it against her. Not fair. Not fair."

Jack nodded. "The two of you worked together in the —"

"The Youth Soccer League. Both our kids belonged."

"Sergeant Silva tells me you know Georgine pretty well."

"We're friends, yeah. You notice I say we *are* friends. I won't back away from Georgine because she's got problems. It's easy to be someone's friend when there's no problems."

"I've got to say I'm impressed with the loyalty of Mrs. Goodfellow's friends."

"Well, why not? Georgine, she's a good, decent person."

"Decent," Jack nodded. "But not so decent in one respect. She has confessed to murder."

Jill did not respond. Obviously, she had no intention of volunteering information. Jack set to work with a series of questions unrelated to the homicide, except that they touched on Georgine's personality.

The unkindest thing Jill said about Georgine was, "Some people find her . . . You know, the type of person who only talks about the kids. But she's steady. You can count on her. When I went through my divorce. Well, it's true what they say. A lot of your married friends. So-called friends. They drop you when you get a divorce. Like it's contagious, or something. So, right when you need friends more than ever. You can't find any."

"Except for Georgine," Jack suggested.

"With Georgine. It was, 'What can I do? How can I help?' With Georgine. If I needed to talk. She was there to listen. Advice? She gives good advice. Georgine is an expert at coping."

"Not so expert. Judging by what happened with her husband."

"Well, I'm not going to pretend I'm sorry about him. If you want my opinion, he married her for her looks. He never cared about Gij. She was an asset. Like a big office or a flashy car. Marrying Georgine was his first career-move."

"So," Jack said, "why did *she* marry *him?*"

"He gave her a good sales pitch. Really, that's it. Georgine and salesmen. They can get her to buy anything. This woman owns three vacuum cleaners. She's trusting. And she believed his promises. Even now. I'll say to her. Why don't you leave him? And she'll tell me how there's good in him. Somewhere. Well, so what? If he makes her unhappy. So what?"

"How did he make her unhappy, Jill?"

"How should I know? I wasn't there. What difference does it make, anyway? She confessed. She told you she did it. So what more do you want?"

"Does Georgine have any other close friends? Maybe a special friend. Girlfriend? Male friend? Someone. A name you could give me?"

"No." Jill looked away. "Can't help you."

Jack studied her through clouds of smoke.

"You've been avoiding me, Miss Roche. And the police."

"Well, I've been busy."

"Failing to cooperate with a homicide investigation. That's a serious matter."

"I don't have to talk to you." She raised her voice slightly. "There's no law that says I have to talk to you or cooperate or answer questions or anything. . . . Is there?"

True enough. Only the grand jury can require people to give evidence, and even then they are not obliged to speak if they feel any threat of self-incrimination. An investigator's authority is largely bluff.

Jack sat back, wondering if Georgine Goodfellow or her attorney had called Mary Antonino and Jill Roche, urging them not to talk, explaining to them their rights.

But why try to stifle the investigation, when Georgine had already confessed? Was it the prelude to a not-guilty plea and some exotic defense, insanity or wife-abuse? Or did Mrs. Goodfellow have something to hide after all?

5

THE victim's parents lived at a farmhouse in old Harwood. Most of their land had gone to a shopping center, though a few chicks still scratched about the backyard. Through the trees could be seen the back side of the mall and three large dumpsters.

A pair of children came running as Jack arrived.

"Have you come to see my grandpa?" the boy asked, ringing the doorbell.

"Know what?" His sister pointed. "We got chickens. And ducks. And cows."

"We don't got cows," the boy said. "We got chickens and ducks, but we don't got cows."

"Well, Grandpa useda have cows." The girl looked up at the visitor. "My daddy died." Too young to understand death, she expected Jack to be impressed.

"I'm, I'm sorry," he stuttered, wanting to say more. Remembering his own children, he wished to comfort these. He thought of saying, things aren't as bad as they seem, kids. But that wasn't exactly true.

Suddenly, Jack Meehan was struck by just how awful their situation was. The real shock would come when they were old enough to understand what their mother had done. He put himself in their place.

My mother and father didn't get along. They fought. Well, how can I say this? My mother killed him. Killed my father. But it didn't have anything to do with me. I was a child.

"Can I help you?" Jack was startled back to the present. A gray-haired woman, adjusting a baggy, flowered dress, stood at the door. Jack introduced himself. "We've been expecting you, Mr. Meehan." But before inviting him in, she leaned toward the children. "Where's Vicki? Eugene, where's your sister?"

"Playing with ducks."

"Well, you make sure she stays in the yard. That's your job today."

She gave a loud sigh before leading Jack through a house furnished with rustic antiques. On the floor, everywhere, were toys.

"God, help me. I'm too old for this." She paused at an oak bookcase, and braced herself with one hand as she caught her breath. "Don't misunderstand, Mr. Meehan. They're good children. But keeping up with the likes of them is a young person's job."

"What are the plans for them?"

"Plans? There are no plans. They'll stay with us, of course. It may be hard, but they're our only grandchildren. Our only link with our son. We won't give them up to her. And besides, she doesn't want them. Or, at least, she doesn't have the nerve to come asking for them." With something like a sneer, she added, "She sent little Eugene a letter, but . . ."

"A letter?"

"I tore it up. He never saw it."

"Did you read it," the prosecutor asked. "What was in it?"

"Some nonsense. Telling the boy not to believe what he was told about her. Trying to make him think she's innocent." The old woman's eyes were clear, steady, and bitter. "What else could she tell him?"

Jack noticed, atop the bookcase, a framed portrait of a wedding party. Georgine, stunning in white, stood with her arm wrapped around James. Beside her stood the prospective grandparents, looking especially pleased.

* * *

Arthur Goodfellow sat in the kitchen beside a huge, wood-burning, cast-iron stove. His large size surprised the assistant district attorney. His hands were particularly big.

"Glad you came, Mr. Meehan. I would've been out to see you if you hadn't come." He pulled a pipe from his sweater pocket. "There were some things I wanted to say. To discuss."

"Well." Jack took a seat. "I'm happy to listen."

"Mainly this." He began filling his pipe. "I've noticed. When you read the papers. I've noticed how you get this or that person sent to jail. And the sentence will be twenty years. Or life even. But, don't you know, in a few years, you find that person is on the street again? Which is because they *say* twenty years, but they don't *mean* twenty years, or anything near that. Well, that's been bothering me. I don't want this woman who killed my son to be on the street again. Ever. At least, not while I'm alive." He lit the pipe. "I don't want to see her face in public. And I don't think I'm being unreasonable."

"No, sir."

Goodfellow puffed once. "There shouldn't be furloughs or work-release. Or any of that nonsense." He puffed again, this time a little harder. "I don't mean to be vindictive. I don't even exactly hate the woman. But. My son is dead. He won't be coming back to life in a few years. He won't be furloughed. Or released. He's dead. He'll never see his children again."

Jack took a deep breath. "I understand."

"You know." The old man studied his feet. "Those news people were here the day after. Never seen people like that. They put a television camera in that window there. A man stood on my hedge and propped his camera in the window. I looked up and he was taking my picture. Damnedest thing, those people. But I let them in. Because I wanted to explain what a fine man and a fine father my son was. I want everyone to know. Because I suspect that's the first thing she'll do. She'll tell lies about him. To make herself look better. It's not enough she killed my son. Now she'll go into court and slander him."

"Unfortunately," Jack conceded, "that's a possibility."

"But we were on television. Weren't we, mother?"

"For all of ten seconds."

31

Goodfellow leaned forward, pointing the pipe at Jack. "I have to do my best by Jimmy. To see that justice, some sort of justice is done here. We don't know what happens to people when they die. Maybe I'm going to see Jim again. And he's going to ask what I did on his behalf. I'm not saying I expect this to happen. But the thought is at the back of my mind. He'll ask what I did. And what am I going to tell him?"

Jack cleared his throat. "The reason I'm here. I'm hoping to build a strong case. So we can be certain she is punished. And that she does go to jail for a long, long time."

Arthur nodded grimly.

"Were you aware that your son owned a handgun?"

"No. I never knew."

"What were his feelings about gun ownership? Does it surprise you that he had a gun in the house?"

"Well." The old man rubbed his chin. "I don't think he was against guns. Years ago. We even did a little hunting. But. I just wouldn't have thought of Jim buying a gun. What was the need?"

"About his marriage. How were they getting along? Were there problems? Your son may have confided in you."

"He never mentioned problems." Arthur leaned away for the first time, looking a little confused. "Now, I keep wishing we'd talked more. Some things I wish I'd said. But, we're just not talkative people, don't you know. Every few weeks they came here for dinner with the children. I won't say they looked terribly happy. But they did seem . . . adjusted to each other. The way couples get. And when this happened. It was like it dropped from the sky. From nowhere." He bit his lip. "I don't know why she did it. I've tried and tried to think why. What justified it? But, I don't know . . ."

The children began screaming outside. The grandmother went to the window and rapped. Her face, in the overcast light, was tight.

"You never know about other people's marriages." She watched the kids. "Even in your own family. Who knows what goes on behind closed doors? She might even have had a good reason to, to be angry with Jimmy. Maybe. But there's one

32

thing I'll never forgive. What she's done to those innocents. I think of that. And I *do* hate her. And I wish her an awful fate."

Jack turned to watch the children. That had to be Vicki, the middle child. Balancing on a fallen log, she looked incredibly healthy. She resembled her mother and perhaps that explained Jack's fascination. He could hardly take his eyes from her.

6

"THIS is what?" Jack Meehan asked. Detective Lieutenant Lyle Sullivan of the state police lifted the slightly overexposed photo from the prosecutor's desk. "This is the closet."

"The closet where Goodfellow kept his gun?"

"Right. The gun. He kept it on the shelf. According to her."

Jack took the photo. "Well, don't you see what's wrong with this?"

"Hey, I didn't take it. That Portugee cop —"

"I'm not talking about the quality of the picture, Lyle. The closet. Do you see what's wrong with the closet?"

"Something wrong with the closet?"

"Do you see a lock on that closet?"

He gave the photo a second, more careful look. "No lock. What of it?"

"Do you have kids?"

"What's the point, Counselor?"

"The mom of the year doesn't leave a gun in an unlocked closet where the kids could get at it."

"So?"

"So? So, Georgine Goodfellow lied about keeping the gun in that closet. And if she lied about that. Maybe she lied about other things."

Sullivan shrugged. "So, she lied. So what? We've still got a ten-page confession with the woman's signature on every damn page."

Jack peered at the photo.

Sullivan insisted, "Maybe there *is* a lock but it doesn't show in the picture. Ever think of that? Maybe she meant another closet. She'd just shot her husband. It was late. She got some little details wrong. What of it?"

"This gun isn't a little detail, Detective. This is a remarkable gun. It's not registered. No serial number. Can't be traced. No one knew that James Goodfellow even owned a gun. And if you'll remember the confession. She says the gun was just there. Appeared in her hand. Or some monumental horseshit like that."

"Yeah?"

"Well, suppose she bought this gun herself," Jack suggested. "Suppose she went out and got it somewhere. For the express purpose of killing James Goodfellow. That makes a big difference. If we can prove she planned to kill him, that'll short-circuit any self-defense, crime-of-passion bullshit."

"Did she also plan to confess? Answer me that. Why would she plan to shoot her husband? And then, afterward, sit in the kitchen. The murder weapon on the table, officers at the door. She does that, she's aced herself out of any inheritance, any insurance, any anything. What the hell kind of plan is that?"

"Well." Jack sat back. "Could be she planned it. But she didn't plan it very carefully. She just had the idea in her head. Shoot the bastard. And she didn't have any idea past that."

Sullivan grunted.

"Another thing," Jack continued. "Really bothers me. I keep thinking how every time I listen to that confession. How there's something missing."

"You mean, some asshole erased part of the tape?"

"I mean she might be telling the truth, as far as it goes. But she's leaving something out. Mainly a motive. An adequate explanation of why she did it."

Sullivan looked more annoyed than ever. "This is a very simple case, Counselor. We've got a body. We've got a gun. We've got a confession. Let's not make a Chinese puzzle out of it, eh?"

* * *

The grand jury sat every Wednesday. In the early morning, witnesses waited on benches in the cold stone lobby, unsmiling, silent, sometimes half asleep.

Jack Meehan took the stairs two at a time. Today, he would seek and gain indictments against a variety of people for a variety of crimes. In some cases, this process could take as little as fifteen minutes. Indicting Georgine Goodfellow for first degree murder, however, would consume hours. Witnesses were to be called, including the accused, and testimony would be an important part of the record.

"Mr. Meehan! Could I have a word with you?"

Jack grimaced, sighting Betsy Levin, the short, plump defense attorney, who straddled the top step. "Battling Betsy," as she was known in the office, was bright and relentless to the point of rudeness.

"Mr. Meehan. Just to let you know, I've been retained by Mrs. Goodfellow."

"Fine." Jack kept walking, wondering, What did I do to deserve this? At their last encounter, an arson trial, Ms. Levin had more or less accused him of suborning perjury. She made no effort, now, to apologize for that slur. She seemed to assume it was forgotten.

"I'm hoping we can discuss what you're calling a confession." She produced a copy. "Georgine Goodfellow's so-called confession."

"Reads well, doesn't it?"

"No judge is going to admit this." She waved the statement.

Jack stopped at the courtroom door and faced her. She was attempting to undermine his confidence in the evidence. "If you think the court is going to throw out a perfectly valid, voluntary confession. Think again, Counselor."

"You call this voluntary? A woman in trauma. Psychologically battered. Handcuffed. Humiliated. Your arm-twisters putting words in her mouth."

"Now wait a minute, Betsy. No one twisted her arm. No one put words in her mouth. And no one. No one put the gun in her hand."

She took a step back, sniffing disdainfully. "You guys kill

35

me. You weren't there. You got a lot of thirdhand information from a bunch of stumblebum cops and you're sure you know everything."

"I'm sure," Jack retorted. "When I've got the lady's signed confession in my pocket. I'm sure."

Jack was prejudiced against defense attorneys. Unlike prosecutors, they did not care about guilt or innocence, only winning, often by loophole or delay. He suspected that some defenders gloried in winning acquittals for guilty clients (including child molesters, drug dealers, and murderers), as if it was a measure of their genius instead of a profound injustice.

With theatrical smoothness, Ms. Levin's tone softened. "If you would only keep an open mind, Jack. Just because she admits to something. That doesn't mean she's guilty. People confess to things they never did. It happens all the time."

"Is this going to be your defense?" Jack smiled. "Listen. Your client planned the murder of her husband. Planned it. Carried it out. Confessed to it. And now I'm going to send her to jail for it. And that's all I've got to say to you on the subject."

Then he noticed Georgine, rapt with attention, perched on the edge of a nearby bench. Dressed in dark colors, Georgine Goodfellow looked both wounded and alluring. Jack almost regretted his remarks. He couldn't take his eyes off her.

"Don't I know you?" the prosecutor blurted.

The woman's face showed a vague hurt, lips parted slightly. "I beg your pardon?" She was practically inaudible.

"Didn't you once live in Merrymount?" Jack asked. "Years ago. Didn't you go to the Watson Elementary School? Live off Beale Street?"

"Don't answer him, Georgine." Betsy moved between them.

"I remember," she nodded. "Yes, I remember you. Jackie Meehan."

Backing into the courtroom, Jack called over Attorney Levin's shoulder. "Lady, you should have stayed in Merrymount." He had to sound tough, because suddenly he felt shocked, and a little sorry for her.

Georgine Bow. Why hadn't he realized? One of the neighborhood kids. Lovely even then. He could remember the games. Relievo. Dodgeball. Georgine Bow, flushed, giggling, out of breath. God, that was her in the hall, all grown-up and waiting to be indicted for murder.

7

"SOMETHING about her face," Jack explained to Frank Mullins. "Something in her face had stayed the same. And when she looked at me. I found myself asking, 'Don't I know you?'"

At the gym, the two men waited a turn on the basketball court. Amid shouts, thumps, and the rattle of rims, Jack wasn't sure his friend could hear.

"She remembered me too. After all these years."

"How well did you know her?" Mullins asked.

"I knew her pretty good. A nice little girl. You know the type. Always careful not to get her clothes dirty. Home by four o'clock. Her father was a photographer. Outside their house was a big sign. Bow Studio."

"And now you're going to send her to prison."

Frank's blunt statement filled Jack with a strange unease.

When their turn came, Jack and Frank joined their teammates beneath the basket. These were pickup games, informal but competitive.

On the court, First Assistant Frank Mullins became the ideal team player. Though small for the game, and a mediocre shooter, he was an excellent passer with an uncanny knack for anticipating the moves of others. In addition, he always knew the score and frequently rescued his mates by citing some obscure rule. Also, he took care to have Jack Meehan on his team.

A starting guard in college, Jack was big enough to play forward in a pickup game. His shot was unspectacular, but sure. More important, he never stopped working, playing defense, rebounding, stealing passes, and setting picks. Occasionally,

37

opponents would say he was lucky, that he landed in the right place at the right time again and again. But it was more than luck.

"This lady," Jack continued as they awaited their opponents. "From what I've heard so far. She could have won the award. Least likely to murder."

"It's always the quiet ones," Frank said.

"And another thing. When she wasted poor Jim. She killed the golden goose. The guy had bank accounts, thousands of dollars. Stocks. Property in New Hampshire. A big chunk of that house was paid for."

Mullins's eyebrows jumped.

"Nothing illegal, as far as I can tell," Jack said. "He had a good business. People working for him. A list of clients as long as your arm. Vico, the electronics firm. The Alden Supermarket chain. Parkside Porsche-Volkswagen. And on and on."

"Is any of that connected to the homicide?" Mullins asked.

"Couldn't find any connection. No. Except, where there's money. Your ears tend to perk up. And something else. This guy is younger than me, and he's worth ten times as much. I mean, I look at my paycheck. It isn't much, and what's there is owed."

"We don't do it for money." Frank took a practice shot. "Job satisfaction."

At home, Jack went to the scrapbook in Rose's hope chest for his sixth-grade class photo. Each student sat at attention, hands on the desk, smiling formally. He saw himself leaning forward, head up, wearing a small bow tie.

Two seats in front was Georgine Bow with a ribbon in her hair, smiling like the teacher's favorite. Her face looked alive, full of hope, and blissfully ignorant of the future. Her face gave Jack a chill.

Assistant District Attorney Jane Christian delivered a freshly typed legal brief to Jack Meehan's desk. "If you get time, Jack. Could you look that over for me? I'd like your opinion."

"Sure, Jane."

Turning, she nearly ran into First Assistant Frank Mullins. "Hello, Jane."

"Uh, hi."

Frank would not move from the threshold, and Jane had to squeeze past. She sprinted down the hall.

"I'd look at Jane's briefs anytime." He gazed after her, longingly.

"What can I do for you, Frank?" Jack asked.

"You know, I like that skirt she's wearing. The way it sort of hangs off her ass."

"You're a class act, Counselor."

Frank produced a final shiver of frustration for Mrs. Christian, then turned to Jack. "Don't tell me you're too busy to have lunch."

But Jack was. In addition to the Goodfellow homicide, he'd been organizing notes and appointments for five other cases. Amid the piles of paper on his desk was a long list of telephone numbers to be called. He had also promised to distribute Flaherty leaflets at a supermarket that evening.

"What'll you do for food?" Frank asked.

"I've ordered out. Pizza Heaven."

"Oh. A gourmet meal. No wonder you won't join me."

It was as Frank departed that she came forward, emerging from the shadows at the end of the hall. "Mr. Meehan." She stood at the threshold. "I'm sorry to bother you. But I was hoping to speak with you."

Stunned, the prosecutor rose. He stared, not quite believing his eyes. "Mrs. Goodfellow?"

Jack removed a pile of books from the chair alongside the desk. "Please sit here, Mrs. Goodfellow."

"Mr. Meehan, I —"

"Be with you in a minute." He pulled a small recorder from his desk, then fumbled through a pile of cassettes before finding a blank tape. Next, Jack called in his secretary as witness, whispering, "Just sit in back. Take notes. And don't make a sound."

Finally, he produced a waiver-of-rights form. "Could you read this and sign it please, Mrs. Goodfellow?" She signed without even looking at it.

A small purse on her lap, Georgine placed her arms flat on the armrests. Her head was high, her eyes remarkably clear and bright. She arched her back slightly when the secretary sat behind her.

"Mr. Meehan, I came here, I was hoping —"

"Before you go on." Jack bent close to the recorder, punching buttons. He was determined to avoid any mistakes. "I want to be sure you know that anything you say may be used against you in court. And, also, if you want, I can call Miss Levin. Because you have the right to have your attorney present. Do you understand all that?"

"Yes."

"And is Miss Levin still your attorney?"

"Betsy doesn't know I came. I wanted a chance to speak with you alone." She gave a worried glance behind her.

"Miss Atwood is my personal secretary. She's very professional, very discreet. And completely trustworthy."

Georgine took a deep breath, unbuttoned her brown, wool coat, and pulled her arms free. Her legs were wonderfully long. At close range, Jack could study her face. The classic high cheekbones, the luminous brown eyes, the fair, flawless skin contrasting with the jet-black bangs.

"I want . . . I hope you will allow me to speak. I don't want to answer questions. I just want to explain something."

Jack nodded.

"Miss Levin thinks I can be found not guilty. She tells me I was psychologically abused. Which, I guess, is true. She thinks I was, in a way, justified. In what I did. I don't know about that."

Georgine made Jack nervous. She had a way of establishing eye contact when he least expected it. Also, he was rattled because this sort of thing just didn't happen. People accused of murder don't drop by to chat with the prosecutor. He had no precedents, and he worried about making a mistake that would violate the woman's rights and exclude her statement.

"As children you and I were friends." She looked down. "That was many years ago. But I remember those times so well." She glanced up hopefully. "We had some, some fun times."

Jack studied his desktop. If she was making a play for sympathy, it would backfire.

"I've been reading. I've been reading the copy of my confession. That night. Well, I didn't make myself clear. You can't read that confession and understand what happened. Or why it happened. And that's what I want to tell you now. Calmly. And completely."

"I can't promise any deal on this."

"I'm not asking for a deal. I just hope you'll be fair. Betsy said you were fairer than most."

"Betsy said that?"

"If I told you how it happened. And if you were convinced. Would you stop this investigation? All this snooping around to the neighbors and so on? I keep seeing poor Sergeant Silva on my street, going door to door like the Avon lady. Would you just accept that I shot my husband? I admit it."

"You mean you'll make a guilty plea?" Jack sat up.

"Yes. I think. I'd be willing to plead guilty to something like manslaughter. Because that's all I'm really guilty of."

"Well. Before I could agree to anything, I'd want to hear your story. And then I'd have to discuss it with others in the office here. And your attorney."

She nodded.

My God, it was like bargaining with a child.

"In fairness," he said. "I have to ask you again. Are you sure you don't want to consult with your attorney now? Or any attorney for that matter?"

With a shake of her head, she said, "All these years. I've pretended that my marriage was happy. To my friends. To my family. Even to myself. What I want to do now. More than anything. Is to tell the truth to someone. Finally."

"When you knew me. In Merrymount. I was happy. At that time, I didn't realize how happy. When you're young you don't think about it. At home, there was a lot of love. And you just assume it goes on like that forever.

"My father. The two of us. We had a marvelous friendship. I can still remember what it felt like to be near him. Like nothing could hurt me. He always encouraged me. He always praised me to the skies. I would have done anything for him.

"When I went with Jim. I saw. I thought I saw a lot of my dad's good qualities. Jim was very polite. And considerate. A little stiff. But, it seemed to me, he was just about the best-looking guy I knew.

"Back then, I thought Jim's parents were strange. You always got the feeling they didn't like you because they never said anything. Jim's father, he has a temper too. The only time you see any enthusiasm is when he's mad at you. I used to wonder how Jim turned out so different. But very soon. After our marriage. I saw. My God. I saw he was exactly the same. That was the surprise of my life. This person who sat in front of our television. Or at his account books. For hour after hour. And didn't smile and didn't talk. And I kept waiting for him to snap out of it. But there was nothing to snap out of. That *was* Jim. That was my husband.

"I had to laugh when the police asked if Jim had a girlfriend. If I did it because he had a girlfriend. If he did. That would have been a hopeful sign. The pattern for our sex life was set at about the first week we were married. If he wanted sex he'd say, 'Let's do it.' Saying 'Let's do it.' That was his idea of foreplay. But then, the sex didn't last much longer.

"And I was so stupid. For years I thought it was like this for everyone. And when finally I'd read a little bit. And talked to my girlfriends. I started wondering about all these, you know, orgasms everyone was having all over the place. I wondered if I'd been doing something wrong. Because at first I thought it must be my fault.

"But, you know, it wasn't me. It wasn't even sex. There's something inside most people. A capacity, a need for others. Except with Jim. With Jim there was nothing.

"I remember when my mom and dad died. Within months of each other. He never comforted us. Even standing at the graves. He never held me or the children. He wasn't trying to be cruel. It's just. It never occurred to him that we might need a little human warmth. What we needed he didn't have to give.

"I never told Jim all these things I'm telling you. It wouldn't have been helpful. He couldn't take criticism. But he knew how I felt. And I guess. Over the years. He got to resent me. What was a sort of indifference. Hostility started creeping in. And he got into this habit, always tearing me down. Blaming me. For everything.

"Like last year. The big fight. He went into a rage. Because his hammer was misplaced. He accused me of letting the kids lose the hammer. I tried to explain. With kids. Those things happen. You can't watch them every minute. But he wouldn't listen. It had to be my fault. I had to admit it was my fault.

"A few days later we found his hammer in the backyard. Near the porch. Where he'd been using it. So, you see, he'd left the hammer out there himself.

"But it was still my fault. Because, he said, he'd asked me to buy him a bigger toolbox. And if I'd bought the toolbox. Then, he could have carried the hammer in it. It wouldn't have been left outside. So, it was my fault still.

"I wasn't able to argue with him. He knew all the tricks. Somehow, no matter how blameless I was. I'd begin to wonder if maybe I hadn't done something awful. I wasn't good at family fights. I had no experience. And my opinion of myself. It started to get lower and lower."

She stopped for a moment, composing herself with a slow, deep breath. "I don't believe in divorce. Or at least I didn't use to. Divorce is a defeat. Giving up. I had a father. I wanted my kids to have a father. So. I kept pretending that someday we would be happy. That Jim really loved us. Only he wasn't so good at expressing it."

She looked directly at Jack. "The problem is. There comes a time when you can't pretend anymore. When the truth just beats down on you so hard you can't ignore it.

"I told the police about the incident at the market. When Jim left me stranded. Because Jim is a busy, busy man. He just forgot me. Like you'd forget your keys or your laundry.

And while I was standing there. Waiting. I realized I was worse off than a servant. Because he wouldn't have forgotten a servant. Servants are treated politely. They get paid. At some point, they go home to people who care about them. And right then, I resolved that we had to have this out. That I couldn't go on, living this way.

"But by the next night. I was still trying to talk to Jim. Because he'd been finding one excuse after another not to talk to me. I put the kids to bed. And I stood at his office door. And I asked him to please talk. He finally agreed. He told me to wait while he got a drink. I thought, Good. We're going to get this settled. Finally.

"I stood in the office, waiting. And I noticed, on the desk. The gun was on it. For some reason. I still don't know why. He had the gun in there. I never liked the idea of a gun in the house. But he bought it. Or got it. From somewhere. After our ten-speeds were stolen from the shed. Usually, it's kept locked in my jewelry box in the closet. For safety's sake. But he'd left it in plain sight. Where any of the kids could find it. And I knew. Come morning. That would be my fault too.

"So, I'm standing there. Waiting again. And he's in the kitchen. I can hear him in the kitchen. Getting his coat from the closet. And his keys. And when I hear him go out. Go out the door. So many things rush into my head. Something snaps.

"I've tried to remember picking up the gun. I can't. All I remember is me coming on the porch. The thing in my hand. Not knowing how it worked. Or if it *would* work. But thinking. Even if it didn't work. Just the attempt. It would change my life. I might go to jail. But that didn't worry me. I felt like I'd been in jail. And if he took the gun and killed me. I was prepared for that too."

She lowered her head and said nothing for several moments. Neither Jack nor his secretary stirred.

"I tell . . . tell you this. So you can stop the investigation. There's no more need. Dragging this on. Which only makes it more difficult for my children. You can stop bothering people in the town with questions. Because now you know the whole story. Complete."

Her voice grew tight. "I'm sorry for what I did. Jim didn't deserve it. He treated me badly. But that was my fault. Because I let him do it." Trembling, she gripped the arms of the chair, somehow managing not to break down.

"My life is ruined. The people I never wanted to hurt are hurt the most. I'm ashamed to face my kids. I keep seeing them, terrified, confused. I see them in my imagination. The doctor gave me medication to take. But I see them, crying, like a bad dream that comes whether you're asleep or awake.

"At night, I wonder if somewhere my mom and dad know what's happened to me. I pray to God they don't. Because it would hurt them terribly." She sobbed. "They wanted my life to be happy."

8

IN the days that followed, the prosecutor picked at Georgine Goodfellow's story. He noted that while she was often emotional, the statement proceeded in a logical, even chronological fashion, climaxing with the murder.

He could find no obvious contradictions or misstatements. And yet, that absence of confusion or oversight unsettled him. Georgine's visit had the earmarks of a performance, something carefully thought out beforehand, if not rehearsed.

Of course, even if her statement was rehearsed, it did not necessarily follow that it was in any way false.

Jack could feel sympathy for the woman, sure. She was lovely, her dark eyes entrancing, her story moving. But he could not forget that James Goodfellow had never given his side of the story. And never would.

Jack played the tape for both Detective Sullivan and Sergeant Silva. "See," Sullivan said. "That answers your problem with no locks on the closet. They kept the gun locked in a jewelry box."

"Yeah," Jack replied. "It's kind of convenient she mentioned that. But then, her friend Mary Antonino must have told her I was asking about the gun, where it was kept."

"Come on, Jack. She's admitted to it twice. Let's wrap this up."

Sergeant Silva impassively listened to the tape. "Well," he said. "I never heard all this about their marriage."

"You don't believe it?"

"It just goes to show you. Even with their good friends. Family. People can hide the truth."

No one caught a detail that intrigued the prosecutor above all others. Twice, Georgine Goodfellow had asked that the investigation be ended. She made a point of it. And Jack Meehan wondered why.

"Did I wake you?" asked State Police Detective Lyle Sullivan.

"I'm in bed." Jack whispered into the phone. "But I wasn't sleeping." He sat up and turned away from Rose.

"You go to bed early," Sullivan chortled. "That'll keep you out of trouble, boy. Do you know how much crime there'd be if everyone went to bed at nine o'clock? I know if I did I'd still be a happily married man." Sullivan sounded a bit tipsy. "The reason I'm calling. I've had something on my desk all day. And I couldn't get ahold of you at your office."

"I snuck out to do some Christmas shopping."

"Yeah, well, I've got information. I knew you'd want to hear it. Because. Frankly. It doesn't make any sense to me."

"What's that, Lyle?"

"You keep going on about the gun. The gun in the Goodfellow case. The gun and the closet. Where did the gun come from? Frankly, I can't see the point. But, anyway, I decided, just because there is that question about the gun. I decided to have ballistics people check it out against recent homicides."

"And?"

"And hold on to your hat. I don't know exactly what it

means. If it means anything. But. The same gun was used six months ago to kill a burglar named Grover Durham."

Jack lowered the phone.

"Are you there?" Sullivan asked. "Hello?"

"There's no mistake about this?"

"No way. We had pristine slugs from both homicides. A perfect match. Twins."

Jack shook his head.

"This Durham thing is unsolved, by the way. One shot to the heart. At close range. Found in his own car. Parked off Sea Drive. Which is where the kids go for the submarine races, in case you don't know. He had money in his glove box. Money on his person. We thought it might have been a contract killing of some kind. He could have been shot elsewhere. Not in the vehicle. Also had a broken neck."

"This is a guy with a record?" Jack questioned.

"Breaking and entering and larceny. Nine total arrests. Three convictions. Twenty-eight years old. City address. No family we could find."

"Well." Jack took a deep breath. "What possible connection could there be between the Goodfellows and a guy like that?"

"There isn't any, as far as I can see."

"This happened when? Last summer, right?"

"July the fifteenth."

Jack thought aloud. "Mrs. Goodfellow claims her husband obtained the gun over a year ago. So . . . Hmmm. That leaves two possibilities. At least two. Either the Goodfellows. One or both of them. They were involved in this earlier killing. Or Georgine Goodfellow is lying about the gun."

"Or she was just mistaken," Sullivan suggested. "After all, it wasn't her gun. It was her husband's. No reason she should know when it was purchased."

"But, Lyle —"

"My guess is. James Goodfellow wanted a gun. He didn't want to bother with a permit. He bought the gun from person or persons unknown. On the black market. And they stuck him with a bloodied weapon."

"What do we know about this Durham?" Jack was annoyed at Sullivan's eagerness to downplay the new information.

"Durham. A small-timer. What we know is basically what I just told you."

"Who handled his murder?"

"Local detectives, mainly. They got nowhere."

"Lyle, do you suppose. In the morning. You could start gathering information on Durham? And his murder. Anything you can dig up. Anything."

A long silence followed.

"Lyle?"

"I don't see the point."

"That's okay. Just do it for me. Humor me."

Detective Lieutenant Sullivan believed that the Goodfellow case was solved. He did not believe in *looking* for complications.

When Jack began reexamining James Goodfellow's financial records, he discovered an interesting thing. Goodfellow held nearly $400,000 in cash, stocks, and equity. But, in checking his tax declarations, Jack could not find the source for all this wealth. Furthermore, much of the cash and stocks seemed of very recent origin.

Jack was no accountant, but experience and instinct told him that this money might be linked to the murder.

He called Sergeant Silva. "Have you heard anything about a connection between the Goodfellows and some sort of illegal activity? Like drugs. Or fencing stolen property. Or anything."

"Well, I'll tell you, Mr. Meehan. I've been asking questions, like you wanted. The neighbors again. People in Goodfellow's office. And I haven't heard word one about anything out of line with them two. Not word one."

Jack explained, in detail, what he'd learned about Grover Durham and the Goodfellows' finances. He asked the veteran policeman to "poke around. I don't know what exactly we're looking for, Tony. Just . . . you know, I got a feeling the gun is a key. If we can find out where it came from. I think it'll go a long way to tying up all the loose ends on this one. I'm thinking that maybe, maybe somebody else is involved. Somebody who doesn't belong. Somebody who has money and access to a gun.''

In his office at home, Jack listened repeatedly to Georgine Goodfellow's latest statements. He listened so often that the words seemed to blur and he heard only the music of her voice, at times so soft and tremulous that the volume had to be adjusted. In this was an intriguing quality at odds with her apparent shyness. Jack hadn't even been conscious of it while they were together. He wondered if Georgine realized how sexy she sounded.

"Would you stop this investigation?" Georgine had asked. "All this snooping around to the neighbors and so on? I keep seeing poor Sergeant Silva on my street, going door to door like the Avon lady."

Jack replayed this remark several times. He concentrated on the inflection in her voice, the rhythm, the underlying tension.

What did the neighbors know?

After the holidays, Jack Meehan went to Harwood and Apple Acres, visiting each house on Wampanoag Road. Most people merely repeated what they'd already told Sergeant Silva. "We didn't see or hear anything until the police came down the street."

When Jack asked about the Goodfellows, the answer was invariably the same. "It's terrible. They seemed nice. Of course, we didn't know them that well."

Donald Garritt, the neighbor who had called the police the night of the murder, spoke in the precise language of a high-tech engineer.

"I heard the noise. What sounded like a series of shots. What sounded like six rounds, approximately. But as I looked over I couldn't see anyone or any movement. And I began to think I hadn't heard anything more than kids' firecrackers. In fact, I was about to return to my reading when I noticed the Goodfellows' front door wide open. On a very chilly night, it was wide open. So, when I called the police, I told them I heard suspicious noises. And that there seemed to be something out of place at the Goodfellow house."

"And the police arrived in about twenty minutes?" Jack asked.

"It was more like twenty-five. Between the time I called and the time the cruiser came down the street."

Jack came to the end of the road, discouraged and eager for the warmth of his car. In bitter cold, his efforts had uncovered nothing new. He studied the Goodfellow home, the station wagon in the driveway. He wished she would come out on the porch or appear at the window. He wanted just another look at her.

He sensed she was inside, watching him. The investigation continuing before her eyes. Was she growing desperate? What was she trying to hide?

At the bottom of the street was a trail through the woods, and Jack decided to follow it a little way. There, the black earth was pounded flat, indicating a lot of foot traffic.

Hands in his pockets, he emerged after about thirty feet. In this older section of the development, the homes were modest Capes, built close together. He went to the nearest one, rang the bell, but got no answer. More wasted time. He was turning to hurry back to his car when an old man waved at him from a nearby porch. "They're not home."

Woodrow Otis retreated as the stranger approached.

"I'm with the district attorney's office." Jack Meehan showed his identification. "Could I have a word?"

"Don't ever let strangers in here." Otis scrambled inside, shut the door, and slid on the chain lock before reopening it a crack. Jack passed his ID in to what was now just a slice of face.

"These days you can't be too careful." Otis consulted Jack's photo ID while keeping a wary eye on the original. "Not with what goes on in the world."

"If it'll make you feel better, telephone my office. They'll vouch for me. Then maybe we can talk inside. It's cold out here."

50

"Last month, an old couple, they were both slaughtered in their beds. Over there by Cobb's Corner. And yonder." He pointed. "A fella was murdered by his own wife. A few yards from where we stand. That was two months ago. A man can't be too careful."

Jack grimaced. The old bastard wasn't going to invite him inside. He curled his freezing hands in his pockets and turned away from the wind. Otis introduced himself in a gush of words. "I am over eighty years old. I might have fought in four wars. But I didn't fight in any. That's how I got to be this old. I live here. Live here with my niece and her husband. Who would like nothing better than to throw me out. Ship me off to some flophouse. Which is what they're planning. Don't think I don't know it."

"Did you happen to know the Goodfellows?" Jack began.

"No."

"You know who they are? James Goodfellow? The man murdered over —"

"I know who you mean," the old man grunted.

"Maybe you remember the night he was killed. Seeing something unusual that night. Anything. October the twenty-seventh."

"Can't help you."

"Think carefully." Jack bounced on his toes to keep the blood circulating. "October twenty-seventh. A Tuesday night. Cold, clear night."

"When it gets dark I go up to my room and watch the television. I keep out of their way when they come home. I'm not giving them any excuse to pack me off."

"So, you didn't see anything?"

"Not at night I didn't."

Jack gave a brusque thank-you, turning just as the old man said, "I see a lot of things. I look out on these woods. Sometimes, in the afternoon, I sit at that window there. You'd be surprised what you see just looking at the woods."

Jack glanced at the woods across the street. "Like what?"

"Like kids. Going in there with liquor. Young kids too. Some of them look about ten years old. And the older ones go in there too, only they bring their girlfriends. I've seen people dump their trash in the woods. Right across the street here. They miss the collection. So they pull over there. And they think the woods, they think it's a good dump."

"Thank you, Mr. Otis."

"And I'll tell you another thing. One of those women over on Wampanoag Road has got a fancy man comes calling afternoons every so often."

Jack moved back to the door. "Come again?"

"In a little foreign car. Parks it right across the road there. And he disappears into the woods. I don't know who he thinks he's fooling."

"What . . . How long has this been going on?" Jack's eyes narrowed.

"All summer. All fall."

"When was the last time you saw him?"

"Haven't seen him for a while. Of course, I was three weeks in the hospital with the high blood pressure. But I'm much better now. Can't have salt on anything. I was never a big eater. But I like a little salt. On vegetables and things —"

"Mr. Otis, have you seen this man since October, the end of October? October twenty-seventh?"

"Couldn't say for sure. Not to the day. But I haven't seen him lately. I'll tell you that."

Jack had his notebook out, pen in hand. Surprisingly, he no longer felt cold.

"Would you have any idea of the make of this car. A foreign car, you say?"

"Right."

"Well?"

"Well, it was foreign, like I say. And black. Color black." The old man rubbed his chin. "The name on it was Porsche." He spelled it. "That's foreign. But I don't know where they make it. Germany or Italy, I'd guess."

"He went down that path. Could you say where he went after that?"

"I could if I could see through trees."

"Could you describe this man," Jack smiled, "in a little more detail?"

"What?"

"More description. The driver. What did he look like?"

"A description? Why didn't you say so? He was. Mostly well dressed. Nice coats. Not tall. With dark hair. I never saw him up close, so I couldn't tell you what his face looks like. He walked like a young man. Not fat. But not thin either."

"Anything else?" Jack asked.

"Ain't that enough?"

"That's fine, Mr. Otis. That's very helpful."

"Well —"

"I might. Someone will call on you again. In the meantime, try and remember any details you can about this man in the Porsche."

"Don't you want the license number?"

"Huh?"

"The tag number. Off his car. Do you want it?"

Jack grinned at his luck. "You remember it?"

"Easy. C-A-C One. I got suspicious with him parked out there all day, so I went and wrote his number down. Once I write a number down, I never forget it."

Departing, Jack said, "Thanks again, Mr. Otis. And I want to keep in touch. So, if your niece does ask you to leave. Give me a call. I can put you in with the right agencies."

"Let her try to throw me out. It's my house."

Retracing his steps on the same path frequented by the man in the Porsche, Jack emerged from the woods at a point only a few feet from the Goodfellow property.

The prosecutor wondered at his own lack of perception. The reason Georgine had tried to stop the investigation, and the missing element in her confession, was staring him in the face.

An accomplice. Georgine Goodfellow had not killed alone.

9

WALTER MINAS HAMPARIAN went to mass on weekdays now. He lived in a condo along the river, a pretty place, landscaped with grassy rises and trees. But he didn't sleep late anymore, didn't even want to. Some mornings, he would sit in the darkened kitchen, elbows on the slick Formica table, waiting for the sun to come up. The idea of electric lights in the morning depressed him.

One day, out of boredom, he walked to Saint Mary's for six o'clock mass. In the back of the crumbling basement church, he followed the liturgy closely, responding to the priest as well as he could. Though he missed the Latin, he enjoyed the service, the cadence of the prayers, the ringing of the communion bells, traditional ceremonies that took him back to his childhood.

Thereafter, whenever he woke early, Walter went to church. Margie, his wife, would have been pleased. At one time, he had loathed these pews, fidgeting in them like a child. Now he found them restful, havens for dreaming where the many hard things he had seen in his life seemed very far away.

Walter left Saint Mary's and drove north to his daughter's house. Janice poured coffee, while he sat with Justin, his three-year-old grandson. "What's doing today, Dad?"

"Working for Kenny today." He winked. "Sleuthing."

"You won't be doing anything too exciting, I hope."

Walt smiled. "The things I do. They barely keep me awake."

Walt's friend Ken Sweeney, a retired city detective, had started a small security business. Mainly servicing high-tech firms, business was thriving. From time to time, a little job opened up for a plodding but honest ex-cop like Walt Hamparian.

The work was far from glamorous, and could even be distasteful. Walt's last assignment had him sitting outside a warehouse all night, spying on Sweeney's own security guards.

"Have you thought about what I said?" Janice asked.

"What you said?"

"About Mrs. Walsh down the street."

Walt grimaced and took a sip of black coffee.

"Come on, Dad. I'm just asking you to meet her."

"You're asking me. Does that mean I have a choice?"

Janice smiled. "It'll be fun."

Retirement weighed on Walt. He spent too much time alone. Occasional jobs lifted his spirits, and it was possible that this Mrs. Walsh might work the same trick.

"This car, Walt. Been checked over twice." Bob Orsino, the service representative, rapped on the hood. "There's not a damn thing wrong with it."

"So, what do I tell them?"

"Just tell them it sounds funny. That's all you have to say. The engine. Tell them the engine makes odd noises." Bob grinned. "We're calling it the Trojan Rabbit."

Walt unbuttoned his coat. Though it was the middle of January, all traces of snow were gone. The temperature in the parking lot of Volkswagen of America, Regional Corporate Office, was over fifty degrees.

"So," Orsino continued. "It's your car. And there are papers in the glove box that say so."

Walt's real car was a full-sized Cadillac. The Rabbit cramped and constricted him like a shirt two sizes too small.

"We've been very careful, Walt. These people are not stupid. The work I've done. Checking repair orders. Collecting coded parts. So far, they've covered all their tracks."

"Maybe they're innocent."

"I hope to God they are. But. The car business isn't like years ago. You got a lemon and you were stuck with it. Today, we warranty everything. Some parts are warranted for two years. If the cigarette lighter doesn't work. We fix it. Or we replace it. Which is great for the customer."

"But a big temptation for the dealer," Walt nodded.

"Exactly. Now, Parkside Porsche-Volkswagen, they do a heavy volume of business. And over the past three years, those guys have filed an awful lot of claims on warranty. Between us, VW isn't making much money selling cars to Parkside. And I've been catching hell about it."

"Well," Walt asked, "why don't you just stop selling to them?"

"It's not that simple. In the first place, we'd lose that area as a market. In the second, if those guys are ripping us off, I've got to know. That's my job." He paused. "I don't enjoy getting people in trouble. Sending, maybe sending some guy with a family to jail. But you can't just let them steal from you. Steal you blind and you do nothing about it."

On the road, Walt liked the car even less than he had in the lot. Everything in it seemed to be made of plastic. Once, pulling alongside a dump truck, he found himself looking up at the trucker's tires. Nonetheless, he remained fairly confident about the job. After all, he'd worked undercover before.

"My daughter," Walt explained to the service manager at Parkside Porsche-Volkswagen. "She says it makes a noise. The engine. A grinding noise."

The man took the keys and hopped in. "Let's take a listen." The car started with one turn of the key.

"She says you can't hear it when it's idling," Walt explained. "You got to be moving."

"I see." They were in the vast maintenance hanger. On the floor were rows of lifts and a backlog of several cars. From the ceiling came snakelike wires, hoses, and cables.

"I don't hear anything, sir." The service manager climbed out to watch the engine as it worked. "Maybe, when the mechanics come back from lunch. I can have them take a closer look at it. If you want to wait. It could be something simple."

"Let's hope." Walt crossed his fingers.

"What do you know about cars, Mr. Hamparian?"

"How to drive them."

The service manager smiled. "Well, you say this noise comes only when the car is moving. That could be transmission trouble."

"Expensive?"

"Afraid so."

Behind the service desk was a plastic sign. RICHARD K. RIPLER, SERVICE MANAGER. Beneath it, Ripler flipped through a loose-leaf notebook.

"As I understand it," Walt said. "Whatever the problem. Even though my daughter bought this car somewhere else. It should be covered by the warranty. In other words, you guys will fix it for nothing."

"Volkswagen pays for the repairs. As long as she's followed the maintenance program and no one has abused the car."

"I'm sure no one has."

Walt sat in the waiting room for nearly an hour. Each time he peeked into the workshop, the little car was sitting exactly where he'd parked it. The mechanics seemed busy with other projects.

At one point, as Walt thumbed through car brochures, a busy young man in an elegant suit burst in. "Waiting for a salesman?" He slapped his hands together.

"Er, no. My car. It's in the shop."

"Any problems? Complaints?"

"Well," Walt said, "I just got here."

"Fine." The man hurried off as abruptly as he'd arrived, and Walt recognized him as Charles A. Carver, president of Parkside Porsche-Volkswagen.

"I'm afraid we're going to have to keep it, Mr. Hamparian." Service manager Ripler arrived moments later, his coat on.

"Oh?" Walt stood.

"Seems to be the transmission. Just what we were afraid of. It may take a day or two just to get the right parts."

Walt grimaced.

"Do you have transportation home, Mr. Hamparian? I'm on my way out, myself. I could give you a lift to the bus stop."

"Fine. I would appreciate that."

Richard Ripler's backseat was a mess of spare parts. He drove a late-model Pontiac, very well cared for, and the clutter seemed a bit incongruous.

Of course, spare parts would figure in any warranty scam. The dealer, claiming he had replaced a faulty carburetor, would need a discarded carburetor to "prove" that the work had been done.

"It doesn't always look that way," Ripler said.

"Excuse me?"

"My backseat. I notice you're looking at my backseat. I've got a '65 Bug in the shop. I'm trying to rehabilitate it with spare parts."

"Bug." Walt grumbled. "I like a big car. A little power. I leave the Bugs and Rabbits to my daughter. My own car is a Caddy."

"You must be a popular fellow at your local gas station."

"Hell, at my age. I can't take it with me." Walt grinned, working hard to ingratiate himself with this fellow, who seemed exceptionally well mannered and polite.

"What sort of work do you do, sir?" Ripler asked.

"I'm retired. I was a patrolman. In the city. Thirty years." Walt had decided to stick to the truth as far as possible.

In a warranty scam, as he understood it, any number of employees might be involved, including mechanics, secretaries, bookkeepers. Certainly, the service manager would have to be in the know. Likewise an active owner. Charles Carver, for example.

Walt studied Ripler carefully. Notwithstanding the stylishly cut winter coat, the tie, the pressed slacks, and the spotless white shirt with a VW logo over the pocket, he had the rough look of a mechanic. And he was self-conscious about his nails. Though manicured, they showed grease underneath.

"So." Ripler stopped at a red light. "You're retired. Why aren't you in Florida?"

"Well, I think about it. Whenever the temperature gets down below freezing. I think about it. If Margie was still alive. We'd probably go to Florida together. She never liked the cold. But now. The only people I'm close to are my daughter and the grandchildren. They're up here."

They stopped at the next intersection, where men, heavy equipment, and a huge hole in the middle of the street had traffic hopelessly snarled.

Walt used the delay for seemingly idle chatter. "Any children yourself, Mr. Ripler?"

"Two boys and a girl."

"It's girls are expensive, as I remember."

"Oh, Jesus, are they ever," he replied. "Ten years old. She's got to have the jeans and the shoes. Whatever the other kids have. She's got to have that. And, of course. The old man." He pointed to himself. "Still hasn't learned to say no."

No doubt Ripler also had a mortgage, dentist bills, Girl Scout dues, and dancing-school tuition. Remembering these expenses, Walt could imagine the part they might play in this business. Those involved in the scam would come to Richard Ripler saying, Keep your mouth shut, take the money, don't rock the boat. And it would be easy for an otherwise decent man to go along. Then they would say, Don't think of getting out now. You're in as deep as the rest of us. You're in and there is no getting out.

"I saw your boss in the waiting room," Walt said.

"My boss?"

"That guy from the TV ads. Carver. Isn't he the boss?"

"He's the boss." Ripler maneuvered past a mountain of brown dirt.

"He's quite a persuasive fellow. On television. I don't like little cars. But listening to him. I want to run down and buy one for myself."

"Yeah," Ripler muttered. "He's persuasive."

Bob Orsino, the Volkswagen service representative, sat at his desk, fingers touching. "I don't trust the police. They're not going to be as careful as we would be. They don't know the situation. They won't have the time or the manpower. I'd like a little more information before calling on the police."

Walter Hamparian, who had just advised Orsino to inform the police, glanced out the window at the threatening clouds rolling in from the west.

"The police," Orsino gestured insistently. "You see, I don't want to call the police. Not until we've got a better idea of what's happening. And, understand, I'm not pals with any of these guys. Far from it. But I don't want the names of innocent people turning up in the papers."

On the desk was the warranty claim for the so-called Trojan Rabbit. While the Parkside dealership had charged VW for replacement of a faulty automatic transmission, the original transmission, secretly coded, was still in the vehicle, untouched.

"Going on the idea that there is wrongdoing," Orsino continued. "Criminality. Well, who is responsible? Which individuals? We don't know. And the minute the police get involved we're going to be fighting that whole dealership. Nobody will talk. They'll have their lawyers, and nobody will talk. That's my worry."

Finally Walt asked. "So. If you don't call the police. Then what?"

"Well, that's why I called you, Walt. Because I was thinking. Where you sort of established a rapport with Ripler, the service manager. Of course, Ripler has to be in on it. But, on the other hand, he's only been working at Parkside two years. So, he probably wasn't in on it at the beginning. You see?"

"No," Walt replied.

"Well, maybe you could sort of talk to Ripler. Feel him out and maybe get him to cooperate with us."

Walt cleared his throat. "Ripler seemed like a decent enough guy, sure. But I was only with him twenty minutes, half an hour."

"But he seemed decent. I've always felt the same thing about him myself."

"Mr. Orsino. I think you underestimate the police and the resources they have for dealing with this sort of thing. I mean, that's their job. There comes a time when you have to call on them. The police."

Orsino wore a dreamy look. He didn't seem to be listening, so Walt tried a different tack. "How about this guy Charles Carver? How about approaching him directly?"

Orsino shook his head. "You can't talk to Carver. At the

best of times you can't. Like a lot of guys from money. He seems friendly and down-to-earth. But if you have to work with him, you get to know he's an arrogant little son of a bitch. You could say he's ruthless. He hates my guts. Well, a lot of people do. People I work with. They don't like me. I know it. It's the nature of my job. Because I've got to be a policeman. Some people, they don't like someone looking over their shoulders. But I don't have to tell you that."

For a long time, neither man spoke. Then Orsino asked, "So, what do you say? Willing to talk to Ripler some more?"

"If that's what you want."

"Just get to know him a little. Be subtle. And if you have the feeling he won't cooperate. Then drop the whole thing. End the conversation and come home. We'll move on to the next step."

"And Carver?"

"Try to stay away from Charles Carver."

In the evening, Walt took Janice's neighbor Peg Walsh to dinner. She did most of the talking, while he pretended to listen. Then, as she grew very animated over something, he realized how completely he had missed female companionship and sharing ideas with someone of his own generation. Slowly, he began to relax, to open up to Peg. And she seemed to be a real find, funny and sweetly sympathetic, as if they'd been longtime friends.

Though he returned home quite late, Walt was still wide awake an hour later. He felt surprised, pleased, and disturbed, all at the same time. Margie would approve, he told himself. Margie would want me to be happy, enjoy life.

Then, why couldn't he be happy without this nagging uneasiness?

He sat in his car in the parking area of Riverside Condominiums, waiting for the light to go out. This was his third visit to Walter Hamparian's home. He had been carefully recording the old man's movements, actually following Hamparian to church one morning.

Snooping after the snoop. It was poetic justice really. And it was as if in studying the person who represented the problem he could find a solution to it.

Sometimes he grew angry, breathing through his teeth. Well, the guy had no right. Holding this threat over his head. I never did anything to you, grandpa.

And what of the people who'd sent Hamparian to interfere in another man's business? I almost feel sorry for those poor bastards. They have no idea what they've gotten hold of, what I might do to them.

Of course, he knew what they expected him to do as the noose tightened. They expected him to lie down and quit. In this situation, anybody else would. Except I'm not like anybody else. Your company agents don't scare me. They just make me mad. They just pump me full of fight.

It was growing cold. He toyed with the idea of turning on the engine for heat. But that might attract attention. Instead, he decided not to mind the cold, to subdue the pain by sheer force of will.

At the right moment, he intended to confront Hamparian, scare him off. The trick was in finding the right way to do this. For example, he could deliver an ultimatum, anonymously, by phone. Or he could be brazen, waiting on the step come morning when the guy opens his front door.

He fantasized about invading Hamparian's condo. He imagined standing over the bed, shaking the headboard until the corporate spy sat up with a scream.

"Good morning, Mr. Hamparian." He would address him in the softest tone. "Now you know. You're not dealing with any ordinary man."

In the early morning, as he drove away, he pictured the comical expression that would spread on Hamparian's face, a look of idiot surprise, of terror. And he nearly laughed aloud.

10

Assistant District Attorney Jack Meehan gagged at the stench of human waste. Breathing in short gasps, as if the air could infect him, he followed the guard down a long, dim corridor past peeling paint and burnt-out bulbs.

Thank God the house of correction in Jack's county, bad as it was, could not match this. Sending people to such a hellhole would keep him awake nights.

Besides the smell, he was struck by the noise and cold. He could hear, beyond the wall, a riot of music and voices. The guard wore two overcoats indoors. Jack kept buttoned up himself.

Accordingly, the prosecutor was not prepared for the administrator's office. Damp with sweat, with his windows open, the acting supervisor sat behind his desk in an unbuttoned shirt. The room smelled of steam, and an ancient radiator hissed and clanged like a runaway locomotive. Jack quickly pulled off his coat.

"Mr. Meehan." The administrator rose. "I'm going to let you use my office. The visiting room. We've got some broken windows in there. This is not the time of year for ocean breezes." He hastily buttoned his shirt. "I wish to Christ I could take some of this heat home with me. My wife. She's got the house so cold. Between this place and my house, it's only a matter of time before I catch pneumonia."

Sitting in the supervisor's chair, the prosecutor waited for the prisoner to appear. Sullivan should be doing this, he thought. In fact, he'd asked the state-police detective several times. "Go down and talk to this guy, Willie Laughlin. See what he knows." Though the veteran investigator always agreed to follow through, he never went.

Sullivan had been only slightly more useful when it came to following up the black Porsche, license CAC-1, which old

Woodrow Otis had spotted in the Goodfellows' neighborhood. The detective had learned that it was registered to Parkside Porsche-Volkswagen, an auto dealership owned by Charles A. Carver.

This was an exciting lead. Though Otis could not positively identify Carver's photo, his description (young, not tall, with dark brown hair) generally fit. Add to this the fact that James Goodfellow had been his bookkeeeper, and Carver had some explaining to do.

Getting him to talk was the problem, and in this Detective Sullivan was no help. "I talked to his secretary," he told the prosecutor. "She says to put any questions on paper and send them through Carver's lawyer."

"That won't do, Lyle. We can't interrogate a piece of paper. He answers questions through his lawyer, we're going to get back ten pages of hieroglyphics."

"Well, what do you want me to do? He won't talk to me."

"Did you at least see him?"

"He wouldn't see me."

"Did you pound on his office door, Lyle? Drop in unexpectedly at his house? You know, there are ways to get people to cooperate."

"Well, I tried the best ways I know. He won't talk to me. And between us, Counselor, I don't see why it's so important that he does. Nothing he can say will change what we already know. That Georgine Goodfellow shot her husband five times. And that she's made a full, free confession."

On his own, Jack had now taken steps to pressure Charles Carver into cooperating with the investigation.

"So this is where they been keeping the heat."

Willie ("Pencil") Laughlin, age twenty-six, swaggered into the supervisor's office, pretending to admire the plaques and photos on the wall. Though he was nearly six feet tall, he weighed only 125 pounds.

"Mr. Laughlin, take a seat."

"Whatever you say, slick." Laughlin slipped into the chair alongside the desk. As Jack introduced himself, the prisoner shifted, fidgeted, could not sit still. He removed his down parka and reached for a stack of mail.

"What is this?" Jack demanded.

"Just checkin. Case there's anything for me."

"Is this what you want to do? Play games?"

"I ain't —"

"I'm a busy man." Jack leaned close. "There's no place on my schedule for assholes."

"Who you calling an asshole? Hey, I didn't come here to be insulted."

"You can leave anytime, my friend."

Dropping the mail, Laughlin leaned back and smirked. His sparse beard could not hide his acne-ravaged skin.

"Let's start again," Jack said. "I want to help you."

"Help me? Right."

"We can help each other, as a matter of fact."

"I got nothing I can do for an assistant D.A. Okay? If I had something, don't you think I would have traded it in before now? You think I like sleeping on the floor?"

"Well, Willie, you wouldn't have to sleep on the floor. You wouldn't have to be here at all. If. If there was somebody could put a good word in with the right people."

He became more attentive.

"You were a friend of Grover Durham," Jack stated.

"Grover?"

Jack leaned forward. "Whatever happened to Grover?"

"Somebody, I don't know. Somebody wasted the poor guy."

"And what do you know about that, Willie?"

"I don't know shit. Honest. I know I didn't do it."

"When was the last time you saw Grover?"

"Hey. Let's get one thing straight here. I don't know what happened to Grover. And besides that, I don't want no part of this. No way."

"All I need." Jack was suddenly inches from Laughlin's ear, his voice barely audible. "Information, Willie. Not courtroom testimony. Just confidential information. Which nobody but me knows where it came from."

Laughlin absently unbuttoned his shirt. "Grover got himself

in some shit. I don't know what. Except it got him killed. And that'll give a dude something to think about. Which is to keep shut."

Jack calmly explained the advantages of cooperating. A federal judge had ruled that the house of correction was overcrowded. Certain inmates would be given early release. Willie could be among the lucky ones. "Out of this shithouse by spring."

Laughlin listened, but still would say nothing.

Jack glanced at his watch. He was due shortly at the district attorney's fund-raiser. The detectives who'd uncovered Willie while investigating the Durham slaying had mentioned Laughlin's weakness for his common-law wife. Perhaps it was time to use this information.

"How's your old lady getting on, Willie?" Jack watched closely for his reaction.

"None of your damn business."

"I guess she's pretty lonely out there. All that time on her hands. Being by herself. Alone."

"My lady, she's cool. Okay? People can talk. That don't mean they know shit about us."

"How many times she been up to see you?"

"Liz don't like this fucked-up place. Okay? Depresses her. I told her, Don't come. *I* fucking told her!"

Jack looked overly sympathetic. "A sad situation. Anytime two people in love are separated. It's not always easy, later on, to pick up where you left off. She's out there. Living on her own. God, I can imagine. It must be hard. I'm a family man myself and I can imagine."

Laughlin scratched his beard while Jack continued to make the case for cooperation. His voice was never insistent, but soft and dreamy, whispering of freedom. "Tell me the last time you saw Grover. Last time you saw him alive. Who's it going to hurt if you tell me that little bit? Talk to me, Willie. Or I'm just going to have to get up and go."

The prisoner's bravado began to wilt. He slumped in his chair. When Jack moved to leave, Willie blurted, "All I can tell you . . . Okay. All I can tell you is. The last time I saw Grover

". . . I, I saw him the day before . . . I was like talking with him one day. And next day. They found him in his car on the beach. But I don't know how he got there. Or who, who . . ."

"Where was he going that night?"

Willie shrugged.

"On a job? Was he on a job?"

"He needed money. He had this house in mind. He'd been watching it a long time."

"Where was it?" Jack demanded.

"I don't know."

"What town?"

"He didn't say," Laughlin insisted.

"Did he tell you anything about it?"

"It looked rich. That's all he'd say. It looked rich."

"Do you know any guys, they maybe had it in for Grover?"

"Not Grover." Laughlin insisted. "I don't know why anybody'd want to do a thing like that to a top guy like Grover. Who never hurt nobody. Who never even carried a gun or a knife or nothing."

"Did Grover ever mention the name Goodfellow? James Goodfellow? Or did you ever hear that name?"

"No."

"Do you know this woman?" Jack showed a photo of Georgine.

"No, but I'd like to," Willie smiled.

"Show a little respect, huh?"

"Sorry."

"How about this guy." The prosecutor displayed a photo of Charles Carver.

Laughlin studied it. "Sure. I seen him on the tube. Selling cars."

"You've never seen him in person?"

"No."

"His name's Charles Carver. Did Grover ever mention that name?"

"No — Well, uh." Laughlin studied Carver's photo more closely. "It's possible."

"What's possible?"

67

Willie's eyes remained fixed on Carver's face. "Maybe Grover mentioned him once. I . . . Maybe I seen those guys together one time. But, you know. I'm a little, you know, hazy."

Jack didn't let the prisoner see his excitement. His voice grew cold. "Don't fuck with me, Willie. I don't like this hazy shit. Hazy. Where I come from, hazy is not cooperation."

Laughlin pursed his lips.

"What do you know about Charles Carver and Grover?" Jack demanded.

"Uh . . . Well, I'm thinking maybe I saw them together once. But —"

"When you saw them together. Where was that?"

"I don't remember. Grover was always hustling shit. He'd go around and see a lot of people. And I'm remembering now that this guy, this guy was definitely one of them."

"And you don't remember where?" Jack was incredulous.

"Okay. Well. All right. Once we went down to a car lot. And I waited outside. While Grover, he went in to talk to the guy. This dude Carver. I saw them through the window. Showroom window. Talking."

"About what?"

"About what? I don't know."

"What did Grover say? He must have told you something. He must have given you a reason why he was going to see this guy."

"Well, maybe, but —"

"What did he say?"

"I, uh, I don't remember." Laughlin looked pained. Jack glared. "Honest, I'm trying to be helpful. But it was a long time ago. Almost a year ago."

For the next twenty minutes, the prosecutor pressed for details. Laughlin was not good at details. Though this link between murder-victim Durham and the owner of the auto dealership was an intriguing possibility, Jack had to wonder if Willie Laughlin had invented it. The man wants a story. Give him a story.

"One more thing, Willie. Did you ever know Grover to steal

cars? Or to deal with people who stole cars? Maybe it was just parts, parts of cars."

"Grover did one thing. Housebreaks. He like specialized."

Jack stood.

"So, I told you everything I know. Now, when am I getting out?" Steam hissed. The prisoner wiped sweat from his face.

Jack threw on his coat. "The thing is, Willie. A guy like you. A guy who goes around passing bad checks. Can I trust a guy like that? I think we'll wait a bit and see how high your story bounces."

In fact, Willie Laughlin's tale smacked of something improvised. And yet, Jack wanted to believe it because it fit so well. Charles Carver was a name that kept coming up. Prior to the murder, his car had been seen regularly in the Goodfellows' neighborhood. James Goodfellow had kept his books.

Was Charles Carver involved with Georgine? Jack examined the possibility. According to James Goodfellow's employees, the boss often worked at home. And Georgine, after all, was kept busy with three young children. This left precious little time for adultery.

Now, here was Willie Laughlin, making the Carver connection more tantalizing than ever, placing murder-victim Grover Durham and the wealthy car dealer together. If true, Laughlin's story established Charles Carver as a common denominator in two homicides, crimes already linked by the same weapon.

"Rich Flaherty is running hard for reelection as district attorney." The mayor bent to the microphone, grinning as he took a thin, gift-wrapped package and passed it down the table to the district attorney, who proceeded to open it. "And your mayor thinks he could use this . . . road map of the District of Columbia."

Smiling, Flaherty held it high.

Laughter swept the hall.

The prosecutor took a deep breath. The room smelled of tobacco and fried chicken. Thank God. Free air. Driving from the house of correction he'd been unable to get that stink from his nostrils, was afraid that it clung to his clothes.

Jack leaned across the table to Rose. "Flaherty wants to see me later. But there's a band. So, if you can survive the speeches. Afterwards, we can dance."

"We can dance." Rose glowed. She loved dancing and Jack was an exceptional partner. In fact, others often stopped to watch them on the floor. Dancing had become a rare treat, and Rose would make the most of the evening.

District Attorney Rich Flaherty, bounding to the rostrum, looked somehow younger and less vulgar than the man Jack saw at the office. Flaherty began by acknowledging the head table, where pols like the mayor and secretary of state sat with a priest, a minister, and a rabbi; as well as with the money men, reliable contributors like attorney H. Bateman Biddle.

Later, they met in a dimly lit back room, amid stacks of cardboard boxes. In one corner, proving his ability to look dignified anywhere, stood H. Bateman Biddle. Skip, to friends.

Frank Mullins hung back. Rich Flaherty took a place near Biddle. And Jack Meehan became the uneasy focus of attention.

"Skip wanted a word with you, Jack," the district attorney said. "I didn't see any harm in a little exchange of ideas."

"An exchange of ideas?" Jack muttered.

Biddle paused theatrically. Arms folded, he peered at the prosecutor with Brahmin disdain.

"What?" Jack finally asked. "What's this all about?"

"I believe you're responsible for this, Mr. Meehan." The silver-haired attorney produced a letter. Jack recognized it as the one he'd recently sent to Charles Carver, urging him to consent to an interview and threatening to call him before the grand jury if he did not. "While those proceedings are secret," he'd written, "even the summons can lead to unpleasant publicity."

Jack smiled uneasily. "I gather you represent Charles Carver."

"You bet your life, I do."

This complicated the prosecutor's job. Attorney Biddle was the district attorney's friend and supporter. Biddle's nephew held a work-study job in the office. Of course, no one would expect favoritism for Biddle's clients. Or anything of the sort. But this complicated the prosecutor's job.

"Where did you get the idea," Biddle squinted, "that my client is uncooperative? That he must be blackmailed into answering questions?"

Jack stole a look at the impassive Richard F. X. Flaherty. "Well. I don't know about blackmail. Let's call it persuasion."

"Let me give you some advice, Counselor. Something I often stress to younger lawyers. The direct approach is always preferred. It may give you some odd satisfaction," he waved the letter, "to harass an honorable citizen like Charles Carver. But it would have been much more effective to simply make an appointment through me."

"The trouble is, I need to speak to Mr. Carver. Not his lawyer."

"And so you would."

"By registered mail, no doubt."

"Let's keep this polite," Rich Flaherty cautioned.

Jack flushed angrily at the rebuke.

"Let me tell you about Charlie Carver," Biddle began. "The sort of man he is. A devoted family man. With roots. Roots in the community. A descendant of the Civil War governor of the commonwealth. Whose friends range from garage mechanics to U.S. senators . . ."

When it began to sound like a courtroom plea, Jack felt compelled to interrupt. "Look, I only care about one thing. Is he going to talk, or what?"

"With counsel present. Certainly. I *would* like to know the nature of the inquiry."

"It concerns the murder of James Goodfellow. Carver's accountant."

For once, Biddle was stopped.

"Your client didn't tell you?" Jack grinned.

Flaherty came to the rescue. "Goodfellow's wife killed him, Skip."

"I see." Biddle nodded. "I see. In that case, if Mr. Carver can offer the district attorney's office any assistance. Well, let me say on his behalf . . . uh. I'm sure he'll be only too happy to cooperate. As I say, make an appointment through me. This sort of thing." He waved the letter with less enthusiasm now. "Totally unnecessary."

"Well." Flaherty rubbed his hands together. "That's settled."

Flaherty and Biddle left together, laughing over something as they reached the hall. Jack remained, staring at Frank Mullins.

"Thanks for the support."

"Hey, don't start on me, Jacko. I had my ass put to the fire on your behalf, just this afternoon. Flaherty wants to know what the Christ is going on with this Goodfellow case. It's taking all your time. You're out chasing people who have nothing to do with anything. I mean, you've got a confession. We know who did it. So, what in hell is holding you up?"

"I know what I'm doing," Jack declared.

"I hope you do."

Astonishing, all the fuss this had created. A modest request to interview Charles Carver. First they balk. Then they sic Bateman Biddle on him. Clearly, Jack had struck a nerve.

11

SUNDAY night was bitter cold. Jack Meehan followed Welton Detective Vito Antonelli into the town's largest park. Police cars were everywhere, on the grass, halfway up the hill. There were so many red-and-blue flashers and squawking radios that Jack was reminded of some sleazy midway. Engines idled, noxious white clouds swirled, and high beams pointed to a wooded spot atop the hill. Most of the state and local police officers collected there, shivering in a silent circle beneath the trees.

"Too many people running around," Jack complained. "Can't we get some organization here?"

"We're doing our best."

Between two trees someone had hung a placard. CRIME SCENE. NO TRESPASSING PER ORDER OF THE WELTON POLICE. Beyond it, the ring of officers parted, discharging a red-nosed priest who seemed grateful to be leaving.

Further on, flashlights zeroed in on the victim, a sight that caught Jack unprepared. He stopped, repelled.

"Something to keep you awake nights," Antonelli said.

The face, drained of color, seemed to have no lips. Worse still, his mouth was wrenched wide open in a horrible, crooked scream, the unnatural expression literally frozen on his face.

"Jesus!" Jack steadied himself, determined to show no weakness before the small-town detective. "Trick or treat?"

"Frozen." Antonelli looked away. "I mean frozen solid. Like a goddamn block of ice. That's how fucking cold it's been."

Husky, gray-haired, rigid, the victim lay on his back, arms bent at the elbows, reaching toward the sky. Traces of crystallized blood could be seen on his face, his hands, and on his black cloth coat. His pant leg was torn and bloody at the knee.

"He put up a fight." Antonelli squatted and pointed. "Dislocated jaw."

A police camera flashed.

"Who is he?" Jack questioned.

"Retired police officer named Walter Hamparian. Lived alone about half a mile from here. Riverside Condominiums. Last time anyone saw him, as near as I can find out, was Thursday night."

The body, bleached even whiter by half a dozen flashlights, looked up at Jack like something not quite of this world.

For a long time the prosecutor stared, unable to think of the questions that needed to be asked.

"He worked part-time for Sweeney Security," Antonelli was saying. "Surveillance jobs."

"Witnesses?"

"None so far. I'm told he occasionally went to six o'clock mass. Like on weekdays even. Saint Mary's. Right down the street. If it did happen on his way to church. Well, it's dark at that hour."

"On his way to church . . ." Shivering, Jack turned away. "God save us."

"There's blood." The detective pointed into the dark, to the sidewalk below. There, a pair of police cars, motors running, flashed blue, then red, then blue. The colors alternately coated the trees. "Starts at the bottom of the hill. There's blood all the way up. Indicating what? Maybe he was trying to run away. Wounds. Uh, looks like stab wounds to me. Multiple."

"What do you think?" Jack looked back at the corpse. "Robbery? They take his wallet?"

"Don't know," Antonelli said. "I wouldn't touch him. With the body in this condition. Who knows? You could bump something and have it snap it off. . . . Well, it could happen."

"I wouldn't want to touch him either," Jack admitted.

How long had Walter Hamparian been here gaping at the sky? In the freezing cold, few had ventured out-of-doors.

"Some jogger found him a couple of hours ago," Antonelli revealed. "One of those lunatics, he's out running when it's fucking forty-below."

A hearse arrived, and two morgue attendants, toting a stretcher, charged up the hill and pushed past police. Despite the crowd, it was quiet. No one talked much. Mostly, people stared at the dead man, keeping their distance, sometimes walking about for a different vantage point.

Jack gave up taking notes. The ink in his pen had frozen. "This guy had a wife? Family?"

"Wife is deceased," the detective said. "He has a daughter. We sent an officer to her house to tell her, you know, what happened."

Better him than me, Jack thought. It suited him fine if the task of prosecuting this crime fell to someone else in the office. One homicide at a time was as much as he could stomach.

"We'll see better in the daylight," Jack said. "You want to put the entire area off-limits tonight. From the sidewalk to the top of the hill. Leave some people here to keep watch. There might still be some physical evidence that hasn't been trampled over."

"My people are doing their best," Antonelli retorted, "under adverse circumstances."

When the attendants covered the victim with a blanket, it was a relief to everyone. The prosecutor pushed his gloved hands deep into his pockets. Jacket zipped to the throat, he wore a hood. Still, as he made his way back to the street, cold seeped in. He counted nine rumbling police cars, state and local, parked all over the hill.

Two young patrolmen approached. Jack stopped them. "Where are you people going?"

"Police business."

"Yeah? Well, I'm the assistant district attorney. And if you've got no duties up there. Then why don't you just stay down here? This isn't a peep show."

At that moment, the stretcher-bearers passed between them. Though the blanket still covered the dead man's face and body, it had fallen away from his hands, which reached out to grasp or fend off the killer, as if the battle had not yet been lost.

Mostly, Bob Orsino looked at the floor. The VW service representative expressed no doubt now. Charles Carver, owner of Parkside Porsche-Volkswagen, had been defrauding the parent company. Orsino cited a three-year pattern of ever-increasing claims on warranty and, more specifically, the claim filed on the so-called Trojan Rabbit.

"What must have happened." Orsino's hands clasped tightly on his lap. "Well. I sent Walter Hamparian to talk to Ripler, the service manager. To feel him out on the idea of cooperating with us. And Walter actually went so far as to telephone Ripler. But. Nothing came of that. Ripler was too scared. And Walter broke off contact without ever even saying straight out who he was and who sent him. Which was the end of Walter's involvement in the case. Or . . . at least. It should have been."

Guilt and anger slowly distorted Orsino's face. "What must have happened. They figured out who Walter was, what he was doing. And it panicked them. Because. After three years. They'd gotten the idea they were safe. They thought they'd never get caught. And Walter panicked them. And they . . . or one of them, killed Walter."

Jack Meehan spoke sympathetically. "Mr. Orsino, I can understand how you feel. But the connection between Parkside and the Hamparian murder. It might seem obvious to you. But in the times we live in. A crime of this sort. It suggests a dozen motives. . . . Well, for example. Ex-policemen often have enemies. Also, you can't eliminate the likelihood that this was one of those apparently motiveless homicides. You know, these so-called psychotics. Finally, there's the most logical possibility. And that's robbery. Because his wallet was taken and found empty in the gutter, about a mile away. The victim alone. Walking. In the dark. It fits the pattern of a series of muggings in the area."

"Those robberies happened two towns away," Orsino protested. "I think they took his wallet to make it look like robbery. Why else did they leave his watch? Walt had a very expensive watch and I'm told they didn't take it. Well, why not?"

"The killer didn't notice it. Or he was scared off by something before he could get it. There are a lot of possibilities here, as I said. And the police have to consider every one of them."

Arms at his side, Orsino drew his fingers into a tight fist. "At first. At first I thought I had no business interfering. Leave it to the professionals. They know what they're doing. But the more I hear. The more I think otherwise. The Welton police went to Charles Carver. He told them he never met Walter. He told them he was in Chicago at the time of the murder. And that's all they wanted to hear. They crossed Carver off their list. And the same goes for Ripler. Who says he was home in bed. And the same is true for everyone at that place."

"I'm sure they haven't crossed anyone off their list, Mr. Orsino."

In fact, Walter Hamparian was the third homicide victim linked to Parkside. By now, several police departments were scrutinizing the dealership, and neither Charles Carver nor his big-time lawyer could stop it. Jack Meehan, meanwhile, was busily collecting information from all the investigations.

Already, the prosecutor had discovered that of twenty full-time Parkside employees only one was known to have a criminal record. Parts driver Paul Barrasso, twenty-six, had been convicted of selling amphetamines to minors some three years before. He'd earned a reduced sentence by turning in his supplier.

"Barrasso," commented one Milham police officer, "he's strictly small-time. In and out of trouble with us since he was eight years old. How he latched on to Parkside is anybody's guess. On the other hand, I wouldn't think he'd have the guts to get mixed up with murder. He's the type, more likely, to rob the corpse." Barrasso's aging grandmother was his less than solid alibi in the Hamparian slaying.

Welton investigators were conceding that Richard Ripler's alibi was not quite foolproof either. The only Parkside employee to have dealt directly with the victim, Ripler had been seen leaving his home for work shortly before 6:30 A.M., the approximate time of the murder. However, the neighbor's recollection was not positive, nor could the time of death be determined beyond doubt.

As for Charles Carver himself, he had indeed been seen in Chicago on the day before and on the afternoon following the murder, which left only the smallest possibility that he had somehow traveled hundreds of miles in between.

And yet, the auto dealer did not behave like a man with nothing to hide. He'd allowed Welton detectives only a brief interrogation. No notes were taken, and Jack doubted that the questions were very penetrating. (Incredibly, the Welton people were convinced that Walter Hamparian had been killed during a robbery!) Significantly, following the murder, Carver had twice canceled interviews with Jack Meehan, despite attorney Biddle's promises.

The prosecutor was increasingly drawn to the theory that the scheme to defraud Volkswagen had evolved into an even darker conspiracy, leading to the murders of Grover Durham, James

Goodfellow, and Walter Hamparian. If Charles Carver was not guilty, he certainly knew more than he was telling.

And fitting in somewhere, somehow, was Georgine Goodfellow.

12

BOB ORSINO stood in the center of the room. Face pale and moist, he seemed to be waiting for something, perhaps an encouraging word from Jack. "Don't blame yourself," the prosecutor obliged. But Orsino winced.

"Exactly what, what caused Walter's death?" he asked.

"Stab wound," Jack replied. "Punctured his heart. Probably would have bled to death in any case. He was stabbed sixteen times."

Orsino looked down. In a nearby office a phone rang, endlessly, irritating. "It wasn't quick then?"

Jack nodded at a copy of the medical examiner's report. "Educated guess is that he was stopped on the sidewalk. By someone. Probably a single assailant. Maybe they exchanged a few words. The killer attacked. Probably with no warning. Stabbing the victim as he stood there. Stabbing him at least once before Hamparian tried to flee. There was blood on the sidewalk. He ran or staggered up the hill, trailing more blood. The victim fell at the top of the hill. He tried to defend himself. He must have fought like hell too. There were slash wounds on his hands. A bite, a human bite mark, believe it or not, on his forearm. Bits of fiber and flesh under his nails. At this point, we believe, the fatal wound was inflicted. He died between six and six-thirty Friday morning. . . . On his way to church."

"Why did he run up the hill?" Orsino asked.

"I don't know."

"Wouldn't he have been more likely to get assistance on the street? A passing car . . . or . . ."

"Could be he thought he could hide in the woods," Jack

78

said. "Could be any reason. I've been doing this work long enough. You get situations where people do things. Under stress. Totally illogical. Totally out of character. And you ask them why. They themselves, they can't tell you why. Civilians have the idea that in a criminal investigation we find a logical explanation for everything. But that rarely happens. There are always things left over. Things that don't fit in anywhere. That don't seem to make a lick of sense."

"A white-collar crime." Orsino stood at the window, which overlooked a brick wall. "It never occurred to me. Never once crossed my mind that this could happen." He toyed with the button of his suit. "Some view you got here."

"Took me five years to get a window." Jack moved quietly for his tape recorder. "I want you to do me a favor, Mr. Orsino. Talk to me about Charles Carver. Whatever you know."

"I don't know all that much. And a lot of what I do know is gossip."

"Gossip too," Jack instructed.

Orsino sat, put on a pair of black-rimmed glasses, and pulled out notes from his own investigation, notes he never once looked at as he spoke.

"Carver has a lot of charm when he's selling cars. But with people who actually deal with him, employees and so forth. He doesn't have many friends. Of course, where he's got all that money. Maybe his friends are rich people. I'm told he runs that dealership as a sort of hobby. He could easily live on what he's got in the bank. Stocks. Trusts and stuff. But he's still a real scrooge. Some of the people he hires. Losers. Because he can get away with paying them next to nothing. He's married. Twice, I think. With one child. He's got a house up here. And he's supposedly got another house in Florida. Palm Beach. Another house on some island somewhere. It was always my impression. Charles Carver. Here's a guy. He's had it all his own way. All his life. He's gotten used to having things his own way. In other words, he's the type, you can't tell him anything."

"And Ripler?" Jack urged. "Tell me about Ripler."

"Ripler. He's older than he looks. He's over forty. The service manager. He's been at Parkside a little over two years. Came from out the western end of the state. Greenfield. Seems like a nice guy. He's always behaved very friendly to me anyway. He's married. Three kids. Lives in Harwood."

"In Harwood?" Jack looked up.

Orsino nodded.

The service representative's information was useful, but Jack would not have a handle on these men until he spoke with them himself. Unfortunately, the only Parkside employees who'd agreed to cooperate with the police had nothing to tell. Ripler, like Carver, was hiding behind his lawyer.

Paul Barrasso, interestingly, had gone to some lengths in refusing to speak with investigators. On the day Welton detectives visited the dealership, Barrasso had locked himself inside the parts wagon.

Charles Carver drove his Porsche to the showroom door. His stylish leather coat was the most imposing thing about him. With longish hair, he looked younger than thirty-two.

Stopping his car on the Parkside lot, Jack Meehan chased Carver into the showroom. Here, he was intercepted by no fewer than three smiling salesmen. "Can I help you?" These men were not easily dismissed.

"Sorry, but I'm not buying today. Really, I'm not. I've, I've got to see . . . someone. Out back." Jack glimpsed Carver slipping into a back room. Pushing past the salesmen, the prosecutor followed him to the repair shop. But in this sprawling, noisy area crammed with cars, Charles Carver had vanished.

"I'm looking for Mr. Carver." Jack approached the cleanest man he saw.

"He was just by here a minute ago." Service Manager Richard Ripler came out from behind his desk. "Uh . . . let me go see if he's in the Parts Department."

Also behind Ripler's desk, perched on a small stool, was a young man with a particularly raunchy skin magazine. He stared at Jack, first in surprise; then his eyes narrowed. "Hey you!" he exclaimed. "You're a cop. Right?"

"No. Sorry. They're never around when you need them, are they?" Jack recognized Paul Barrasso from his police photo.

"Don't tell me you're not a cop. Why else were you sitting out front all morning? We're not stupid here, you know." The man gnawed at his lip. He was slovenly, with dirty trousers, grease-stained hands, dark, uncombed hair, and the beginnings of a beer belly. "I keep telling you guys. You guys stop pestering me. I'm going to call my lawyer if you don't stop pestering me!"

"Whatever you're hiding, friend. It's safe from me."

"I ain't hiding nothing!" Shouting, Barrasso rose from his stool. "And I'm not answering questions. So don't bother to ask any. I know my rights. And I don't got to say one word if I don't want to. And I don't."

"You could've fooled me." Jack managed a cocky smile. Yet, he had the feeling of being threatened. Work in the shop had stopped. It seemed everyone was watching him. It was all a bit bizarre.

"Mr. Carver isn't in the shop." Service Manager Ripler had returned. "He was here a minute ago. But, I don't know where he went. Try his office out by the showroom."

Parkside Porsche-Volkswagen had the relaxed atmosphere of an IRS auditor's waiting room. The receptionist was as tense as the others. "You can't see Mr. Carver without an appointment. I'm sorry, but those are the rules."

"The problem is," Jack maintained, "whenever I make an appointment Mr. Carver is always unexpectedly called away. I thought maybe this time I'd surprise him."

Jack handed over his card. The receptionist carried it into Carver's office and returned moments later. "Mr. Carver is unable to see you at this time."

"Suppose we talk through the door. He doesn't have to actually see me."

"Mr. Carver says to call his lawyer."

"Hey, Charles Carver!" Jack shouted.
The receptionist gasped.

Frank Mullins led the way to the Muffin House, grumbling as Jack Meehan explained why the apparently clear-cut case of James Goodfellow's death wasn't clear at all, how it had branched out in odd directions.

"The murder weapon ties Grover Durham and James Goodfellow together," Jack explained. "Goodfellow kept the books for Charles Carver. At the same time, by the way, there was an unexplained increase, a significant increase in Goodfellow's bank balance. Carver's Porsche was seen near Goodfellow's home all summer and fall. According to Willie Laughlin, Carver also knew Grover Durham. Finally, Walter Hamparian is murdered while investigating a warranty fraud at Parkside. So. We have three murders, plus various felonies. And the single link appears to be Charles Carver."

"And what does Carver say about all this?" Mullins asked.

"Well, you were there when Biddle promised Carver would talk to me. I'm still waiting. At first, he put me off. Then, today, I got a registered letter from Biddle. His client will not answer questions under any circumstances. Any attempts to ask questions will be followed by a suit for harassment. And he gives the excuse that he can't talk because he's being investigated in this warranty fraud."

"You've decided Carver is involved in warranty fraud?" Frank asked.

"Not just me. The Milham police. And Volkswagen of America are looking into it."

"He's got stocks," Frank mused. "All that shit. How much is he worth?"

"Lots. He's got, he's got houses everywhere."

"Well then, why should he bother? Warranty fraud. I mean, why take the risk?"

"If you don't think you're going to get caught. There's no risk."

"But," Frank scoffed, "such a piddling amount."

"Look. With some guys. There's no bag of money too small

they won't stoop to pick it up. And from what I've heard. Carver is one of those guys."

The first assistant winced. "You know, Jack. I remember your report about this guy in the house of correction. What's his name? Laughlin. This guy who puts Charles Carver and Grover Durham together. I remember you said, for all you knew, he was bullshitting you all the way. Would have said anything to get himself out of the can."

"Sure, but that was before —"

"And when, when Hamparian was killed. Wasn't Charles Carver out of state somewhere?"

"Chicago, yeah."

Mullins grimaced. "And there's no doubt who killed James Goodfellow. I mean, we have Georgine's confession."

Jack could not answer.

"It seems to me," the first assistant concluded, "you've got three unrelated homicides with coincidental ties to Charles Carver. In fact, all your suspicions stem from the premise that Carver was bilking VW on warranties. Something no one has proved. Something that might not even be true. But even if it is. I mean, you're talking about a penny-ante white-collar crime that's going to bring a suspended sentence at best. And for this they murder people? Come on, Jack. That's not even logical."

At a break in the traffic, Mullins dashed across the street, with Jack right behind him. Frank had made a good point. For a moment, Jack wondered if he might not be right.

"Now wait a minute." The prosecutor suddenly caught up. "It doesn't have to be logical."

"What?"

"See. It only has to be logical in the mind of the killer. And you take a guy like Charles Carver. Somebody who tries to build an image of himself as Mr. Solid Citizen. Dedicated to propriety."

"This sounds more like you," Mullins muttered.

"A guy like that. Looking at a felony charge. He might panic. He might overreact. Do something illogical."

"This is Charles Carver you're talking about? The knife-wielding millionaire?"

Jack gestured earnestly. "Consider the sort of people Carver associates with. The sort of scumbums he hires at his dealership. I mean, even the guy who drives his parts truck has a record. Now. Accept for argument's sake that Carver did business with Grover Durham. A known felon. Well, that raises the possibility that he uses people like that. Criminal types. He associates with criminals and he uses them."

"Uses them for what?"

But Jack couldn't say. His theory was half-formed. Convinced that Parkside Porsche-Volkswagen was at the center of a murderous conspiracy, he could not offer a particle of real evidence suggesting which individuals were involved or how. Likewise, he believed that Georgine Goodfellow had not killed her husband unaided. In support of his belief, he could cite only her gentle temperament, the mystery of the twice-used gun, and the sightings of Charles Carver's Porsche in her neighborhood.

Nonetheless, if he lacked the facts to prove a link between these crimes, Jack trusted that a connection would be found. Something, or someone, would break. He resolved to be patient. To wait.

Within a week, his patience paid off.

13

"You know what? I don't think I should even be here."

The voice, from darkness, would not stay in one place. Jack Meehan grew annoyed, then wary, chasing Paul Barrasso, who evidently wanted to be coaxed into talking.

"This was your idea," Jack said. "You called me. Remember?"

It was probably a mistake to be here alone with him. At the same time, he couldn't waste an opportunity like this. Jack's only precaution had been to leave a sealed envelope on his desk, explaining where he was going, who he was going to see. Well, that seemed adequate. Until he got here and realized how dark and isolated the meeting place was.

Milham police officers had laughed at the idea of Paul Barrasso as a killer. They hadn't heard him threatening Jack Meehan that day at the dealership. Nor had the parts driver explained his abrupt about-face, except to say, "Things look different now."

"Just what's going down at your place?" Jack asked.

"Well. I don't know. Really. I don't know a lot about it."

"Here's what I know, Mr. Barrasso. Here's what I know. I know someone has been cheating on warranties. I know that. Can't prove it yet. But it's only a matter of time before the indictments come down."

"Yeah." Barrasso ducked behind the shuttered refreshment stand. Jack followed. The beach was deserted; the lake, by moonlight, a mix of water and ice. But Barrasso was forever looking about as if he expected something to come out of the forest and pounce on him.

Jack tried to envision this garage rat paired with Georgine. Beauty and the beast. It was inconceivable.

"What we need to hear," Jack continued. "Who's involved in this scam? Who gets the payoffs?"

"Not me."

"You drive the parts wagon. With a warranty fraud. They need spare parts."

"Hey, look. I pick up the parts it don't mean I know what they're for. I ain't no mechanic."

"Remember the investigator from VW who was killed in Welton?"

"What? Yeah. So."

"Here's your problem, Paul. When the day comes. When the Welton Police start making arrests on that one. How are you going to convince them you're not involved? This is homicide, remember. And you're the only guy over there with a felony record."

Barrasso looked thoughtful, as though he'd already considered this problem.

Jack came closer. "Cops aren't any different than other people. They want things easy. Once they get a load of you. Oh, boy. That's easy. The junkie did it."

"I ain't no junkie. And I didn't do anything."

"Talk to me, Paul. Be smart. Separate yourself from those guys. You don't want to go where those guys are headed."

"I . . . I don't know. Like. What's in it for me?"

"You'll get consideration, Paul. And let's face it. You're going to need consideration. Somebody in that shop committed murder. Maybe there's a bunch of people involved. Don't get fished up in the net."

The parts driver did not argue the premise, as though conceding that someone from Parkside had indeed murdered Walter Hamparian. The prosecutor sensed that Barrasso knew more than a little about it.

"You be my informant, Paul. I can take care of you. I know you're afraid. You're afraid and you need somebody to look out for you. Somebody to confide in. Well, I'm right here."

Barrasso moved away, then back again. Back and forth. "All I know is. That place . . . it's fucking crazy."

"You mean Parkside?"

After a long pause, Barrasso said, "Shut off the tape recorder."

"Sure. I'll do that if you want. But. I think the tape recorder is your best protection." Jack pulled the device from his pocket and held it up. "Look. You see it's on. The 'record' button is depressed. The little wheels are turning. And now I'm repeating on tape what I told you when we started this conversation. Nothing you say will be used or can be used against you in court. I'm treating you as a confidential informant. I won't reveal your name to anyone without permission."

The witness thrust his hands into his pockets. Breath came like steam. "I . . ."

"What's there to be afraid of?"

"That place is crazy. He's killed people before this, you know. I don't want him to kill me. He would kill me. If he knew I was here with you . . ."

"Who?"

"Look. You didn't get any of this from me. But. Even before. There were stories. Rumors. About him killing people. Someone. Something from years ago. I heard he even had clippings, newspaper stories about it. Which, I thought that was bullshit. Until he showed them to me. Like he was proud, you know? He does these things. Then, he's got to tell somebody. Because he's so proud of himself. Strange. But, I'll tell you. He's got people in there scared shitless." Barrasso turned away and then turned back. "You know Carver."

"Carver?"

"Carver's fucking unreal. He's got so goddamn much money. And there's no rip-off he won't try. He clips VW whenever the repair shop is down and he's got mechanics on their butts. Like. One day I come back to the shop late. Everybody's gone home. I hear this god-awful noise. So's I go into the shop. There's Carver in his suit, standing there. And Ripler in this car. Foot to the floor. Fumes everywhere. And the engine screaming. When they see me. The two of them get all flustered. Ripler starts explaining real fast. How the engine's shot. But it ain't shot bad enough to be covered by the warranty. Though it should be covered. So, these two beauties. They're going to fix it so it is. I just nod. You know. Whatever you say, boss."

Barrasso walked back and forth again. "Carver. Carver wants everyone scared. That's how he got himself into all this shit. Have you talked to my boss? You should talk to Mr. Carver. Look him over real good. All the shit he's into."

"For instance?"

"You should know. How about withholding? Sales tax? Did you check to see how much money Carver owes the fucking government? Creditors? People got to beg him for their money. He don't pay out one cent until they send the goddamn sheriff to his door. He cheats customers. Inflates repair bills. Turns back odometers. Sells demos for new. That's just the way he does business. If I did that I'd be back in the county jail. But I don't have lots of money. You guys. You don't seem so interested in crooks when they're also rich. You're a great bunch of detectives, you guys are. Like. You say I'm the only man in the shop with a record. You've got this guy committed something like first-degree murder. First-fucking-degree murder. Look him up. For cry eye. How about *his* record?"

Jack was nodding, trying not to seem too astounded by these revelations, wondering how much was true. "What do you know about the murder of James Goodfellow?"

"Who? Oh, the bookkeeper. I heard his wife did it."

"There hasn't been any talk? Maybe about Carver and —"

Suddenly, Barrasso leaned forward and grabbed Jack's wrist. He had a surprisingly firm grip. Jack recoiled at the feel of callused, dry skin.

"You better understand. This is all confidential stuff I just told you."

"Of course."

"My name. My name better not get out."

"I promise —"

"If my name gets out. If people find out I talked to you. Well. Jesus, they just better not. Hear me? They just better not."

Jack Meehan believed he was driving aimlessly. Lost in thought, trying to evaluate what Barrasso had told him, he was surprised to find himself in Harwood.

Georgine Goodfellow's neighborhood was not far away, and Jack felt an impulse to drive down her street. He wanted to sit outside her house and watch the big front window.

What is Georgine doing now? Is she walking to the window? Is she staring out on the street? What is she wearing? Is her face tense and frightened? Or are her eyes unblinking and confident?

The prosecutor sat at the top of Wampanoag Road, wondering if the sight of Georgine could help answer his questions about these brutal killings. And yet, the urge to drive down her street was so strong he did not completely understand it.

At home, the prosecutor listened to the Paul Barrasso tape again and again, just as he'd listened to Georgine Goodfellow's statements. Jack was not brilliant. He'd earned his degree by attending evening classes at an obscure university. Ivy League types, the Bateman Biddles, could sometimes intimidate him.

But Jack compensated with hard work. On an important investigation, he did extensive interviews with witnesses and took voluminous notes. On his own time, he rewrote the notes, and organized them in a workbook. Over the course of an investigation and trial, he might rewrite this several times.

"It helps me to remember," he once explained to Rose. "In court. You don't want to be confused over even the smallest detail. And you never, ever want to be surprised."

Occasionally, the constant review paid unexpected dividends, and Jack gradually came to see what had not been apparent earlier. On paper, for example, small inconsistencies and unresponsive answers raised questions of their own. On tape, meaning could be gleaned from tones of voice, inflections, and the slightest hesitations. Jack could sometimes sense where evasions had been made.

Taking off her coat, Rose came into the office.

"Late night?" Jack looked up.

"Oh, that class never lets out on time."

"How was it?"

She shrugged. "Not very interesting. I've got to stick it out. I need the credits." She glanced at the sprawl of notes and documents on the desk. "You look like you've really been at it tonight." She touched a photo of Georgine. Provided by the elder Goodfellows, it showed the accused woman at her best, smiling with joy and energy, eyes wide and shining. Standing on a porch, with one hand on the rail, Georgine pointed slyly to the photographer.

"I've never seen one case take up so much of your time," Rose said. "It seems like every spare minute —"

"Well, I wouldn't spend the time if I didn't think it was important." Jack slipped the photo into a folder.

After Rose left the office, Jack realized he'd been a bit short with her. It was the same old problem, actually. They barely saw each other. Eating supper alone, resentments built up.

In the past, they'd talked out their difficulties. All this work takes us toward an easy future. A cottage on the Cape. Vacations in the islands. Jack himself had often predicted that good times were not far off.

From the darkened bedroom at the end of the hall he heard Rose calling good-naturedly, "Get in here."

He looked up. "What?"

"Get in here and do your duty."

"I did that an hour ago."

"I wasn't here an hour ago." She pretended alarm.

"Well, yeah. I got tired of waiting and I had to go ahead without you."

"What?"

"Oh Rose," he muttered to himself, "sometimes I worry about us."

"What'd you say?"

He wanted to say that these are dangerous times. We've got to be careful. People with the best intentions, in perfect circumstances, can drift apart.

"Come to bed," she sang out. "I'll show you some quality time."

Jack was already putting his papers away.

He was cold to the bone. Creeping through someone's yard, he'd squatted behind an evergreen across from John Meehan's house. He studied the second-floor window where John's head could be glimpsed, probably bent over a desk. Mostly, there was nothing to see, but he could imagine the desk piled with notes, photos, lab reports.

God Almighty! What he wouldn't give to get in there, to rummage through it all. How much did the prosecutor know?

Suddenly, Meehan stood. Oh God, if he'd been a marksman with a rifle he could have finished the investigation right there. One shot. *Pow!* Glass shatters. Man drops from view. Case closed. He wondered why prosecutors weren't murdered more often.

Joints aching, he knew he couldn't remain here another minute. Yet he did, waiting until Meehan put out the light. As he crossed the street, he worked out the stiffness in his legs and back.

He paced off Meehan's front yard. At the side of the house, he made note of the basement windows. Old and cracked. A firm push could pop them open.

In the backyard he stepped over a child's tricycle and climbed the porch. Satisfied that none of the neighbors had a good view of this door, he studied the lock. Inside, the illuminated clock shone dimly on two tiny winter coats hung on the wall. Below these, he made out kids' boots and mittens.

It all felt wrong. Just wrong. In an instant, he decided that there was a better time and place. And he hurried away.

Just as he'd waited for Walter Hamparian, he now waited out successive evenings in a car parked in the sprawling lot behind the district attorney's office. Pretending to read the newspaper, he was ever watchful, noticing, for example, when the county employees quit the building and where John Meehan parked his car.

After a week, he knew the schedule. Meehan would appear at five o'clock, or a few minutes earlier; often with coworkers, laughing, smiling, careless, once even walking right past him in the car. The prosecutor was so punctual you had to wonder if he was one of those clock-watchers, a guy who never works late, never gets caught in deserted parking lots.

But the killer was patient, willing to wait, to return night after night. If he could manage it here, in their own backyard. Jesus, what a fright it would give them all! They'd think a long time before they came bothering him again.

John Meehan's punctuality did not last. During the second week the killer looked up from his newspaper, startled to find the parking lot almost empty and Meehan's car sitting by itself in a far corner. All the lights in the building were out, save one over the alley.

Working late after all, John? Well, I can guess what you're doing up there.

Folding away the paper, taking measured breaths, the killer remained quite still. It was essential to be cool, purposeful.

The parking lot was shut off from the main street and was bounded by other darkened office buildings. The killer began to realize that he would never have a better chance.

At around 6:30 P.M., the assistant district attorney, an active, fit-looking man, left the building. Of course, Meehan had been up there trying to unravel these murders. According to Biddle the guy didn't think about anything else. In fact, everything would be going smoothly now, except for this one pain-in-the-ass prosecutor.

The killer was startled at the quiet. The loudest sound was his own rythmic breathing and Meehan's shoes *click-clicking* on the pavement as he passed.

Out of the car, leaving the door slightly ajar. The killer's hand went to his pocket and the weapon. He fell in behind his target. And experienced a moment of near panic as Meehan seemed about to turn. What the hell do you want? Meehan would say, looking him right in the eye.

But it didn't happen. Meehan went on, head down, deep in thought.

Sorry it has to be this way, John. If you'd only left me alone. All I ever wanted was peace.

Anger doubled his resolve. They must think I'm a fool. I'm just going to sit back and let it happen?

God, that Meehan is big. Well, it doesn't matter. Because you can come up from behind. And before the guy knows what's happening. It goes in. It goes in like nothing.

If you do it right. This time. If you do it right. Meehan drops. Onto the tar. Finished. With little fuss or pain. And you walk on as if nothing had occurred.

In the half dark, just a few paces behind now. Trying to get a breath. Stomach a little queasy. Ignore all that. So much can go wrong. A car might pull into the parking lot, the glare of high beams catching the glint of the blade just as the body crumples. Don't think of it. Be bold! Take a chance.

Getting closer. Size up Meehan's walk. Broad back measured by a tan overcoat. Smell of deodorant or hair tonic. Still doesn't notice me. Doesn't know death is here.

Grip the weapon. Ready to thrust. Underhand. Into the back.

Smashing through. And if the man turns. The man won't turn. But if the man does turn. Do it! Do it anyway. Inches from his face. Eye to eye. Gut him.

He stopped in shock.

Meehan walked on, oblivious.

Just a few feet away, a man and a woman in the front seat of their car pulled from an embrace and looked directly at him. They were not happy at being seen.

Change directions, but keep walking. Thank God the knife is still in my pocket. No panic. Be casual. Thank Christ I saw them.

And what if he hadn't? Suppose he'd killed Meehan in front of two witnesses? He could hear the screaming. Careless! Stupid! Oh, he'd been so close to disaster. His hands shook. He hurried back to his car as John Meehan drove away, ignorant of his deliverance.

Well, maybe it was a blessing, a sign. He admitted now what he'd refused to face before. Killing an assistant D.A. would be an awful mistake, a tactical blunder. Like killing a cop. Far from frightening them off. They'd never leave it alone. Track you to the ends of the earth. God, his hands wouldn't steady. God.

The cool was gone. That night with Grover Durham. Lying abed. Hearing noises downstairs. A break-in! So smooth, so calm. His pulse never varied. He got his gun and did what had to be done.

Why was he such a wreck tonight?

He felt the weight of the knife and began to compose himself. Incredibly sharp. Leaves a wound like a paper cut, only deep. He imagined that the severed blood vessels held together for a while, out of habit. Until pressure forced blood everywhere. Which was probably why poor Hamparian had taken so long to die.

He could still feel his revulsion at the first blow. He could close his eyes and relive the whole thing. He hadn't imagined it would be like that. An unworldly, horrible sensation. After the initial resistance, he was stabbing . . . nothing. A spirit. Water was the answer. People are mostly water.

And, as he had tried to recover from the shock, staring at the dripping weapon. Suddenly. The son of a bitch. Hamparian got up.

The killer pursued, ferociously, slashing, jabbing. But the old guy moved so far. So fast. You wouldn't think he had such strength. The chase was exhausting. The killer's throat burned in the cold. But he kept lashing out, chopping. Until the blade caught hard bones, jarring his hand. A whirl of churning limbs and spitting blood. Loud gasps for breath.

The man finally dropped for the second and last time.

Even then, Hamparian reached out. A dead man yanked furiously at the killer's hair, pummeled his face, jabbed his gut with a stick. Why wouldn't Walter just quit?

Finish the bastard! He stabbed and slashed with one hand. Formed a fist with the other. Swinging. *Crack!* Breaking the old guy's jaw, then falling on top of him, exhausted.

At the peak of the hill, he finally rose up and rammed the blade home. As deeply as possible. To be sure. While sounds he could never forget came from the dying man's throat.

14

"Let me get this straight." Sergeant Tony Silva wheeled his car onto the highway. "You've got an informant who says Georgine Goodfellow didn't kill her husband?"

"No, no." Jack Meehan chose his words with care. "This guy. The informant. He's connected to the auto dealership where Goodfellow did the books. And it seems Goodfellow isn't the only homicide victim to have a connection with that place. Our informant fingered a guy, the owner of the dealership, a guy named Charles Carver, who he figures is capable of murder. Well, all I'm saying. Since the victim was Carver's employee. Since Carver's car was often seen in the area. We ought to look into whether this Charles Carver had anything to do with the death of James Goodfellow."

"This is Charles Carver, the guy on TV?"

"The same," Jack nodded.

"And your informant. He's reliable?"

"Well," Jack admitted, "as a matter of fact, we had a problem with some of what he said. Uh, he told us Carver had a record. That he'd been involved or convicted in a previous murder. But, the thing is. Carver doesn't have a record. Of any kind."

"Maybe you should go back and talk to this informant some more."

"Yeah," Jack agreed. "I intend to do that."

Tony concentrated on the road, squinting. "So. Why do we want to see Mrs. Goodfellow? There can't be any doubts about the case against her. It's an airtight case."

"That's not the point, Tony. You take the fact that people doing business with a certain auto dealership start getting murdered all over the county. That's got to be more than a coincidence. Add to that another oddity. Two homicides and one gun. At a time when Mrs. Goodfellow claims the gun was in her husband's possession, it was used to kill this character, Grover Durham. Well, how does she explain that? I'd like to hear her explain that."

"But she's confessed —"

"Her confession isn't good enough. Not for me. I keep getting the feeling. The more I listen to that confession. I think she's leaving something out. She's protecting somebody."

Jack watched the trees fly past, bare branches. "I've listened to her statement so many times . . ." He felt the cold window with his fingertips. The whole truth. How close could he get to it? He sensed only that he hadn't gotten very near.

"You know what I want, Tony? I want to hear her say . . . I shot my husband."

"She already did say it. She said it on the tape."

"Did she?"

Jack Meehan and Tony Silva were on Georgine Goodfellow's front porch for more than ten minutes, ringing the bell and pounding on the door.

"She's not home," Tony said.

"She's home. Her car's here." He peered in the narrow window at the top of the door, but saw only indistinct shadows.

"She don't want to talk to us. Why should she talk to us?"

"You watch. I bet she does."

Jack knocked again. It was warmer now, the world was defrosting to something brown and damp. In the woods at the end of the street, a layer of fog rose from the ground.

When they'd given up, had actually walked down the porch stairs, a noise came from inside. "There she is." Jack skipped back.

Shielding her face with one open palm, blinking, head down, Georgine no longer resembled the smartly dressed woman who'd visited Jack's office. In a bathrobe, hair disheveled, pale, she resembled the police mug shot taken immediately after the murder. Seeing her this way, Jack was momentarily speechless.

"What?" she demanded.

"Uh, Mrs. Goodfellow. I think you'll remember me. John, well, Jack Meehan. The assistant district attorney. Sergeant Silva and I wondered if we might have a word with you."

"What?"

"If we could come in?" Jack pulled out his Sony lest there be any claims of impropriety. She stared at it.

"I don't know about this."

A whiff of her breath bent Jack slightly backward. "You don't have to talk with us. And I should remind you that anything you say can be used against you in a court of law. And, if you do decide to speak with us. You're entitled to have your lawyer present. Do you understand all that?"

She was motionless, leaning on the doorframe, seemingly asleep on her feet. Jack, worried that she might suddenly yank the door shut, stuck his foot against it.

"Do you understand, Mrs. Goodfellow?"

"You told me all that . . . before . . . last time. I'm not stupid, you know."

"I have to be sure," Jack said. "Each time. That you understand your rights."

"I understand my rights. Okay? And I have the right to remain silent. Silent. The right to be treated like shit. And the right to remain silent."

Jack cleared his throat. She still hadn't exactly looked at him. "We have a few questions. Serious questions. About the statement you gave at my office. And the statement you gave to Sergeant Silva. I know you're very anxious that we get the truth down. For the record. And we wondered if you could hear us out. Just, just listen to our questions. And answer them if you like. And if you'd rather not answer them, any of them. Fine. We won't pressure you. If you want us to leave at any point. Just say so. And we'll leave."

She never actually invited them in, but shuffled off down the hall, leaving the door open. Jack and Sergeant Silva looked at each other, then followed.

Jack was impressed with the Goodfellow's dream house. The furniture included genuine antiques and artful reproductions. The rugs were Persian. In the foyer, a small oil portrait of Georgine emphasized her dark eyes and blue-black hair. The fireplace brickwork occupied half of the living room wall.

Yet, scattered everywhere were dishes, coffee cups, and beer cans. A slice of pizza on an end table showed traces of green mold. The place smelled bad. Clothes, papers, and magazines littered the floor. The blinds were drawn, the television was playing "General Hospital" at high volume.

Moving slowly, Georgine turned off the set. Next, she cleared the newspapers and the remains of a sandwich from overstuffed chairs on either side of the hearth. "Please sit down."

Glancing at the floor, she was startled by the accumulated litter, as if she'd never noticed it before. She began, suddenly, to clean it up.

"Can we help?" Jack placed his recorder on the coffee table.

"No, thank you." When she bent for a dish, her bathrobe fell away and one full, fair breast peeked into view. Without much hurry, she straightened and adjusted the garment, giving

Jack a stare that was oddly defiant. He looked away, blushing.

Georgine's burst of energy had little effect. She soon surveyed the mess and sighed. "Why am I doing this? I don't care what you think of me."

Unconsciously, she toyed with the wedding ring on her finger.

"Would you like to get dressed?" Jack suggested. "Maybe you'd feel more comfortable."

Georgine gnawed on her lip. "I'll get dressed," she said, as if it was her own idea.

Once her bedroom door had closed, Sergeant Silva whispered, "Phew. What a pigsty."

Jack leapt up and began gathering papers and magazines, stacking them neatly on the hearth. Quickly, he pulled the blinds, parted the curtains, and opened a window.

"Lady drunk," Tony muttered. "Disgusting."

"Well, are you going to just sit there are are you going to help me?"

And they ferried a load of glasses and cups to the kitchen, which was a shambles, the sink piled with dirty dishes.

When Georgine returned twenty minutes later, the living room was still not clean, but it was somewhat neater. She looked about uneasily, embarrassed.

Georgine herself had undergone a small transformation. Hair combed, she wore black designer jeans and a white cotton blouse that complimented her figure. Jack tried not to stare. Her complexion was rosier now, her eyes awake.

"Why don't we sit down?" Jack said.

She went slowly, cautiously to the couch.

"When was the last time you got out of here?" Jack sounded friendly.

"I don't get out enough. That's what Betsy keeps telling me. I should get out. Get out more."

"You should. Stuck indoors all day. That's not healthy."

"Not healthy." She nodded. "Not healthy. I'm touched, Mr. Meehan. Your concern for my health." She looked straight ahead. "I'm going to get a drink. Does anyone else want a drink? I'm going to have one."

"None for me," Jack said.

"I'm on duty," Tony said.

"Well, I'm going to have one. Is that okay? I'm only having a beer. Okay?"

"Entirely up to you, Mrs. Goodfellow."

From the kitchen came the sound of a pan bouncing on the floor, then the rinsing of a glass. Finally, the pop of a beer can. Tony looked at Jack and shook his head.

Returning, she sat erect and took ladylike sips of the beer. She sipped nonstop.

"Mrs. Goodfellow." Jack's voice was toneless. "Are you aware that your husband's gun. The weapon you used . . . you know. Are you aware that it was once used to kill an ex-convict named Grover Durham?"

She put down the glass and looked nervously from one man to the other.

"Are you aware of that, Mrs. Goodfellow?"

"No."

"Does the name, is the name familiar to you? Grover Durham?"

"No. Should it be? I didn't — Is that — Are you accusing me . . . of something?"

"Not at all."

"It was Jim's gun. I don't know, I don't know where he got it. If it was used . . . what it was used for. I don't know."

"Of course," Jack said, "he had the gun for a short time. Relatively. Less than a year, you said."

"About a year."

"And you're sure of that? No doubts at all?"

"My husband owned the gun for one year. No longer. And whatever it was used for before that, I don't know."

"The problem is, Mrs. Goodfellow. The murder of Grover Durham took place over the summer. This past summer. While the gun was supposedly in your husband's possession. In this house."

She took a quick swallow of beer. "I thought . . . I thought this questioning. I thought it would be about my statement."

"What we're asking," Jack said, "is related to your statement. It's related to your statement about the gun. You told us

99

your husband obtained the gun a year ago, for protection. Well. Imagine our surprise. We find out it was used during the summer to kill someone."

She studied her beer.

"Mrs. Goodfellow?"

"You . . . you don't like me much, Mr. Meehan."

"Personally? I, I don't dislike you. No."

"The reason I say." She took another swallow. "I say it. Because I've been cooperative, cooperating with you. Talking. And I asked only that you be fair. And you have me, charged me with first-degree murder. When you know it wasn't. It wasn't anything planned. Except, now you come. You want me to admit to another murder." She was close to tears.

"No, ma'am. I've only come for some sort of explanation."

"Explanation? How can I explain when the gun, it didn't belong to me. And you know that, Mr. Meehan. You know that!"

She looked straight ahead, composing herself. "It doesn't matter. I'm resigned. That you'll do what you want. To me. Men take me from this jail to that. And I tell myself. This is the rest of my life. Men deciding where I should go. What I did wrong. What's to happen to me." She took a gulp, draining the beer. Suddenly, she reached out. "My glass is empty."

Tony went to the kitchen for a refill. Georgine stood unsteadily as if to follow, perhaps to get away from the questions. And Jack began to wonder why she had even allowed them in. For that matter, why had she confessed? He could think of only one reason.

Sitting again, she leaned forward, put her open hands together, and looked down. "The kitchen's a mess."

"I wouldn't worry about it."

"It doesn't matter, this house. I have to sell it. I can't get at his money, you know. I have to sell the house. But, they, they won't give you what it's worth. When they know you have to sell. I'm going to sell the station wagon too. Get a little car, a used car. There's an advantage to my situation, you see. You don't have to think ahead very far." She gave Jack a self-pitying smile that caused him to look away.

"Jim's car. That mostly belonged to the bank. I got a few

dollars for it. He had a lot of life insurance. But I'm not eligible for that. Maybe the kids can get it. Betsy wrote their grandfather. Told him to get the kids a lawyer to look after their interests."

"They're nice, cute kids," Jack said.

At last, her eyes opened fully. She came forward to the edge of the couch. "When did you see them?"

"A while ago."

"How did they look?"

"Fine. They were fine. Playing with the animals. At, at their grandfather's house."

It was the first time he'd ever seen Georgine really smile. A spontaneous glow of joy. She rocked back slightly. "I'll bet Nicole. Nicole was in her glory. Did they ask for me? Well, I suppose there's no reason why they should. But they looked okay?"

"They looked fine. And the middle one. Vicki. She looks like you, as a girl. It's almost eerie. She made a deep impression on me when I first saw her. But, at the time, I didn't understand why."

The smile drifted into an expression dreamy and pleasant. What clear, smooth skin, Jack thought. Despite himself, he wanted to touch it, could imagine the tips of his fingers on her cheeks. And when, suddenly, she looked up, it was as if she'd forgotten all her troubles. She gazed warmly at the prosecutor.

Pretending to be unmoved, Jack looked at his recorder. "Don't you visit your kids, Georgine?"

She frowned. "I don't want to."

"But . . . it must be awfully tough on them. Losing father and mother both."

She bit hard on her lip. "No, no. They're going to lose me eventually. Better this way." She looked up at Tony and snatched away the glass of beer. "What are they saying about me in town, Sergeant?"

"What?"

"You know. How I drink. I'm a lush. How I killed my husband. And I don't care about my kids, I dumped my kids. And . . . what else, Sergeant?"

"I haven't heard —"

"You know, Mr. Meehan. I walk into the drugstore and they pull their kids away if I get close. I'm such a horror. A terrible, evil bitch . . . Well." She took a swallow of beer. "Maybe they're right."

"Charles Carver."

"What? Is that a question? Charles Carver. My husband. He was one of my husband's clients."

"Did you ever meet him?"

"A few times. To say hello. He invited us to a party once and wound up selling Jim that car we couldn't afford. Jim said he'd have to do Carver's books for two hundred years just to pay for the thing."

"Did Carver ever come here?" Jack questioned.

"Here? No."

"You're sure?"

"Well, yeah."

"Ever meet a man named Richard Ripler?" Jack watched closely. "Or Paul Barrasso?"

"Not that I recall." She never flinched.

"They both work at Carver's dealership."

"It was Jim's car. He had it serviced. I wasn't allowed to drive it even. So, there's no reason I would know the names of those people."

"Your husband was well off. Took in a lot of money. Over the last few years, especially."

"I should hope so. He worked hard enough."

"Did he ever speak to you about dishonest business practices at Parkside Porsche-Volkswagen?"

"No," she said flatly.

"Did you ever overhear —"

"Jim never talked business at home. Years ago, I tried to show an interest in his work. But, my God, accountants' shoptalk . . ."

"Mrs. Goodfellow, was your husband blackmailing Charles Carver?"

She laughed. "You." Georgine pointed. "These questions. These aren't the right questions. About my statement. You're not so honest as you pretend, Mr. Meehan." She shook her head. "Betsy was right. She said I was crazy to talk to you. She wouldn't want me talking to you now, you know. She says. First off, she says you only care about putting people in jail and making yourself look good. And second, you're a man. And you're like all men. Your idea of a woman is, How can I use her? Men are users. But they can't help it. That's just how they were made." She went back to her glass. "Like Jimmy."

"Still can't forgive him," Jack prodded.

"I guess I hurt him more than he hurt me. And I'm not angry at him. And I don't hate him anymore. I can see now that it was my own fault. I could have left. Years ago. I could have left. I wish I could forgive myself. For not leaving."

Jack spoke softly. "What happened the night your husband was shot?"

"I told you."

"You know, I've listened to both your statements. Listened again and again. And it's like, every time, it's like I missed something. Like there's something you're not telling me."

"Everything I told you," she raised her voice. "Everything I said was true."

"My concern is with what you didn't say."

"If you have specific questions —"

"Who shot your husband?"

She gave him a sideways look.

"Who did the actual shooting? Pulled the trigger?"

"I already told you."

"Oh, these tapes. Sure, you say you killed your husband. You make a point of saying it over and over. But. Something curious. No place do you say the words *I shot him*. It's always *I killed him*. Never *I shot him*. Almost as if, consciously or unconsciously, you avoided saying it."

"Killed. Shot. It's the same."

"It isn't." He pulled a transcript from his pocket and fumbled in vain for the appropriate page. "Even where you talk about the shooting. You describe it. You say this happened. And that happened. But you never say *I* did this. Or *I* did that."

"I'll say it now. I shot him."

"How many times?"

"I don't remember. Six. Five."

"And the last shot. You shot him in the head?"

"In the . . . yes."

"From less than a foot away?" Jack pointed his index finger about eight inches from the woman's forehead. "This close?"

She stared at it. "Yes."

"And you . . . held the gun. He was still alive?"

Her eyes grew wide.

"Isn't that right? He was still alive?"

"I . . . I . . ."

"Did he try to avoid the shot? Did he move?"

She closed her eyes. "I don't remember."

"Or did he lay still and make it easy for you?"

She came abruptly to her feet. The empty glass fell. They heard it roll across the floor. "Leave me alone, leave me alone." She moved away, turning her back on both men.

"I . . ." Jack stood. "If you'd like a minute to, to catch your breath . . ."

"You promised to leave if I asked. Well, I'm asking now."

"Don't do this, Georgine."

She gave a violent shake.

Tony tugged at Jack's sleeve. Time to go.

"It's stupid," Jack argued, retrieving his tape recorder and coat. "To spend one day longer than you have to in prison is stupid." He cursed himself for pushing too hard. Dozens of questions still begged to be answered. "I wish you'd reconsider. I don't know if you're trying to shield somebody, or what, but . . ."

At a distance she followed them out. And though Jack coaxed and stalled, Georgine did not say another word.

"You don't think I was too hard on her?" Jack muttered as they drove back to the police station.

"Too hard?"

"Well, I tried to shake her up. Get her to tell the truth. Which is in her own best interests. But, someone in her situation. Alone in that house day after day. You wonder about her grip on reality. How's she going to react?"

"She seemed better by the time we left," Tony said. "When we got there. Jesus, what a sight."

"What do you think overall? What do you think of her responses to my questions?"

"What do I think? Well . . . To be honest. If you want my opinion. I think you're barking up the wrong tree, Counselor."

Jack straightened the front of his coat, asking, "How do you mean that, Sergeant?"

"I mean, after talking to her. I can believe that woman shot her husband. Just like she says in her confession. Anybody who can live like that. In all that swill."

"You think because she's a lousy housekeeper —"

"I think she's crazy as a bastard," Tony replied. "All that ranting and raving about men. Men are users. To listen to her, she's going to like the woman's reformatory."

"Well, I disagree, Sergeant. She's not crazy. Far from it. Take the way she mixes the lies in with the truth. Mostly she tells the truth. That, what she said about men, how she feels used by men. Well, I can believe it. At the same time, it becomes part of the motive. For the murder of her husband. Another excuse to take her story at face value. Because she's desperate for us to believe she acted alone. She pulled the trigger. With no help, no accomplice."

"Because she did," Tony argued. "She killed her husband. All by herself. And now she's got the guilts. And wants to be punished."

"For someone who wants to be punished, she seems plenty interested in a light sentence. She's still complaining because we've indicted her on murder one."

"But if she didn't do it, Mr. Meehan, why confess at all?"

It was a question, Jack decided, requiring more thought.

Leaving the Harwood police station, Jack Meehan drove aimlessly. He found he could think better on empty country roads, taking routes he did not know, half hoping to lose himself.

Did Georgine Goodfellow have a lover?

She'd told Silva and Sullivan that sex held no interest for

her. And yet, with her eyes and body, she was sexy without even trying. You could almost smell it on her.

Georgine Goodfellow and Charles Andrews Carver. Why had Jack been so timid in exploring this possibility, so reluctant to pair Georgine with anybody?

Carver, working his warranty scam with James Goodfellow, meets the accountant's knockout wife. The man who'd "gotten used to having things his own way" decides he wants Georgine. Lonely, impressed by his wealth, she responds.

Inevitably, James finds out. He vows to blow the whistle on Carver's illegal operation, to take the children from Georgine. For the adulterers, James is a problem that must be eliminated.

Charles pulls the trigger. Georgine pleads guilty to manslaughter and serves a short or suspended sentence. Then they live happily ever after. Except, judging by Georgine, it hadn't gone completely according to plan. With the prospect of a suspended sentence fading, had the man abandoned her?

Jack stopped at a sub shop for supper. Eating a meatball sandwich in his cramped Chevette, he began to realize that Frank Mullins would pick apart this last scenario.

In the first place, little connected Georgine Goodfellow and Charles Carver. It couldn't be proved that they were even acquainted. Sure, the Porsche had been seen in the area, but there might be a dozen explanations for that. And the eccentric Woodrow Otis was not a very reliable witness.

Furthermore, the prosecutor could find no place in his theory for the Durham and Hamparian murders. Almost certainly all three killings, on Charles Carver's doorstep, were closely related. More than likely they stemmed from the warranty scam. Solve one and solve them all.

Jack tried to sort out his impressions of Georgine Goodfellow. She talks and talks. But her face, her hurting eyes, something pleads, Don't believe, Don't believe you've heard it all.

For some reason, Jack remembered what she'd said about her loving relationship with her father. Mr. Bow. Dimly, there was something he knew about this. But it went so far back. He couldn't . . . quite . . . grasp it.

If he put aside her present difficulties, which were enough

to unhinge anyone, the picture Jack had formed of Georgine was of a shy, vulnerable, even sweet-tempered woman. Connecting her to murder weapons, illicit affairs, or any of the shenanigans at Parkside Porsche-Volkswagen seemed like a bad joke.

What haunted him finally was the love and pride she showed at the mere mention of her children. How she spoke a name, *Nicole,* lingering on it, as if she'd been waiting days for the excuse to say it aloud.

15

ON Wampanoag Road, the house looked cold and dead. "Oh, Christ," Jack grunted. The big station wagon sat in the driveway. Why were all the lights off? Perhaps he had gone too far with Georgine.

"What do you want now?" Her voice was muffled.

"Please open up, Mrs. Goodfellow. It's John Meehan again. I'd just like one quick word with you and then I'll be on my way." He leaned close and lowered his voice. "It's pretty important, Georgine."

She pulled the door open a crack.

"I came back to see if you were okay. When we left, you seemed a little upset. I got to worrying. What with the things we talked about, the things I said —"

"I'm fine." The door swung wide open. "As you see."

By porch light, she did look fine. Her eyes clear and bright, she smelled of perfumed soap.

"Are you expecting company?"

"Is there something I can do for you?" she asked.

"You're right. It's none of my business. I was just concerned. See, I was in the neighborhood. Came by and all the lights were off."

"The living room light is on." She pointed.

He walked past her to the living room. Cleaned, it looked

like a different place. Lined up neatly on an end table were four medicine bottles. Pills and capsules were collected in a big pile. He might not have noticed them, except they were beneath the only light in the room.

"I'm cleaning out the medicine cabinet." She stood behind him. "Old prescriptions. Dangerous to keep around."

He nodded. Sweeping up the pills and capsules, Jack marched to the kitchen and washed them down the sink. The kitchen, he was surprised to see, had been cleaned as well.

"You didn't have to do that," she said.

"Like you said. Dangerous to keep around."

She looked at the floor. "Don't judge me. You don't know what I've been through."

She might scream rape now. And, Jesus, would Jack be in a lot of trouble. In fact, it was insane to even be here alone with her. But, oddly, this did not occur to the normally cautious prosecutor until much later.

"Explain this one thing for me and I'll go away. I'll leave." He held out his open hand. "Tell me why you won't see your children."

She shuddered.

"Why won't you see them?"

"Because . . . I told you, for their own good."

"Don't say that," Jack replied. "This is no good for them."

"Seeing me would only confuse them."

"And they're not confused now?"

She closed her eyes.

"You know what I think, Mrs. Goodfellow?" He waited until she looked up at him. "I think maybe you just don't want to see them."

"Yeah, that must be it."

"If you really wanted to see them. Well, they're not far from here. Are they?"

"I'm not going to talk about it."

"You get all sad-eyed when anyone mentions them. That's just an act, right?"

She complained, "It's all been so easy for you, everything —"

"The bottom line is. You just don't give a shit."
"What do you know about it?"
"You're after the house. The money."
"And I thought you'd be fair. Ha!"
"So what if your kids cry themselves to sleep."
"Bastard!"
"It would have been kinder if you'd killed them too."
"Shut up!" She spit the words into Jack's face. Suddenly, inches away, was a Georgine he hadn't seen before, her face distorted by rage, teeth set, lips curled, her complexion as red as blood. Both fists came up quickly.

Shocked, Jack remembered that no one knew he was here. He took a step back and braced himself. But for what? By now she was weeping. "Why?" Tears ran down her face. "Why can't you leave me alone? Don't you think I want to see them?"

"Then do it."

"I can't. I can't because I want him to think I don't care. I want him to think that those children mean nothing to me."

Jack held his breath.

It was some moments before she asked, "Can't you figure it out? You're so smart. You know so much."

"The man who shot your husband? Is that who you mean?"

She tilted her face upward. "He kills people, you see. He doesn't care. He just kills them. Like he killed Jim. He had the gun in his coat. All the time he was talking. Had the gun in his coat pocket. We didn't know he had it. Until . . . The whole thing, it was over in less than a minute. Everything blown apart in less than a minute. And there's no way, no way to fix it up again."

"Are you going to tell me his name, Georgine?"

"He told me not to say anything about him. About his being here. Not one word. He said it was for my own safety. And the safety of my children. See, I have three children. He could kill one. Just to make his point. He's capable. So, so I've done all this. Kept shut. My mouth shut. Stayed away from the kids. Like I didn't care. And I let everyone know. So he'll know too. And I don't have to worry. They'll be safe. They'll be safe."

"Tell me what happened."

"I've told you too much already."

"If it's a question of police protection."

"Don't make me laugh."

"Just tell me who this guy is and I'll have him locked up within the hour," Jack promised.

"Yeah. Until some judge lets him out." Breathing hard, she dropped slowly to one of the kitchen chairs. "I saw him kill my husband. Shooting, shooting. To make sure Jim didn't have a chance. Then . . . He just turned away. Like it was nothing. My husband's, his, the back of his head exploded all over the lawn. And he acted like it was nothing. Took my arm and brought me inside. Sat me right here. Right at this table. He told me. Very calm. He told me what story to tell the police. Said I'd get off easy. He's saying all this like there's no question I'm going to do it. Like people usually do what he asks. I keep nodding. Agreeing. Because I . . ." She began to cry. "I didn't want him to kill me too. All the time. The gun was on the table between us. It's the only thing I could look at. My mouth so dry. I couldn't, couldn't stop shaking. I kept wondering, you know, why is the table moving? Like. Rattling. I, I didn't even know I was doing it myself."

Jack wanted to reach out and comfort her. Instead, he looked away, forcing himself to remain cool, professional. It could be an act. It could be. But if it was, it was a masterpiece. He asked, "Mrs. Goodfellow. Georgine. There's no tape recorder here. No witnesses. Just you and me. And all I want is the name."

"No . . . I, I don't know his name."

"Is it Charles Carver? Or any of the names I've mentioned? Ripler? Barrasso?"

She shook her head. "It was someone. Someone neither of us ever met. Ever saw before."

"I won't send an innocent person to jail. But I can't just take your word for this. Because, frankly, it's a pretty wild story. And if I'm going to believe it. I've got to have proof. Evidence. Give me a description at least."

"No. I can't. I can't say anything."

"We prosecutors have confidential sources," Jack insisted. "It's not a new thing. We're experienced at keeping that sort of arrangement secret."

"No."

"Look, Georgine. Here's my problem. Even if I believe that this man, this unnamed man pulled the trigger. How do I know that you weren't in cahoots with him? That you aren't his, his lover? Or that you didn't hire him to do it? How do I know unless you tell me more?"

"Mr. Meehan, I don't care what you know. Or don't know. Right now I have one aim in my life. To keep my kids safe. Nothing else counts."

"You could go to jail for a long time."

"Well, you know, I don't see any other choice."

"I want you to understand," Jack said. "You're not the only person who'll suffer. We think there's been another murder connected to this case already. A retired policeman named Walter Hamparian. Maybe you read about him. A grandfather. But he didn't look like anyone's grandfather after he'd been stabbed sixteen times."

"I don't want to hear about it."

"That's the third killing connected to this case."

"One of my babies won't be the fourth."

"Tell me why this man killed your husband."

"He didn't say."

"Why didn't he shoot you?"

"I don't know. . . ." She sniffled. "I could only think. Keep him away from my children. I'll do anything you want. But in the name of God, don't touch my children." She stared at the prosecutor as if pleading for his understanding and sympathy. Jack's detached, professional voice caught in his throat.

"Sometimes I wish I died with Jim. You know? This isn't much of a life."

"You don't want to be thinking like that."

"I was going to take those pills today. After you and Sergeant Silva left. But I didn't want to be found with the house that way. I know it sounds ridiculous. But we were so proud of this place. I didn't want everyone saying it was a mess. I didn't want to die like a pig in all that dirt. So, I decided to clean up first. Straighten up. And I worked all afternoon. After you left. And pretty soon. Taking pills. I didn't feel like it anymore. But I don't know why not."

Though Jack had every intention of hurrying back to Rose, he moved reluctantly to his car.

Once inside, he was unable to take his eyes off Georgine's porch light. Of course, he felt real sympathy for her. Anybody would. Nothing wrong in that either. Many of the people he'd sent to jail over the years were pitiable in one way or another. You still did your job because the system, people's safety, depended on it.

He felt sorry for the woman. Which is why he considered the idea of going back inside and explaining himself. I know I sounded, well, at times . . . cruel. I'm not that way. Don't think I'm that way. Sometimes you need to be ruthless to get at the truth.

God, it was exciting just looking at her, her womanly figure, her quivering lower lip.

You don't have to be afraid of me, Georgine. I haven't judged you. I'm in no position to judge anyone. My life hasn't been as easy as you think. I've had to make compromises all along the way. Sometimes, just to get by, you have to do things that are beneath your dignity, that you'd just as soon forget.

For the first time, the prosecutor entertained the possibility that Georgine was entirely innocent. Her story required proofs, of course. But it meshed with findings in the Parkside killings, raising the possibility that James Goodfellow had been murdered because he knew too much about Charles Carver's sleazy dealings. The killer, furthermore, could even have been a contracted hit man.

The prosecutor put his key in the ignition just as the last light went out. Now, he thought he saw her, a faint shadow at the window, watching him. Why didn't he go? Drive away?

Well, he was worried about her. Of course. After finding those pills and hearing her story he had good reason to worry.

Perhaps he'd better check again to be sure she's all right. He won't go inside. He'll merely knock on the door.

I want to be certain you're okay. Are you sure? I could make arrangements. Someone to look in . . . I don't know, something.

The prosecutor shivered. Quickly he buttoned his coat against the cold.

Don't press it, chum. Back to earth. Put your mind on business. Remember that poor son of a bitch lying on the front lawn. Evaluate Georgine's story tomorrow. See if you still feel sorry for her in the daylight. And one other thing. Don't go near her again Ever.

16

"THE lobster special looks good." Jack Meehan held up his menu.

"Yeah, well . . ." Frank Mullins peered impatiently across the crowded restaurant. "They're not going to take our order until the girls get back."

No sooner had the Mullinses and Meehans sat down than Rose and Cathy hurried off to the ladies' room. For Jack, this was a chance to talk a little business, and he waited until just the right moment to say, "Have you, uh. Have you come to a decision?"

"A decision?"

"About, you know, about what we discussed all afternoon. My interview with Georgine Goodfellow."

"I'll say it again, you're going to get yourself in trouble, approaching her like that."

"But the substance. What she said. Have you thought about what she told me?"

Frank snickered. "Hey. First she killed him. Then she didn't. Just another broad can't make up her mind."

"Okay," Jack conceded, "her story has a lot of holes. But there's *something* about it, Frank. And it explains the odd things she's said and done up till now. Like falling all over herself to confess. Then complaining because she isn't charged with manslaughter. It's as if, by pleading guilty, she mainly wants to stop any further investigation."

"Do you suppose it's possible. That she pleaded guilty because she *is* guilty?" The first assistant was smiling. "Come on, Jack. You've heard people recant confessions before. They get close to trial. Close to prison."

"But that's just the point. Because she hasn't recanted anything. Even though she changed her story. Even though she claimed someone else killed her husband. She refuses to say it for the record. She wouldn't let me put it on tape. Wouldn't sign anything. And I gave her every opportunity. In court, under oath, she plans to stick by that original confession."

"I'll bet she does."

"If you'd been there, Frank. If you'd seen the circumstances, the way this all came out. She didn't want to tell me."

"I can hardly believe what I'm hearing, Jack. This is a classic jailhouse alibi. I didn't do it. Some man dropped over and *he* did it. Some one-armed man, no doubt. A few weeks ago you would have laughed at a story like that. But with this Goodfellow thing. It's like you've gotten emotionally involved or something. Emotionally involved and it's affected your judgment. Now, that can happen sometimes, to the best of us."

Jack gave a derisive snort.

"Look, partner. I'm only telling you what the district attorney is telling me. He wants to know why a signed confession isn't enough for you. Why are you still poking around in this Parkside business when, after all these weeks, you haven't found a single witness or a single piece of evidence to connect it to the Goodfellow murder? And besides that, between us, he's wondering why, in the middle of an important election, why a prominent homicide is allowed to drag on and on."

"It's going to take as long as it takes," Jack insisted. "Elections don't enter into it."

Smiling, Frank raised his eyebrows. "Blasphemy." He was only half joking.

"Oh, I had a good time." Rose yawned contentedly on the drive home. "Why don't we do that more often?" She leaned on Jack and smiled up at him. For the first time in a long time her husband had seemed happy and eager to please her. Dancing, he'd been attentive, holding her tight, often pressing his face tenderly against hers.

Cathy Mullins snoozed in the front seat beside Frank. Very drunk, she revived enough to ask, "What's next?"

But they were going home. Both couples had waiting babysitters, charging by the hour.

"Anyway." Frank was enthusiastic as they stopped for a red light. "I heard some good news today." He took a quick peek back, smiling. "Remember the conversation we had a few months back? Jack? Remember we were talking about the district attorney? Going to Congress? Going to Washington?"

"I remember." Jack put his arm around Rose.

"Remember how I said you wouldn't be left in the lurch. I said Uncle Flaherty would take care of you. Remember I said that?"

"What's this?" Rose asked.

"Talk," Jack replied. "Just talk."

"Well. Just talk." Frank nodded. "I brought that up. Maybe I had a reason. Maybe I had something in mind. Like the arena. The new arena they're building downtown."

"You've lost me," Jack said.

"The new arena will be built and administered by the arena authority. And that authority. It's going to need the usual complement of staff attorneys. Guys who'll be working for a quasi-public operation. Which means their salaries have got to be competitive with private industry. Let's say double what your average assistant D.A. is making. And Jack. If you want to interview for one of those jobs. Well, I can get you an interview."

Rose sat up. "Sounds interesting."

"This job." Frank pushed through the intersection as the light turned green. "Let me tell you about this job. If I didn't expect to be going to Washington myself next year. I might take this job myself."

"Twice what I'm making now?" Jack was skeptical. "Who am I supposed to kill, Frank?"

"Why do you take that attitude?"

"Because they don't just give those jobs away. Those jobs are promised out. People who've got connections. People who've made big contributions. There's no reason they're going to give a job like that to me."

"What are you talking about?" Frank exclaimed. "You have connections. You work for Rich Flaherty. And Rich is a close personal friend of the man whose say-so is filling those jobs. The Speaker. Now. Rich wants to take care of Jack Meehan. Because you've been a good soldier, you've been loyal."

"But . . . I'm the type of lawyer . . . Probably what they need is someone experienced at corporate law. Or real-estate law. That sort of work. They don't want me."

"Hey," Frank spoke up. "Why don't you let them decide if they want you or not. Just go put your name in."

"Yeah," Rose said. "Just go put your name in. What have we got to lose?"

Jack quickly saw that this was an argument he could not win. He agreed to take the interview, while putting the whole matter from his mind. Frank seemed delighted.

Rose undressed for bed. The prosecutor pulled the covers to his chin and concentrated on his wife as she wiggled out of her slip. But when she hurried off to the shower, Jack was left alone to deal with Georgine Goodfellow.

Night after night, he remembered that look on her face. In the kitchen. Only for a moment. But there was murder in her eyes. And he wondered if that was the only honest thing she'd given him, if he'd been fooled as his superiors now implied.

In the dark, Jack replayed the whole encounter. The pills, the tears, the pleading glances. Suppose it had all been carefully planned, to win sympathy and blunt his work as prosecutor. Suppose all that vulnerability had been a pose masking a shrewd, duplicitous, and increasingly angry individual.

Was it an accident when Georgine all but fell out of her bathrobe? And when she put on the tight jeans and the flattering white blouse. Could she be ignorant of the effect?

Jack felt he'd been extraordinarily fair-minded in dealing with this woman. It galled him to think she'd taken advantage of that. I trusted you. I took you at face value. Now, I need to know. Have you lied to me? Is Frank right? Are you just like all the others? You did it. And now you're trying to con and whore your way out of it.

Don't lie to me, Georgine. Don't make that mistake. I'll punish you for it. I'll bury you so deep you'll never see those kids again.

The scream sent him leaping from the bed.

"Rose found it," Jack Meehan recounted glumly. "I was already in bed. She went into my office to check the heat. And. All over the floor. The place was a mess. Ransacked. Papers thrown, thrown against the wall."

"You're lucky," Frank Mullins grinned. "When my house got broken into. You should have seen what they threw against the wall."

Jack continued, "Probably happened during the day. Rose and I were working. The kids at school. I think he got in through a cellar window. That was the opinion of the police. He took a small portable television. And my camera."

"Robbery," Frank nodded.

"The police are calling it a robbery."

"There you go."

"Except for the tape." Jack loosened his collar. The courthouse seemed overheated today. "Tape recording I made. Of an interview with a witness. Potential witness in the Goodfellow case. Named Paul Barrasso."

Mullins eyebrows bounced. "A witness to what?"

"The point is, this guy said some very incriminating things

117

on tape. Incriminating not himself. But other people. Now, I left that tape on my desk. It was still there last night. Whoever broke in. Listened to it."

"How do you know that?"

"Same way I know it wasn't a robbery. That little tape recorder. Worth over a hundred bucks. But you can carry the thing in your pocket. So, why didn't he take it? Lying in plain sight? I'll tell you why. Because, leaving it made a point. That he'd been in my house. That he'd been through my papers, everything. And anytime. He can come back."

"Who?" Mullins asked.

"I don't know who."

"Well, who is it Barrasso incriminates on the tape?"

"Charles Carver," Jack replied.

"Oh, Christ . . . Incriminates him how?"

"Barrasso says that Charles Carver is, well, crooked. And he might be capable of murder. Barrasso. He's maybe got more to tell. But the thing is. I promised him confidentiality. I gave him *my* word, in fact. Now someone. They've heard the entire conversation. Like they were standing next to us the whole goddamn time."

"I think you're jumping to conclusions, Jack. If the police are calling it robbery. Well, they know their business."

Jack tensed. "Something like this. I never thought. I've never heard of it happening before. And I'm wondering what sort of person we're dealing with here. Breaking into the house of an assistant D.A. to fish for evidence. I mean, talk about balls." He turned to the first assistant. "I can't find Paul Barrasso. I stopped by his apartment this morning. Left a note. A warning. Told him to call me. But he hasn't called. No one's seen him. He's . . . disappeared."

At the Meehan house new locks were ordered for the doors and windows. An earsplitting burglar alarm was installed. Local police agreed to make frequent runs past the house. Finally, to the delight of the children, Jack vowed to buy a watchdog.

In fact, the prosecutor no longer felt secure in his own home.

Frank Mullins could not convince him this was merely "the way everybody feels after a housebreak." Obsessed with the safety of his family, his children, Jack began to understand Georgine Goodfellows's story. If you'd seen a loved one suddenly, brutally murdered, wouldn't that leave you terrified beyond reason? Wouldn't you endure anything — shame, loneliness, prison — to prevent it from happening again?

17

THE old woman opened her door slowly. "Yes? Oh God, what are you?"

Jack Meehan displayed his ID. "I'm with the district attorney's office, ma'am. Could I come in? It'll only take a minute."

She looked him up and down. "What for?"

"Just to ask a few questions."

"Well. You can come in." She seemed to know the reason for Jack's visit. "But don't expect I can help you."

Jack sat uneasily on the edge of the couch. The old woman took an overstuffed chair. The furniture was worn, the apartment cluttered.

"I've come about your grandson, Mrs. Ready. Paul Barrasso."

"Well, I didn't expect I was the one in trouble."

"Now, I haven't said anything about trouble. I just want to talk to him."

"What's he done now?"

"He's not in his apartment. He's got mail piling up. And he hasn't been seen at work for days. The upshot of this. I want to talk to Paul. But I don't know how to find him."

"He don't tell me where he's going," the grandmother said.

The prosecutor had a bad feeling. It wasn't reasonable for the guy to just vanish without a word. Jack couldn't forget the tape recording, Barrasso pleading for secrecy.

"Mrs. Ready. I don't want to worry you. Or frighten you. But I'm afraid that Paul might be in some kind of danger."

"Doesn't surprise me."

"Paul has been known to keep bad company," Jack said.

"Most of his friends are scum, if that's what you mean."

"Right. Only now. I'm afraid. I've heard rumors. Some of his friends, er, acquaintances. Some of them might be after him. In order to do him harm. And the only reason I want to see Paul. Is to warn him."

The grandmother began rocking in her chair. Her face tightened, her eyes clouded.

"Have you any idea where Paul might have gone?"

"I . . ." She sighed.

"Maybe he didn't tell you where he went. But maybe you can guess."

She took a deep breath. "A few days ago. Paul came by here to pick up a pair of skis. Certain things he keeps here because his apartment is so small."

"Skis?"

"I thought he was back by now. I haven't heard from him. But that doesn't mean anything. He wouldn't have called me, the little bastard."

"Yeah. If he went skiing. Where would he go?"

"Well. There's only one place he could afford to go. A cottage I own in Acton, Maine. He'd stay there. Ski in the White Mountains."

Mrs. Ready gave the address. All at once, she overflowed with information, revealing that Paul had lately seemed edgy, not himself.

"That boy was always too much for me. I had no business. At my age. Raising another child. But I was left with him, and what choice did I have? I couldn't control him, you see. Even back then, I couldn't control him."

At the door, she added, "Paul's always been troublesome. But, you know. Despite it all. He's not a bad boy. He's broken the law, I know. But. He never hurt anyone. He's got a good heart. Underneath it all."

* * *

120

The assistant district attorney left for Maine early the next morning. He went out of a sense of responsibility to Paul Barrasso, a man once convicted of selling drugs to minors.

Well, it wasn't fair. Messed up by a freak incident, a million-to-one shot. Although . . . he might have been more careful. Didn't have to leave the tape lying in plain sight. Could have locked it up. Could have returned it to the office. But who could have predicted this?

Now, Jack's imagination wouldn't leave him alone. He saw Paul Barrasso cowering in the Maine woods, pleading for his life. And as he dies he thinks of the prosecutor who'd made so many promises, who'd insisted it was safe to tape everything, who'd fumbled away a man's life.

The Ready cottage, surrounded by forest and other cottages, was on a lake at the end of a dirt road.

Jack bluffed his way in. "I've just come from seeing Mrs. Ready, the owner."

"Oh, sure. Come in." The hesitant, bearded man introduced himself as Roger Forgette. He led Jack past the narrow kitchen to a large room where several sleeping bags were spread around a wood stove. The place was surprisingly neat, though all the furnishings were secondhand and the linoleum was beginning to turn up in places.

A young girl in the corner looked up from a paperback. Nervous, Roger ignored her, inviting Jack to sit on an old couch. Next, he opened a window, a clumsy effort to reduce the scent of some controlled substance.

"You're a friend of Paul Barrasso?" Jack began.

"Well." The young man scratched at his lumberjack shirt. "Actually, my brother knows him better. He's really a friend of my brother's. He invited my brother up here. But Ronnie, he couldn't come. So, I came instead. Brass said that was okay with him."

"Brass?"

"Paul. You know, Barrasso. That's what everyone calls him. Brass. Anyway, Brass says I could come. He says anyone could come. Open house. So. We had a bunch of people up here for a while. But most of them went home. And the rest are skiing now."

"Is Barrasso here?"

"He was here the first couple of days. But he's gone now."

"When did he leave?"

"Monday night. I think it was Monday."

"Did he say where he was going?"

"No," Roger answered.

"Did he say anything? He must have said something to someone."

"Not really."

"Had he gotten a message then? A phone call? A letter?"

"Could have." Roger nodded. "If he got a call. It would have been on the pay phone down the market. There's no phone here."

The prosecutor leaned over. "Didn't anybody wonder where he'd gone? I mean, it's been two days. Your host. He just walks out and never comes back. Didn't that seem a little odd?"

Forgette shrugged. "Not for Brass. I mean. If you knew what Brass is like you'd probably stop looking for him. The guy invites you to his cottage. And he wants lots of people around. So he invites lots of people. Then, he starts hitting on everyone's girl. Eating all the food. Drinking all the beer. Which he didn't pay for none of it. He fought with most everyone here. So, when he left. Right? When he left no one was sad he didn't come back. Were they, Caroline?"

The girl looked up from her paperback. "Who's that?"

"Paul Barrasso."

"Oh. You mean the groper."

Where the main road skirted the lake was a general store. Jack Meehan showed the clerk a photo of Paul Barrasso. "Maybe you took a call for him Monday."

"Nope. Don't remember that I did."

Jack gazed out on the parking lot, beyond the dumpster, to a fat, rusting Buick. It looked familiar. Of course, he'd seen

Barrasso's car once. In the dark. Near Blue Pond where the two men had made the tape recording.

"What do you know about that heap over there?"

"Yeah." The storekeeper came to the door. "That old thing. Been sitting in my lot a few days now. I thought it belonged to one of these cottages down the road here, else I would've had it towed away."

Unlocked, the car was piled with empty beer cans and had almost no gas. There was no trace of blood, no sign of a struggle. Paul Barrasso's registration shared the glove box with a small quantity of hashish. The trunk was empty, the battery dead, and the right rear tire flat.

A day later, Jack Meehan, accompanied by police, entered Paul Barrasso's Milham Square apartment. Just under the door, where Jack had left it, was a note warning the informant that he might be in danger. There was a chance Paul had seen it on his return from Maine.

Yet, a very sophisticated stereo was found among the piles of dirty clothes, dirty magazines, and cupcake wrappers. If the parts driver had run away, it seemed unlikely he would have left behind an item that could so easily be converted to cash.

Where was Paul Barrasso? Jack liked to imagine that the informant had seen his message. Or had seen the killer coming. And fled. Into the woods. Hiding. But Barrasso had left no clue to his whereabouts, no reason for optimism.

In the Parkside case Jack now counted a possible *four* homicides. He was close to giving up.

18

THE Speaker stood, extending his hand, as Jack Meehan entered his office. A handsome man, his perfectly tailored blue-gray suit coordinated with his silver-blue hair. Ironically, at less than five foot eight, the man retained an aura of power, a larger-than-life quality Jack had never glimpsed on the evening news. By comparison, Rich Flaherty seemed small-time.

"Have a seat, Jack." The great man smiled, blue eyes twinkling. Jack, who knew all about politicians and their tricks, felt an air of well-being. He'd come to the statehouse expecting to be interviewed by some flunky, expecting to be patted on the back and told, "Don't call us. We'll call you." Now, sitting in this office with its historic portraits and huge windows, he found the prospect of doubling his salary almost real.

Surprisingly, the Speaker began questioning the prosecutor, not about his job or professional qualifications, but about his children, Karen and John. This went on at length. "What are their ages? What do they like to do for fun?"

Jack soon felt so at ease that he actually showed his wallet photos. The Speaker of the Great and General Court sat up, enthusiastic, as if Jack had done him a favor by sharing them.

"You know, Jack." He studied each photo as he spoke. "I have a preference for family men in government. I have no use for these town-house professionals with their Cuisinarts and poodles. Those birds don't have to concern themselves with the future. They'll leave nothing behind. (Beautiful children. God, you're a lucky man.) It's my opinion that this arena must be built and administered with an eye toward the long haul."

"Well," Jack nodded earnestly, "with two preschoolers I expect to be hauling for some time to come."

The Speaker chuckled. "And you work for Rich Flaherty? Did you know that Richie and I were state reps together? Many years ago. And, I kid you not, that man always had a reputation for attracting the best people to his staff."

Of course, all this qualified as politician's bullshit. But the Speaker, his clear, blue eyes twinkling, was able to make the most clichéd flattery ring true. Jack beamed.

"Well," Rose asked, "how did it go?"

Jack smiled across the dinner table. "I give old Frank credit. When he arranges an interview he doesn't fool around. Your husband spent the afternoon with the Speaker himself."

"You got to meet the Speaker?"

"Well, to be accurate. It was more than I just met him. We had a long chat, actually."

"A chat?"

"Yeah. The two of us."

"About what?" Rose asked.

"Well, believe it or not. We mainly talked about Karen and John."

The children grinned with pride.

"Karen and John?" Rose asked. "Is that a good sign?"

"I think it shows they've already made a decision."

Suddenly, Rose broke into a triumphant grin. "Do you know what this means, Jack? Doubling your salary. Do you know how this is going to change our lives?"

"I said they've already made a decision, Rose. But it could be they've decided not to give me the job."

"Oh, no. You deserve this job. It's a reward for all the years you've worked so hard."

"But —"

"You've done favors for those people. Lots of favors. And you did good work at the office. You've been conscientious, God knows. And now, after all the years when nobody seemed to care. They've finally recognized it."

"All I'm saying, Rose. Let's not celebrate until after they've offered the job. And after I've accepted."

"After you've accepted?" She looked surprised. "Of course you'll accept."

"Of course I'll accept. But, what I'm saying. You know. Before I accept. I do have obligations."

"Obligations? What does that mean?"

"Just. I'm involved in a very difficult case. The Goodfellow thing and —"

"Well, so what, Jack. You're not indispensable, you know."

"I'm not saying I am. I'm just saying it's a difficult, complicated case. And it would take a long time for a new man to catch on to all the subtleties."

"Someone else can do it." She raised her voice. "You have your own problems. Let someone else deal with that."

"Well." He turned to the kids. They were quiet, curious,

understanding only that their parents were deeply concerned about something. After a moment, Jack conceded, "Maybe you're right, Rose. Maybe you're right."

Admittedly, he was drawn to the idea of leaving the D.A.'s office, where a small mistake can be a matter of life or death. The arena authority offered him real money for the first time in his life. And he had made a hit with the Speaker. The people on the Hill behaved as if the job already belonged to Jack Meehan.

Jack wondered if common sense demanded that he quit the Goodfellow prosecution. At times, his efforts seemed to have done more harm than good. He remembered Frank Mullins's charge that he'd become "emotionally involved." The words made him more than a little uncomfortable, as if there might be some truth in them. Perhaps a more detached investigator would have been more prudent, would not have compromised his source.

The disappearance of Paul Barrasso hadn't exactly made the Parkside matter a priority. "It's odd," Frank Mullins agreed. "But remember. This guy is a bum. And dropping out of sight without a word. It's a thing bums do."

Grandmother Ready, who appeared one day at the Milham police station to claim Paul's stereo and clothing, more or less agreed. "You watch," she told a detective. "One day he'll come waltzing back like he's never been gone."

"You mean he's done this before?" she was asked.

"No. He's never left me before. Except when he was in jail. Paul's a homebody. That's how come I know he'll come back. You watch."

Jack Meehan could not dismiss the possibility that his carelessness had killed the parts driver. It was one factor that kept him active in the investigation.

Her face thin and lined, Barbara Ripler looked older than her husband. Soft-spoken, she invited the assistant district attorney into the living room, then kept him waiting alone for several minutes.

If Jack had doubted Richard Ripler's involvement in fraud, those doubts fell away now. The service manager lived in a large house on a landscaped lot just over the Harwood line. Inside, the furnishings were of high quality — kept like new in clear plastic covers. Out back, a stockade surrounded the pool.

"Nice place," Jack began, trying to control his envy.

"Thank you."

"When I drove up here. You know, I thought I must have the wrong address. You *are* the auto-mechanic Riplers?"

"My husband is the service manager at Parkside Porsche-Volkswagen. Dick is not a mechanic. He's a white-collar man."

Jack had scarcely begun to explain his visit when they were interrupted by screams and shouts from the second floor. The prosecutor sat up, listening closely to what seemed to be a fierce family squabble between brothers. It ended with a loud thump, as if a body hit the floor.

Nervously, Mrs. Ripler cleared her throat.

"Are they going to be all right up there?"

"Perhaps you'll get to the point of this visit, Mr. Meehan."

"Well, yeah. It's the service manager." Jack paused, looking about the room in awe. "Only in America! Me, I had to be a lawyer."

"I beg your pardon?"

"I can't stop myself from asking, but did one of you inherit a fortune? Win the lottery? What?"

"If you're asking how we can afford this house. Well, we're hardworking people, Mr. Meehan. We both work. We save our money. And we pay cash. Never buy on credit. That's what Dick always goes by."

"Well, my hat's off to you both. If you can do all this by paying cash, God bless you."

Mrs. Ripler winced when the battle on the second floor resumed. "I'm sorry, Mr. Meehan." The plastic covers crackled when she stood. "You'll have to excuse me for a moment."

Left alone, Jack could hear more shouting, angry teenage voices and Barbara Ripler's occasional, timid tones. It all ended with a slamming door.

Balancing a notepad on his knee, Jack concluded that the Ripler household was a bit odd and unusually tense. He decided not to produce the tape recorder until Barbara relaxed and answered a few questions — assuming she'd ever sit down long enough to hear them. In fact, she did not return for nearly twenty minutes.

The prosecutor was impatiently consulting his watch when the woman reappeared. "Sorry to keep you waiting."

"No problem. We'll get right to it." Looking at his notes, Jack was startled by a deep, male voice.

"Is there something I can do for you?"

The astonished prosecutor looked up to find Richard Ripler at the threshold.

"I . . . I was just asking your wife . . . asking your wife some questions." Jack stood, struggling not to seem like a child caught with jam on his fingers. Now, he understood why he'd been left sitting here so long. Barbara had phoned for help, and her husband had rushed home from work.

"Haven't I seen you before?" Ripler asked. "Didn't you come by the dealership?"

The prosecutor introduced himself and offered his hand. Ripler hesitated before accepting it. The grip was firm. He looked Jack in the eye, his expression evidently lacking hostility or anger. Wearing a bright blue parka, he was remarkably well groomed. With his tie and pressed slacks, no one would have guessed that he spent his days in a garage.

"I'd hoped your wife could answer some of our questions."

"Questions?"

"About . . . well." Jack turned away from Barbara, who was no longer pretending to smile. "Actually. Since you're here. A lucky break, really. *You* could answer my questions."

Short, well built, Ripler fit Woodrow Otis's description of the "fancy man" in the Porsche. But then, Jack reminded himself, so did Charles Carver. It was a pretty vague description, after all.

"I wish I could help you," Ripler said. "Unfortunately, I've been advised by my attorney, Mr. Clinton Perry, not to answer any questions. I've already explained that to the police."

The prosecutor shrugged. "Nobody tells me anything." He'd recognized the attorney's name, a member of H. Bateman Biddle's firm. Was everyone at Parkside represented by Biddle? Was this the way Charles Carver kept tabs on people?

"I'm sorry you went to all this trouble for nothing, Mr. Meehan."

Jack mumbled, "I'm pretty bummed out about it myself." He was being shown the door, though Ripler remained polite.

"I understand you're looking for a new man at your place." Jack stopped.

Ripler looked uncertain.

"Parts driver?"

"Oh yeah," the service manager nodded. "The other guy quit."

"Did he quit? Or is he just gone?"

Ripler started to speak, but checked himself.

"You met Walter Hamparian. As far as we know, you're the only Parkside employee who dealt with Walter."

"I told you, I've been advised by my attorney not to —"

"Hamparian's dead. And your parts driver. He goes off to Maine. And never comes back. And the bookkeeper shot to death. The body count rises. But all anyone's got to say is, No comment. Just leaves me wondering about you people. Leaves me curious as hell."

"Why do you say *you people?*" Ripler's lip twitched. He'd been holding the door open for Jack. "Let me tell you something." He closed it. "See, I'm a married man. With kids. With responsibilities. You can see that. If it was just me. Maybe I'd feel different. As it is, I keep my mouth shut. Mind my own business. Let me explain what's going on. Maybe you'll understand. I come into a job situation. Things are done a certain way. Maybe I don't like it. The little things they do to cheat people. Maybe I don't like that. But I'm the new guy. Am I supposed to complain? Get on my high horse or something? Would you? They'd just laugh you right out of there."

"It's more involved now than just cheating a few people," Jack replied.

Ripler bowed his head, moving closer, lowering his voice.

"One day. When we woke up here. Things were out of place. What was latched. All of a sudden it was unlatched. Certain things, not valuable things necessarily, but things you couldn't miss, they'd disappeared. Someone had come in my house in the night. I didn't see them. I didn't hear them. But they made sure I found out about them. And I got the point."

"Did you make a police report, Mr. Ripler?"

"What? Do you think I'm crazy?" Suddenly, the door swung open. "Please don't come here again, Mr. Meehan. It's dangerous for me and my family. And a waste of time for you."

According to Detective Lieutenant Sullivan, Charles Carver's second wife lived out of state, while the first, Mrs. Jean Carver, was so detached from her husband that she was not worth interviewing. She lived in a modest neighborhood near the Merrymount section, where both Jack Meehan and Georgine Bow had grown up.

It was while ignoring Detective Sullivan's advice, driving to Jean Carver's home, that Jack impulsively detoured to his old neighborhood. After so many years, finding his way about was difficult. Inevitably, the landmarks had changed or vanished. He was dismayed to see the ancient school with its huge windows replaced by a structure of poured concrete, practically without windows.

His former home was unrecognizable, having taken on aluminum siding and a new front room where the porch had been. He remembered playing ball with his dad in the side yard. Only now, he was astonished to discover there hadn't been any side yard, just a grassy alleyway.

The Bow house was more familiar. Two evergreens in the front yard had once seemed huge. After more than twenty years, they still looked huge. The white sign with black lettering, BOW STUDIOS, was gone. However, the metal poles it had hung from remained, anchored in concrete, rusting, and about to be engulfed by one of the trees.

The house had fallen on hard times. Badly in need of a paint job, it seemed uninhabited. Had it somehow caught Georgine's bad luck?

As a child, he rarely went there. Georgine's mom always had treats for the gang. But Jack could still feel the burden of good behavior. Mr. Bow was in his darkroom. Or Mr. Bow was in his studio. Don't make noise. Don't disturb him.

Heavyset, silent, Mr. Bow kept away from everyone.

Sitting in his Chevette outside the old place, the assistant district attorney couldn't be sure what he'd gotten hold of in remembering this. Or if it made any difference that Georgine had lied about her father.

The lovely Jean Christoforo Carver could be sharp and pleasant at once. "So." She smiled at the prosecutor. "You're digging the dirt on Charlie."

"That implies there's dirt to dig."

"Oh, come on. There's always dirt. If you go looking for it. The question is. With Charlie. Why do you want to look for it?"

About thirty, with a lush figure, dark eyes, and red hair, Jean sat near the window in the sun room.

"How often do you see your husband?"

"Ah, well . . . My ex-husband. Ex. I don't see him very often. Maybe twice a month. When he comes for Cheri. Our daughter, Cheri."

"I gather you'd just as soon not see him."

"No," she said. "Not at all. We just . . . we have very little in the way of common interests. Aside from Cheri and the business, we have nothing to talk about."

"The business?"

"I'm a part owner of his car dealership. So is Cheri. Not that I have anything to do with the place. Every so often I get a little check. But. Like I wasn't consulted about the sale. Charlie has the right to sell my share along with his share."

For a moment, Jack was uncertain about what he'd heard. "You said *sale?*"

"That's right. But I wasn't consulted."

"Oh, right. You mean the sale of the dealership."

"It was a shocker," she replied. "Charlie. After all these years. Building up his reputation. Turning the thing into a real

131

money-maker. He just gives it up. I guess he decided sitting in the sun somewhere would be more fun."

Jack was nodding, as if this information did not surprise him. Yes, of course, that sale. "By the way, has he found a buyer yet?"

"No. But he will. And Charlie will get top price. Because he's nobody's fool when it comes to business. People think he inherited all his money. Well, he inherited a fancy name and very little else. What Charlie did, he went right out and worked and worked. Until he had as much as everybody always thought he had. He's a whiz with money, that man."

"A whiz with money," Jack observed, "but not with you."

"My marriage." She looked away with a coy smile. "Is my business."

"What I'm interested in. It isn't so much your marriage. It's your ex-husband. I'm always curious about successful people."

"Right. You want to know all about Charlie. But you won't tell me why you want to know. I'm sure it's more than curiosity."

Jean had a model's face, smooth, confident, with knowing eyes. Jack told her, "My investigation concerns allegations revolving around the Parkside dealership. Allegations of fraud . . . and murder."

The word *murder* caught her off guard. She was plainly shocked, did not even bother trying to hide it. "Charlie wouldn't be involved in . . ."

"He hasn't said anything to you?"

"Not about *murder* . . . or anything."

"You don't seem too surprised. I mean, sure, you're surprised. But you've always had that feeling, Jean. About Charlie. That he might be capable of murder."

"No."

"You've seen him. Episodes. Where he could be violent."

"I suppose, what? You mean that thing in Key West, years ago? Who told you about that? It was an isolated incident. I mean, it was hard for us at the beginning. His family was against the marriage. Against me. I wasn't rich enough or something. I wasn't rich at all. But. Any marriage. Where the couple is young. You get so you lose your temper. You just want to kill — Well, not literally kill. But strike. Strike out at the other person. And that's what happened. I threw something at him. And he threw something at me. But. I recovered. And it never happened again. And. I forgot it. Forgive and forget. Forgive and forget."

Generally, Mrs. Carver tried to put her ex-husband in the best light, which was not surprising considering their financial ties. Nonetheless, the prosecutor felt he'd made headway, particularly with the reference to Carver's violent streak.

"Do you know your husband's current, second wife?"

"Never met her."

"Then maybe your daughter. She's met her? Talked about her?"

"All I can tell you," Jean replied. "They don't live together. Haven't for years. Whether they're friendly, I couldn't say. But they don't live together. In a way, it's kind of sad. Poor Charlie. All that money. All alone in the big house."

19

First Assistant Frank Mullins was conceding nothing. But as they sat in the office library, Jack Meehan could not help but feel vindicated by this turn of events. Of course, the prosecutor remained polite as the suave H. Bateman Biddle swapped compliments with Frank. In fact, Charles Carver's lawyer had come hat in hand, oozing good fellowship.

"Several people have made noises about the House seat," Biddle was saying. "But it's my feeling that noise is all it will amount to. A few months from now we'll have to be calling him Congressman Flaherty and he'll be impossible to live with."

"It's looking good," Frank agreed. "He's got the organization. He's got the name recognition. And he knows how to shake that money tree. With a little help. With a little help from his friends, of course."

Biddle permitted himself a small smile. Glancing at Jack, he said, "We got off on the wrong foot last time, Jack. I'm afraid it was my fault."

"I'm sure you were just doing your job. Skip."

"As you were doing yours. And doing it well." Smiling, he lightly patted his styled silver hair. His clothes, Jack mused, probably cost more than my car. "Since our first meeting," Biddle said, "the situation has changed. The murder of Mr. Hamparian has changed it. And at this time my client is eager to cooperate fully in solving this brutal, senseless crime."

"But," Jack mumbled to himself.

"However. My client, out of deference to his family and his standing in the community, cannot forsake his constitutional protection against self-incrimination. Consequently, he faces a dilemma. How to shield himself against prosecution for lesser transgressions while cooperating and telling the police everything he knows about this hideous killing."

A deal. Jack gave Frank a triumphant look. Just the fact of this meeting indicated that Charles Carver was up to his roof rack in this dirty business. Biddle was now conducting damage control.

"Well," Jack said, "the problem with offering immunity. How do we know your boy isn't implicated in the murder himself?"

Biddle looked astonished.

"Let me make a suggestion," Frank eagerly interjected. "We can protect ourselves. We can give immunity conditionally. In other words, we accept Charles Carver's statement that he is innocent of any involvement in homicide. Then, if we discover later that he is culpable in Hamparian's murder. Or if we discover that he's lied to us, or misled us in any way. Then, the entire agreement is null and void. And we proceed against him. At the same time, everything he's told us remains admissible in court. So, you see, it's a deal by which we can't lose."

Biddle wasn't objecting, or attempting to obscure this proposal, or bargaining for a better one. All of which led Jack to believe that he and the first assistant had hashed it out pretty thoroughly beforehand.

Jack began, "Well. We don't want to be in the position of buying a pig in a poke. How do we know Carver's information is even worth bargaining for?"

Biddle nodded. "Charles Carver has always been a bit of a rogue. In this case, he's proved to be a bit of a fool as well. But he's by no means a murderer. In the course of running his business, in the midst of a bad recession, he cut a few corners in order to survive. Nothing serious. Practices that skirt the law. Borderline misdemeanors."

"You mean felonies," Jack retorted. "Defrauding Volkswagen of America."

"Nothing violent," Biddle added hastily. "Nonviolent. And the important point is this. That several people within the organization, the business. Several people were involved in this illegal activity. And it was here that the real problems began. Because one of these men appears to have panicked, behaved irrationally, once Walter Hamparian, the VW investigator, came on the scene. Acting on his own. Let me stress that. Acting on his own, this man decided to speak to Walter. To scare him off perhaps. And, evidently, one thing led to another. And evidently matters got out of hand. Evidently."

"Richard Ripler killed Hamparian," Frank revealed.

"My client was not involved in any way. He did not participate in the murder. He did not direct it. He did not acquiesce in it. He did, in fact, make an effort to stop the man."

"I guess calling the police wasn't part of that effort," Jack noted.

Biddle leaned forward and lowered his voice. "Richard Ripler is a violent, unpredictable man. With the result that those in the know are too frightened to bring their suspicions to the police. Excepting my client. Charles Carver will cooperate. Desperately wants to cooperate. Even at considerable personal risk."

Biddle began to sound ironic. "It's a situation where Charlie imagined he was being smart. Indulging in a little white-collar crime. Well, he outsmarted himself. The whole thing blew up in his face. Now, he's chased by homicide detectives. His life is threatened. I told him. I told him just the other day,

'Charlie. I hope to God you've learned something from all this.' "

Jack questioned, "Are you telling us that Charles Carver can identify Ripler as Hamparian's murderer?"

"He can't give direct evidence. He is not an eyewitness. But he has quite a story to tell. He will fill in the gaps, get you pointed in the right direction. And believe me, you want Ripler in custody as soon as possible. He is dangerous."

"The murder of James Goodfellow," Jack continued. "Did Ripler also kill Goodfellow?"

"I can only tell you this," Biddle declared. "James Goodfellow, according to my information, was not involved in the warranty fraud."

"Was not?"

"As regards the Goodfellow slaying. I'm sure my client will be happy to tell you whatever he knows as soon as this nuisance threat of prosecution is removed."

"Why is Carver selling his business?" Jack demanded. "Does he see some advantage in more portable assets?"

"You have been busy, Mr. Meehan. Well, that sale is nothing more than a smart business move. Charlie has an unerring sense in business matters. He sees scandal coming. In a few months the name of Parkside VW might be significantly devalued. If you're hinting that my client might be preparing to leave the area, run away. Well, why should he? Outside of this petty scam, Charles Carver is an innocent man."

"This is nothing more than his latest con." Alone with Frank Mullins, Jack was making no effort to hide his opposition to Biddle's proposed deal. "I don't care what arrangement Carver agrees to. Once we grant him immunity. Even conditional immunity. Well, from then on he's our guy. On the record, he's our guy. If we have to turn around and indict him for murder. We look like a bunch of assholes in court."

"But Carver isn't suspected of murder." Frank smiled like a man with good cards in his hand. "And there's nothing to suggest he should be."

"No? Nothing to suggest? I've got a briefcase full of notes that suggest a lot to me."

"I've read your report, Jack. You've done a lot of work. No question, you've proved me wrong about a lot of things on this case. But. So much of what you dug up just hasn't checked out. I'm afraid."

"Hasn't checked out?" The prosecutor grew hot. "For instance what? What hasn't checked out?"

Frank consulted a loose-leaf folder on his desk, turning pages while holding up one finger. "Okay, here." He pointed. "You had this business about money. James Goodfellow having all this money."

"Right. Yeah. Money the books couldn't account for. Thousands of dollars which appeared out of nowhere. Well, it must've come from Parkside. The warranty scam. And if it did. Then Carver lied when he told Biddle that James Goodfellow wasn't involved."

"It came from the sale of the Goodfellows' farm."

Jack was momentarily speechless. "What? How do you know that?"

"Lyle Sullivan. I asked him to look into it for me. He found out that Goodfellow was given a substantial share of the proceeds when his father sold the farm. There's what? There's a mall there now, I think. The taxes were handled by the family attorney. Paid separately. Which is probably why you missed it. You're a lawyer, Jack. Not an accountant. It was an understandable mistake."

Jack took a deep breath. "Okay. That's a small point. But I had plenty more than that. The car. Carver's Porsche. What was it doing in the Goodfellow neighborhood all summer? Isn't that just a little bit suspicious?"

"Sure it is," Frank agreed. "But you got one thing wrong. It's not Carver's car. It's a company car. Registered to the dealership. Usually, Carver drives it home. But everybody at Parkside has used it at one time or another. And why it was seen in that particular neighborhood I can't say. But maybe somebody's got a lady friend around there, just like old man Otis said."

"Maybe it's Carver," Jack insisted. "For all we know his lady friend was Georgine Goodfellow."

"Charles Carver can provide witnesses. His secretary for one.

137

Who'll swear he habitually spent his entire workday on the premises. Didn't go out for lunch even. So, if someone regularly took that car to the Goodfellows' neighborhood. Evidently, that someone wasn't Carver."

"Where'd you get all this 'reliable' information? From Skip Biddle?"

Waving the folder, Mullins stood and came around to sit on the edge of his desk. "I'm no more anxious than you are to make deals with a killer. So, I took steps to check your information. Yes, I talked to Skip Biddle. But police records told me this. Your informant. The guy who fingered Carver and then disappeared. What's his name? Barrasso? He told you that Carver had a record. A murder conviction, yet. Well, as a matter of fact, no Parkside employee has ever been convicted of a felony. With the exception of Barrasso himself."

"I know that," Jack conceded. "But a guy like Barrasso. You don't expect his information is going to be perfect. He's going to forget things and exaggerate and even lie. But I think most of what he told, what he said about Charles Carver. I think it was the truth."

"Pretty lame, Jack."

"How about the gun, then? You can't excuse that away. The Goodfellow murder. The Grover Durham murder. Same murder weapon. Now, explain that."

"It has to be a coincidence. James Goodfellow bought the gun on the black market. And he got stuck with a used gun."

"Oh, stop it, Frank. Is it a coincidence that Grover Durham did business with Charles Carver? I've got a witness. Willie Laughlin. Who saw them together. Don't you understand, there are too many links to Carver. Too goddamn many coincidences."

Mullins went to the outer office. He asked his secretary to find Detective Lieutenant Sullivan. "I saw him in the building this morning, Mary. See if you can track him down."

"What do you want with Sullivan?" Jack nearly stood.

"He's going to clear up this Durham business once and for all." The first assistant sat and put his feet up on the desk. "Heard anything from the arena authority?"

"The what? Oh, no. Not yet."

"Well, you will, Jacko. And I've got a feeling you're going to like what you hear. I happen to know the Speaker called Mr. Flaherty to thank him for sending you over."

"Well, you know, thanks for getting me the interview."

Mullins grinned. "Glad to help. Glad to help."

Detective Lieutenant Lyle Sullivan arrived, Danish in one hand, coffee in the other. "What's up?"

"Jack wants to hear about William Laughlin."

"Oh, yeah." Sullivan nodded. "I was over the house of correction to see old Willie a few days ago. At Mr. Mullins's request. To pin, to pin Willie down on his story. Get some details of this meeting between Grover Durham and Charles Carver. We went at it for more than an hour. It was very difficult to get anything out of him. Dates. He don't remember dates. Or weather. Or time of year even. I'm saying, 'Well. Maybe you don't remember anything cause this never happened.' And I huff and puff about obstruction of justice. And say, 'Boy, are you in a heap of trouble.' And pretty soon, the little cocksucker, he admits it."

"Admits what?" Jack questioned.

"Admits. That he don't know Charles Carver except he's seen him on television. He admits he made up the whole thing about going along with Grover Durham to Carver's dealership. He made that up. Because it seemed like what the assistant D.A. wanted to hear. And Willie, he wanted to get out of jail."

Mullins grinned. "You were right about Laughlin in the first place, Jack. Just a not-so-smart con artist. Just happens he was telling you what you wanted to believe. That Charles Carver was the villain. And Georgine Goodfellow was as pure as Ivory Soap."

20

IN his office, the prosecutor organized his work for the day, carefully arranging his notes on the desk. Then he sat motionless, devastated.

At the end, Mullins had admitted that links between three

murders might be more than mere coincidence. "But where's the proof?" he had asked. "You can't give me a good guess at what the connection is. And I need proof in this office."

Increasingly, the target of Jack Meehan's work had been Charles Carver. Yet, Mullins had picked that evidence apart. It seemed that fraud was Carver's only crime.

If Carver was telling the truth. If James Goodfellow hadn't been involved in the warranty scam. It left the obvious motives for his murder: jealousy, hatred, anger. It left Georgine Goodfellow, accomplice or no, as guilty as sin.

Well, so what? If Georgine is guilty. Why should that bother you?

Jack stared at the chair where Georgine had sat. He could remember her looking down all the time, seeming frightened, vulnerable, pathetic. But it had been an act, a woman's trick. And it was time to stop excusing her.

He knew positively that she'd lied to him that night in the kitchen. In spite of her rage and grief, she'd had enough presence to invent, obscure, to lie. Well, it wasn't even logical. A man comes from nowhere. Kills her husband. Threatens her. And on account of that Georgine is prepared to keep silent, to go to prison, to go through hell. There had to be more to it.

She lied to me. Damn her!

The prosecutor walked to the window and stared. He did not want to work today. Go home. Lie in bed. Eat something. And maybe the world won't look so grim and pointless.

In the afternoon, Jack's depression hung on. He stared at the wall for hours. His secretary even remarked on it.

"I'm just a little tired," he explained. "I've been working too hard. I guess."

It was odd and disturbing the way he could close his eyes and see Georgine. He could remember the way the room smelled when she was here. And when he resolved to put his mind to other things — he could not.

The phone call from the Speaker's office came a few days later. Almost dizzy with excitement, the prosecutor instantly accepted the position at the arena authority.

"We'll want you in two weeks," said the Speaker's man.

"Two weeks? I've got work here —"
"Never mind that. It's all been arranged."
"Fine." Jack replied without thinking. "I'll be there."
Rose was thrilled. "Now aren't you glad you listened to me and took the interview?"

Unhappily, as the Meehans celebrated with dinner at an expensive restaurant, Jack was already beginning to have doubts. Had he left Georgine in the lurch, betrayed? As with Barrasso, he'd promised to help, had seemed to care. Was it all a lie?

Rose did not share his misgivings. "They can get along fine without you," she insisted during a tense moment over the salad. "It's time to think of yourself for a change. To think of us. Your family. This is a great opportunity. We don't get chances like this every day. Do you want to spend the rest of your life brooding over the job you didn't take?"

In the days to come, Jack began finding brochures scattered throughout the house, promoting vacations in Hawaii, real estate, and smart cars. Rose no longer argued the merits of his new opportunity. The question was closed. Certainly, he would take the job.

For his part, Jack Meehan was not immune to the lure of money. He daydreamed about a new Mercedes. It would be fun to push the Chevette off a cliff. Lately, he'd been meeting a lot of people, people of his own generation, people who seemed to live at a much higher level.

Well, what's wrong with me? Why don't I drive a Mercedes? If I don't begin to climb now, perhaps I never will. In a few years the kids will need money for college. Is it wrong to consider our future?

Mrs. Janice Price looked too young to be the daughter of Walter Hamparian. She sat in the office chair, hardly moving, not once raising her voice. But she fixed Jack with an accusing look that was all the more withering for her outward calm.

"My children are with a sitter. I paid for a sitter so I could come here and talk to you."

"You needn't have," Jack replied. "If you'd telephoned —"

"I'm sure you'd rather I telephoned. I'm sure you'd prefer

to deal with me that way. But I wanted to see you when I spoke. I wanted to see your face."

"I was about to say, Mrs. Price. If you call. Let me know when you want to see me. I'd be willing . . . Well, I'm sure someone would be willing to drop by your house." Jack smiled sympathetically. "We want to be helpful."

"That's fine. You say you want to be helpful. Fine. But my father has been dead two months. With nothing. Absolutely nothing done about it."

"Uh . . . these things take time. . . ." Jack groped for the right words, the right tone. But this was a no-win conversation, one he wished he could have avoided. "Don't think for a minute, Mrs. Price, that nothing is being done. There are state-police detectives on this. Plus local police. And just recently, for example, just recently we've had someone come forward who might have information. He wants immunity. And we're pursuing the matter."

"Who is it?"

"Well, of course, I can't tell you his name. You can appreciate why, being the daughter of a police officer."

"I can also appreciate a brush-off when I hear it. I've been to the Welton police. And I've been to the state police. And I got the same runaround there."

"There's no runaround, Mrs. Price. The fact that your father was a police officer has made his case a top priority around here."

"Don't patronize me, Mr. Meehan. I'm not stupid." One side of her mouth turned up in a sort of grimace. She looked down at the floor and didn't speak for some moments. "My father. You should have met my father. Everyone loved him. Everyone. I don't say it because I'm his daughter. It's true. He was a special sort of person."

"I've heard that."

"My father." Her eyes were shining. "They smuggled him past the Turks when he was an infant. The only surviving child of eight. My father always taught us. It's a miracle. An act of God that our family exists at all. God worked a miracle to give my father life. No one had the right — after all his years. At a dangerous job. No one had the right to . . ." She swallowed hard, her face flushed.

Jack was waiting for the proper moment to explain. Mrs. Price, nothing is more important than finding and convicting your father's killer. But today's the day I'm supposed to give my notice.

"I was there when your father was found, Mrs. Price. We're. None of us. Casual about this case. Believe me, the police are working very hard —"

"If they're working so hard. What have they found out about his appointment? I told them about it. But I could see at the time it was going in one ear and out the other."

"Appointment?" Jack was confused.

"On the day my father was killed he was expected at my house for lunch. But he had to cancel a few days before. He said something had come up. An appointment. I didn't ask him anything more about it because I figured it was none of my business. But then, after what happened. Don't you see? The person who made that appointment was obviously the same person who killed my father."

"Well . . ." Jack shrugged. "I really don't think you can leap to an assumption like that."

"I can tell you who *wasn't* meeting my father." She reached into her bag for a long list of names and numbers that filled both sides of a sheet of typing paper. "I've called all these people myself. All my father's friends. Our family. His business associates. Every name in his address book. I've called them all and none of them made that appointment."

Jack accepted the list, which included hundreds of names.

"Since none of these people made this appointment, Mr. Meehan. Who did?"

"Uh . . . Anybody could have, I'm afraid. Even somebody coming to read the meter."

"I called the gas company and the electric company," she retorted.

"This appointment might have been with a friend of your father's. Someone whose name wasn't in his address book. Someone you don't know. Maybe even a lady friend."

The suggestion made her angry. "It was the killer."

"Mrs. Price, you're asking us to make an assumption based on no evidence whatsoever. Now, we don't work that way."

"It's because he's rich," she sneered.

"Excuse me?"

"Charles Carver. I know the whole story about him from Mr. Orsino there. Carver made that appointment with my father. He denies it, of course. But he wouldn't face me to deny it. Had his lawyer write me a letter."

"Again. You haven't given me any proof, evidence."

"Don't think you're fooling me." Mrs. Price nodded at Jack and lowered her voice. "See, my father was a police officer, Mr. Meehan. So I know a little bit. About crooked judges and crooked lawyers. And how if you've got enough money you can buy your way out of anything."

"Mrs. Price." Jack looked down at his desk and then back to the outraged woman. "I shouldn't even be discussing an investigation in progress. But I'm going to tell you that Charles Carver was in Chicago at the time your father was killed. And he's got witnesses and documentation to prove it."

"Chicago is only five hours away by jet. Have you thought of that?"

Jack didn't answer. Pointless to argue with someone as emotional, as obsessed as this lady had become. He glanced at the incredible list that represented so many tedious hours on the telephone. Mrs. Price, he wanted to say. Go home to your family and forget all this. You're not doing anybody any good.

And yet, he wondered about Walter Hamparian's appointment. Why hadn't he heard of it before?

"No one cares," Janice Price concluded. "I talk to them and I can tell. They're all the time hoping I'll go away. So they can sweep my father's murder under the rug. No one cares, Mr. Meehan. No one."

The prosecutor could not reply. He stared at the envelope on his desk. It contained his resignation.

Once Janice Price had gone, Jack Meehan was on the phone to Detective Lieutenant Lyle Sullivan. "What do you know about a meeting Walter Hamparian was to supposed to have had on the afternoon of his death?"

"Oh. You've been talking to the formidable Mrs. Price."

"Well. I was just curious to know. Is there anything to her story?"

Detective Sullivan chuckled. "I'm sure there's something to it. Something like the old guy didn't want to go to his daughter's house for lunch. He doesn't like her cooking. Or the kids drive him nuts. So he said he couldn't come. And he made up an excuse so's not to hurt her feelings."

"That's what you think?"

"That's what I think."

"Mrs. Price, she thinks Charles Carver murdered her father."

"Well, she must've got that off her Ouija board. Because she hasn't an idea when it comes to evidence."

"Yeah, that's what I told her," Jack replied.

"Anyway, I thought you were off this business, Counselor. I thought we laid the Charles Carver theory to rest the other day."

"You know, I was thinking. Just in case. Has anyone checked the phone records? If someone made an appointment with Hamparian. The chances are they made this appointment over the phone. Now, Carver was supposedly in Chicago during this time. So, if he made the appointment. If he had called Hamparian. The hotel might have a record of it."

Sullivan muttered. "The Hamparian homicide isn't even our business. It's an active investigation of the Welton Police Department."

"You know, Lyle, you worked real hard undermining me with Mullins the other day. Now, you could work the other side of the street a little. You could do this for me. Call Chicago. Check the phone records."

"Well, tell me this. If Carver made a phone call from Chicago. Well. How does he turn around and kill Hamparian in Welton?"

"Mrs. Price reminds us that Chicago is only five hours away by jet. Suppose Carver came back here on Thursday. Killed Hamparian on Friday morning. And returned to his hotel in time to check out by late Friday afternoon."

"Busy guy."

"And then there's the other possibility. That Carver didn't have to kill Hamparian. He got someone to do it for him."

Detective Sullivan more or less agreed to call Charles Carver's Chicago hotel. The prosecutor found Sullivan's attitude particularly aggravating. Sullivan had made up his mind that the Goodfellow murder was solved, and that the Hamparian homicide was none of his business. He was indifferent to any information that tended to contradict these conclusions.

Hanging up, Jack Meehan grew silent, reflective. He'd just taught himself something. Perhaps he too was guilty of taking a one-sided view of the problem.

From early on, he'd made the assumption that everything flowed from the warranty fraud, one small crime leading to larger ones. Well, it seemed logical at first. The bookkeeper had been killed. An investigator stabbed to death. An alleged participant in the fraud, the parts driver, had disappeared. Finally, even the wild card, Grover Durham, had a criminal record, making his involvement in the scam a possibility.

And yet, despite all of Jack's digging, there was no hard evidence linking either James Goodfellow or Grover Durham to the fraud. Furthermore, Walter Hamparian's detective efforts had gone nowhere. The old man had not been a threat. Finally, fraud is not exactly a hanging offense.

So, why were these men murdered? Was something else at work here, some factor not yet considered?

The prosecutor had to readjust his thinking. He'd swallowed whole the tale of Grover Durham meeting Charles Carver. He saw now that Willie Laughlin's story was jerry-built, full of holes. As Frank Mullins had said, Jack just wanted to believe it, to believe a certain set of facts. Now he must see the matter without prejudice. Face the truth, even if the truth hurt.

Then, Jack Meehan had an exciting revelation. He could not prove the common thread, the motive that ran through each of these homicides, as Frank Mullins had demanded. But for the first time, he knew what that motive was.

21

ACROSS the vast, flat athletic field, she was a tiny figure. She sat on a bench beside a heavyset woman, watching the children as they climbed the jungle gym and sailed to dizzying heights on the swings.

When she rose to leave, the children gathered round, urgently, closer and closer, clinging to her coat. She bent to kiss and hug each one. Probably, they were all teary-eyed.

Finally alone, making her way back, she signaled for the police dog that had been chasing pigeons across the muddy brown soccer field. Flushed, she seemed preoccupied with her own sadness. Until, that is, she reached the parking lot and found Jack Meehan beside her car.

"How?" Georgine Goodfellow seemed angry and alarmed. "How did you know where to find me?"

"Sergeant Silva. He's been looking out for you."

"You mean he's been spying on me."

"He's been looking out for you," Jack repeated.

The dog, growling, showed an unfriendly interest in Jack. Georgine held its collar.

"I'll tell you," Jack said. "Let that dog run. And we'll talk."

She looked away. Wind blew her hair about her face. "Just. I don't think that's a good idea."

"What?"

"Talking to you is not a good idea for me."

"You talked to me before," Jack said.

"Things were different before. Betsy. My lawyer gets furious when I talk to you. She says I have nothing to gain and lots to lose. Besides. I already told you enough. Too much, really."

"Now, Georgine." Jack bent toward her. The dog rumbled. "We both know you're lying."

"Why —"

"We both know you've been lying all along." Jack unbuttoned his coat.

"No."

"I stuck my neck out for you. Everybody told me. Stop screwing around. Just put her away. But I tried to do right by you. And all I expected, all I wanted in return. Was for you to be straight with me."

"I have been."

"Don't lie! Goddammit!" His voice rose. "I still want to help you. But if you don't stop lying to me —"

Suddenly, the dog barked and snapped at Jack, barely missing his fingers. She pulled the animal back while the prosecutor tried to calm himself. He was almost shaking with rage. He could not explain this outburst.

After a few moments, he said quietly, "Tell me again about your father, Georgine."

"My father?"

"You told me before about your father. This warm, wonderful relationship. You and your father. Except you forgot something. I knew your father. Just a little bit and years ago. But I knew him. And he wasn't warm and wonderful. The fact is, you were afraid of your father."

"That isn't true."

"Kids have a good instinct for that stuff. I remember. In those days. Going to your house. Not often. But whenever we went. I was uncomfortable. We all were, us kids. And we picked up on it from you."

"This is ridiculous," she said. "I loved my father. And he loved me."

"That may be, Georgine. But the fact remains. Whether you admit it to yourself or not. You were afraid of him."

"I ought to know how I feel about my own father. Why am I even arguing about this?"

"It wouldn't matter," Jack said. "Wouldn't be important. Except for this. A woman who has a good relationship with her father. In my experience. She's one kind of woman. And the woman who isn't comfortable with her father. She's, she's something else. Less confident. Less sure of herself. More likely to get stuck with some bum and figure that's all she deserves, all she rates. And if she does leave. It's usually to go from one bum to another."

"What you're saying means nothing to me."

Jack smiled. "There was something else you said. At the end of the first interrogation. Something you said in passing, like you were talking to yourself. And you were so clever about your lies. Describing the killing exactly as it happened. But leaving out one little detail. The detail that someone else was there and pulled the trigger. You never told any lie you didn't need to tell, Georgine. So, when you made this remark. When you made it. I'm guessing it was the truth."

Jack's voice deepened. "You were complaining. Something about all this misery because in your whole life you'd made one mistake. One mistake. And what I want to know now." He moved closer. "What was the mistake? You say you didn't shoot your husband. It wasn't that. Not your marriage either. Because your marriage produced three beautiful children. So it wasn't that. And I'm asking, what was it, Georgine?"

She wouldn't look at him, but gazed across the field.

"You know what I think? I think you had an affair with someone. I think that was your mistake. Your one mistake. An involvement. A thing with someone. And it caused your husband's murder."

She turned her face away, shaking her head.

"I don't know his name," Jack persisted. "But he's one of the boys over at Parkside. Whenever he came to see you. He drove the company car. Parked it over on the other side of the woods. Maybe you called him. Yeah. Maybe you called to let him know when the coast was clear, your husband gone to work, the kids shipped off to the grandparents. But whoever this guy is, I've got a pretty good idea he killed Walter Hamparian. Grover Durham. Maybe Paul Barrasso. And, with your help. James Goodfellow. He left you holding the bag on that one. Told you to plead guilty to manslaughter. Or self-defense. Or something. Anyway, he told you you'd get off. Maybe he promised to marry you somewhere down the road. And you believed him. Except, after all this time, Georgine. Do you still think it's going to work?"

She looked up and wet her lips. "You. If you only knew how wrong you are."

"Go ahead," Jack dared. "Tell me how wrong I am."

She watched the dog racing across the field. "I need a drink."

The bottle was in her car, under the seat.

"It was a mistake. The worst mistake of my life. I met a man. And he set out to win me over. A whole campaign like. And by the time I realized what was happening. It was too late."

"He won you over?"

"He was always full of compliments. He'd say kind things, things I never heard at home. He had a way about him, you know. A nice smile. Charm. You're probably thinking I was depressed or something. And what he said was just flattery. The bored housewife story. And you've heard it before. But."

She paused, remembering, nearly smiling. "Other guys, lots of guys, have come on to me before and I just put them off. He looked at me. I could, you know, feel it. With the wide shoulders and the muscle tone you can see right through his shirt. I guess I'd always been aware of it. Without admitting it. To myself. How much I liked men like that. Was drawn to them.

"One day. While Jim was at work and the kids were with Grandma. He took me for a drive. It was early summer. I can still remember how everything you looked at was green. Like green was the only color in the world. And he stopped. On some winding road somewhere. Near a pasture with horses and cows. I did say no. Told him no. But he kissed me anyway. And after that. I just . . ."

"What?"

She stared at the bottle and shrugged. "He told me not to do anything. To sit back and relax. And he started massaging my face. And worked down." Her fingers slid down the neck of the bottle.

"We don't need all the details," Jack said uneasily.

"He told me later he actually studied, took a course in massage. Because he knows how important that is to a woman. How guys make the mistake, thinking women have erogenous zones. But, he says women just *are* erogenous. And, well, I've never had an experience like that. He could just touch me. Touch me a certain way. And that was all it took."

There was a dreamy, though somber, tone to these recollections. She gazed skyward, eyes unfocused, seeming to forget Jack, who sat silently, occasionally biting his lip.

"There was never a bit of room in that damned car. But in the beginning it didn't matter. Because while I did him. What seemed important. What he seemed to care about. Was me. All the time. Saying, 'Let me see your face. Look up and let me see your face while you do that.'"

Jack, sitting in her car, could imagine this all too vividly, had to remind himself to stay detached. But his hands were balled into fists and he wanted to smash at something.

"A couple of hours later he asked me to marry him. He had it all planned out. You know, like he'd been thinking about it a long time. Both of us would get quick divorces in Haiti. Then we'd get married down there. I said we'd have to wait and see how things worked out. He didn't like that. But I managed to send him home happy."

"Jesus, Georgine. A guy like him. Jesus."

"I was weak. I was weak. Not to blame Jim. But I need help to be strong. I need to feel, to know somebody cares. And then I'll always be right. Nothing could turn me. If I hadn't felt so alone.

"And I could only think how all my life. I'd taken care of people. My husband. My kids. And I love my kids. But for once. I was going to take care of me. Myself. Before I was too old. I was going to have something I never had before. . . . It was stupid. Selfish. And I guess I got what I deserved. And more. By the second week. What with all the lying and deception. Making love in a parked car began to lose its appeal. I found I disliked myself. And after that it all soured fast.

"He was very demanding. I was to be available three and four times a week. And I'd tell him no. That was too much.

Jim was home a lot. Jim would find out. After a while. I got the idea. He *wanted* Jim to find out. Jim was the big issue. Whether I was still doing it with Jim. All summer long. Whenever I saw him. I got the third degree. If I said no, he complained. I was lying to spare his feelings. And if I said yes, he'd get enraged. Positively enraged. At Jim.

"I found out. Just like he was crazy in love with me. For no reason. He could hate people. Passionately despise them. People he'd never even met. It didn't seem like he had a good grasp on reality, you know? Like. For example. Toward the end he was very insistent I tell Jim about us. Because he had the idea Jim was going to graciously step aside. Well, I had no intention of telling Jim. But I'd pretend like I was just waiting for the right time to do it.

"Another thing. He talked all the time about reincarnation. How he'd lived all these lives, you know? And usually, he knew me in each of them. He said that was the reason for our love at first sight. Because down through the ages. In different times. We'd search until we found each other. And we'd fall in love. Again and again.

"I don't know." She shook her head sadly. "Once I got away from him, I could think. Think clearly. And I started to realize he was completely insane. And I should break it off. I hinted around on the phone one day that maybe we should let things cool down. He told me he'd rather see both of us dead than keep apart. I'm thinking, Okay, Georgine. This is where you get off. Only it wasn't so easy.

"By fall, I was missing our appointments. Making excuses. I thought, well, now he'll get the message. Instead. One afternoon. With the kids in the backyard. He barged into the house. Unannounced. Uninvited. He had to talk. He wanted to show me these old newspaper clippings. About a killing. A murder. And him. They had his picture. And the victim's picture. He put his finger on it and said, 'I killed this man.' I was terrified. Not just that he'd done such a thing. But why did he want me to know? He talked about the pressures on him. He said, 'I have pressures on me now that you couldn't begin to imagine.' And as we talked. For no reason at all. He took out a huge

152

black gun and put it on the table. Between us. He didn't mention it. He just took the thing out. It was there awhile. And then he put it away.

"That night. I told my husband. Which wasn't easy. But I was scared half out of my mind. Afraid for my children. Jim was hurt. Like you'd expect. But, later, he said how maybe some of it was his fault. He said he wanted to save our marriage and that he'd help me.

"I saw then how I'd exaggerated all Jim's flaws. How I'd become obsessed with what was wrong in him. Totally ignoring what was right. His generosity. Loyalty. And so forth. I realized I'd always been a little spoiled, expecting things to be perfect. But things don't go perfect for anyone. My life wasn't perfect. But I had so much to be thankful for. And I prayed to God. Please, help me put right this one mistake. And I'll never complain again. . . ."

She suddenly looked up, eyes wide and moist, as if to ask why God hadn't listened. So completely alone, Jack thought. He wanted to reach out and reassure her with a touch, an embrace. But such a gesture might easily be misconstrued.

"Jim was good. I'm sure now he knew all along what was going on. Was only waiting for me to come to my senses. He talked about going to the police or going to court against this guy. But when I pointed out what that would mean. That everything would become common knowledge. Spilled all over town. Well. Neither one of us wanted that.

"He decided I should call and break it off. A clean break. I wasn't sure. But Jim stood over me while I dialed. On the phone. That bastard. He wouldn't give up. He kept insisting I wasn't acting of my own free will. Like Jim was making me say those things. I denied that. I swore I was doing what I thought best. Then, he started saying, 'Jim's there. Isn't he? Your husband, he's there.' And he says, 'Put Jim on the phone.' I looked up at my husband and said, 'He wants to talk to you.' And even while I'm saying it I realize what a stupid, stupid thing I'm doing. Once he knew Jim was there he became more convinced than ever that I'd been forced to make the call.

"All week, he kept telephoning me. At all hours of the day.

Even late at night. Once, at two o'clock in the morning. Always talking ragtime, how he wanted to see me. To set up a meeting, including my husband. He wanted us all to talk this out. Like we were, all three of us, going to a marriage counselor, or something. I begged him. Please, leave us alone.

"The next morning a sand and gravel truck dumped two tons of crushed stones in our driveway. We woke up to it. Rocks piled six feet high. They said we'd ordered it. After we got the mess cleaned up. Which took all day. Jim drove to his house and left a note in the mailbox threatening legal action. I guess . . . that was a mistake.

"Within the hour he came to our house. My husband didn't want to deal with him. And Jim tried to leave. He followed. Out the door. Saying, in a voice. I can still hear it. Very calm, almost friendly voice. Saying, 'Let's talk, Jim. Let's work this out together.' "

For nearly a minute, she didn't speak. Head down, she suddenly, carefully, placed the wine bottle on the floor. Jack was about to say something himself.

"After," Georgine said. "After he murdered my husband . . . he brought me into the kitchen. He acted so calm. As if what had happened. As if we'd both planned it out together. Only one time he showed . . . emotion. He got mad at Jim. For trying to destroy our love, he said. For causing the killing. He was mad at Jim, if you can follow this, for 'forcing' his own murder.

"He said I should blame it on an intruder. A burglar. And that if his name became involved. They'd crucify him. Because of his past. He just assumed I'd cooperate. So, so sure of himself. And I figured. To be that sure. He must know something I don't. I just better do what he says.

"I took the blame on myself. Because no one would believe that foolish burglar story. And I was afraid. If the police started investigating. They might find him. And if they did. And if he got the idea I'd betrayed him. God knows what he'd do.

"Even after I was arrested. Sitting in the police station. And for all the days after that. I had the feeling. Like anything I said or did would get back to him. And I could be dead in a minute. Just like Jim. It's funny too. Because he abandoned me. Completely. I haven't spoken to him since that night."

Drained, Georgine exhaled, gripping the bottom of the steering wheel with both hands, staring out over the hood.

"I would have told you all this last time. The whole truth. But I was afraid. I thought you'd get the wrong idea. You'd think because we were lovers. You'd think we planned to kill Jim together. But then. You come back. And I find out you think that anyway. So, I decided I might as well tell you. And maybe you'll understand what I'm up against."

She looked glumly at the floor. "I'll go to jail. In a way, I deserve it. I didn't hold the gun. But if I hadn't taken up with him. My children would still have a father. . . . Only, only I don't deserve to go to jail for years and years. And not see my babies again. I didn't mean to hurt anyone."

"I, I can help you," Jack said. "But, for God's sake, no more lies, Georgine. Tell me everything. Please. Every detail. Every name. Now."

She sniffled. "Oh, sure. You want me to tell his name. And if you believe me. Even that won't be the end of it. Next, you'll want me to testify in court. And I won't. I've said enough. Risked enough. Just sitting here with you is a risk."

Her resistance astonished him. Didn't she realize that among all the police, judges, and lawyers awaiting her, only Jack Meehan wanted to help? God, that was as obvious as the look on his face. Why couldn't she see it?

For a moment, he thought to appeal to her, one human being to another. To do something dramatic. To engulf her in his goodwill. But he wasn't sure how, and the idea left him oddly frightened.

"If I talk against him," she said. "Well. These things have a way of leaking out."

Jack shifted uneasily, remembering the Barrasso debacle, how that statement had *leaked out*. He had the unsettling feeling that Georgine was referring to it.

"Has it occurred to you, Georgine. Once we have his name. We can bring him in. Get him off the streets. I'll see to it personally that you're protected."

"Aren't you forgetting? He's killed before. And that didn't keep him off the streets."

"Well. Neither one of us knows the circumstances of that. Obviously, someone screwed up somewhere."

"No shit."

"With your help," Jack insisted. "We'll have enough evidence this time to put him in prison forever."

"Prison is not forever," she replied. "Don't you read the papers? What he's got planned for me. If I help you. That's forever. Because he'll be loose again. On parole. Or furlough. Or work-release. So many excuses they've got for letting people out. They'll find one for him. And laws and evidence and rules. He won't be hassled by all that. When he decides to kill me, he'll just kill me. The way he killed those others." She looked directly at Jack. "Don't tell me these things can't happen, Mr. Meehan. Because they do happen. They have happened."

She sat back, voice soft, resigned. "I see what you want. You want me to trust your courts and judges. Well, I know how that works. When I'm murdered too, everybody goes around for a week saying how terrible. And after that, no one can remember my name. Well. No thanks. I'd rather stay alive."

Then, unexpectedly, but matter-of-factly, she said, "Maybe you think I deserve to die."

"Come on, now." Jack smiled. Yet, he wondered, how am I coming across? Stiff and officious? Just a different kind of cop? She doesn't trust me, otherwise she'd cooperate.

The prosecutor had always prized his cunning as an interrogator. In court, more than once, his apparently plodding manner had gained admissions from witnesses who'd sat down intending not to make them. What was the best approach here? Georgine was like a lost soul, tumbling away from him. Perhaps he could shock her back.

"You still care for this man."

"No."

"You still feel something for him."

"Hate," she said. "Fear."

"Something else. He has some hold on you. Or you'd tell me his name."

"I hope I never see him again. I swear it. I'd rather be dead than have him touch me."

Jack spent a lot of time just staring, hoping she would feel obliged to fill the silence. That never happened. She seemed accustomed to silence.

"You think staying quiet keeps you safe?" Jack said softly. "If you took a vow of silence you still wouldn't be safe. Because he can never be sure. Understand? Anytime. You might decide to cooperate."

"I won't."

"He doesn't know that, Georgine. And the problem for you. Is this. You don't have any easy choices. But I'm telling you what I honestly believe. Your best chance. Your best chance is with me."

"With you?"

"Come down to my office. We'll put you on a polygraph, a lie detector."

She stared at the bottle on the floor, a sleepy look coming over her.

"A polygraph's not admissible in court, understand. But we tend to trust it as an investigative tool." She hadn't moved. He couldn't be sure she was listening any longer. "The test can tell us that your story. Your version of your husband's death is true."

"Oh."

"And if it is. If the lie detector exonerates you of direct responsibility. And I'm satisfied. I'll drop all charges. And if you want to cooperate then. Fine. You can expect us behind you one hundred percent."

She looked outside and suddenly her expression softened, the lines around her eyes seemed to disappear. "You never give up," she said softly.

"I want to help you, Georgine."

She gave him a quick look, smiling slightly but warmly. It

was an abrupt swing of mood, perhaps an effort to escape the prosecutor's demands or to put Jack off balance. Still, he enjoyed her smile.

"I remember when we were kids," she said. "You always got your way. It's, I mean, you were never nasty about it. You just never quit. Until we all played the game the way you thought we should play it."

"You have a better memory than I do."

"I never forgot you," she declared.

"Georgine, I just want things to be done right. To be fair."

She sighed, leaning on the headrest. "It was fun. We had fun in those days."

"It was a long time ago."

"I often wonder how my life would have been different if my family hadn't moved away. It's not good to be uprooted. To be tossed into a new high school and have to make new friends. I liked the friends I had before. And if I stayed. With my friends. Friends who really cared about me. I wouldn't be in this trouble now, I think."

She slumped in Jack's direction, as if to lean on his shoulder. He kept his distance, yet he wondered if it wouldn't be smart to play on her loneliness, her idealized vision of the past. He might win her trust by pretending to romance her. Or would that tactic backfire?

She closed her eyes for a moment, her face relaxed, and Georgine was even lovelier and younger-looking than he'd realized. Jack decided she would never look better for as long as she lived.

"You were right," she was saying.

"What? I was right about what?"

"Seeing my kids. It was a good idea. To talk and hear them laugh. Hear them call me." She looked at him. "A little thing like that. You don't even give it a thought. Until you're alone for so long with no one to call you."

Georgine. Jack wanted to call her, to hold her, to acknowledge feelings he'd tried until now to ignore. But, God, he was frightened. I love Rose. I didn't ask for this. And the ice-cold hands, the throbbing knees, the erection, it all seemed like a bad joke, a rude surprise.

Desire left him confused, alarmed. And yet, he felt something besides desire that disturbed him even more. Conceivably, it went back to their days in Merrymount. He'd always liked Georgine very much. It hurt to see her suffer.

He was torn by the thought of leaving her alone to spend the night in that empty house. Far from pretending to romance her, he dared not even touch her, knowing he would be unable to stop.

The prosecutor was uncomfortable, hot and constricted as if his clothing had shrunk. He'd been a fool, assuming that this sort of thing only happened to people like Frank Mullins, who went looking for it. Jack loved his wife, deeply. Surely, it was not possible to feel so much for another woman.

This isn't happening, please.

"Is something wrong?" Georgine asked.

"I . . . I just remembered something." Jack pressed against the door, as far from Georgine as he could possibly get. Grasping the door handle, he wanted desperately to put his feet safely back on the ground.

"I wish you'd think it over." Struggling for control, his voice went perfectly flat, formal in tone.

"What?" Georgine sat upright.

"Uh. What I said about the polygraph."

She stared at him until Jack looked down at the floor.

"I should be going," he said.

"Sure . . . sure . . ."

"Let me suggest. That you discuss this, what we've talked about. Discuss it with your attorney."

She looked outside, apprehensive, as clouds helped bring on an early evening. The beginnings of panic were at the edges of her lips and in her eyes. The prosecutor's hot and cold manner had frightened her.

"I can't stay," Jack repeated.

"I . . . I have to find my dog."

"He's right outside the door, Mrs. Goodfellow." When Jack stepped out, the panting animal leaped in.

She patted it. "Good boy." She pulled the dog close, her head against it's huge, powerful neck. "They told me not to get him. They said. Someone said. These dogs can turn on you." She gave a hard squeeze. "Do you think this fella's going to turn on me, Mr. Meehan?" The Alsatian's tail thump-thumped on the seat.

"Tell Betsy what we talked about," Jack instructed. "Tell her about the polygraph. Betsy will look out for you."

Driving home to his wife, Jack remembered Georgine saying, I need help to be strong. I need help. To know someone cares. The prosecutor, fearing he cared too much, left it now to Betsy Levin.

"Have you told?" Rose asked once they were both under the covers.

Jack rolled over. "Have I told what?"

"You know, given your notice, told them you're quitting. The arena authority gave you two weeks. Well, a week's gone by already."

"Yeah . . . I'll tell them tomorrow."

"What's the delay?" she asked.

"Oh, well, I've been real busy. Besides, they know already. The guy from the Speaker's office told me everything's been arranged. Giving notice is just a formality." He chose his words with care here. Too little information might make Rose suspicious. And too much would surely have the same effect. Not that there was any reason for suspicion.

"I've been running around," he explained, "trying to get my work in order. You know, presentable for the next guy."

"That Goodfellow murder again."

"Well, yeah. That too. Or. Uh, mainly that. The, uh, the Goodfellow murder. Right."

After a pause, Rose said, "If it's so important, it's too bad they didn't give you more time to finish."

In the living room, behind the couch, was a rolled-up Oriental rug. Of course, with the new job, the Meehans could well afford it. Jack was in no position to ask his wife to take it back.

Rose talked of interrupting her studies for a year. "So we can spend more time together." The extra money, she explained, would make all the difference. "No more running around like crazy people, breaking our backs for a few extra dollars. For the first time, we'll be financially secure."

For Jack, the new job marked a logical progression in his career. He'd worked very hard. More and more, he realized that he deserved this step up.

Only, what would become of Georgine when he left the office seven days hence? Here was the rub that kept him awake far into the night. He liked to imagine that his replacement would be as diligent as he had been. In fact, Frank Mullins had hinted at taking over the case himself.

Jack could not bear the thought of Georgine in prison. She'd be so different after that, harder and older.

It wasn't fair to Rose, the way this woman haunted him. But Jack seemed unable to control his imagination. Uninvited, images of Georgine came to him. He could hear the loving things she wanted to tell him. Could see her looming over him, lips parted, naked, her plump white breasts swaying, sliding across his body. Looking up, he would be a little intimidated because he could see Georgine and nothing else.

For all that, the prosecutor was, by nature, a wary man. Even Georgine Goodfellow could not break down his defenses. Some part of him remained always the skeptic.

I never forgot you. She'd practically made a play for him. In the car, he was almost certain he could have had her right there. What did it all mean? Was she somehow seeking refuge in memories of happy childhood? Or was she afraid and grasping for Jack's affection as a buffer, lest she fall back under the influence of her lover, her husband's killer? Or, finally, was she simply using Jack Meehan to escape punishment for her crimes?

The prosecutor was intrigued by her description of the murder's aftermath. The killer hadn't simply left Georgine. He had "abandoned" her. *Abandoned.* It was an odd choice of words.

"You still feel something for him." Jack had tried to shock her. "I'd rather be dead than have him touch me," she had replied, rather extravagantly. Did the lady protest too much? Georgine had loved this fellow, and he had *killed* for her. The possibility of ties between them was real, even if Jack Meehan did not want to believe it.

161

22

MARY ANN PEASELY, the supervisor of passenger operations, slowly shook her head at Assistant District Attorney Jack Meehan. "You want an ID for a passenger on either an inbound Thursday afternoon flight. Or an outbound Friday afternoon flight. Two months ago. I mean, seriously, do you know how many thousands of faces we've seen since then?"

"I've got a good feeling." Jack waved Charles Carver's picture. "Somebody might remember this guy."

"I hope you realize how time-consuming this will be. Those who might have seen him. You're talking about pilots, flight attendants, boarding personnel, security, tickets and reservations. A couple of dozen people."

"I'll need all their names. And fast. I've only got a week to see as many of them as I can."

Jack met with several people that afternoon. In the supervisor's office he displayed an eight-by-ten glossy of Charles Carver and reminded each that the weather had been well below freezing on both of the days in question. He showed newspapers, borrowed from the library, saying, "Here's what was going on in the world on those days."

The results were disappointing. No one could be certain he or she even remembered the day. "There wasn't anything special about it," said one.

A security officer, however, did recognize the photo. "Sure. This is the guy sells cars on TV between the wrestling matches."

In the late afternoon, Jack called the Palm Beach and Key West police departments, seeking information, even gossip, concerning Charles Carver. "I know the guy," one sergeant explained. "He's a solid citizen type. Plays racquetball sometime with the chief."

As he listened, disheartened, the prosecutor noticed a letter on his desk from the Michigan Shores Hotel in Chicago. Phone wedged beneath his ear, he tore the envelope open. Incredibly, Detective Sullivan had finally made a contribution, for here was Charles Carver's Chicago telephone bill. Jack was so excited he hung up on Palm Beach in midsentence.

One by one, the prosecutor ran down the numbers Carver had called. He discovered that several calls had been made to an airline ticket office in Chicago, several to his dealership, four to the home of Richard Ripler, and one to Walter Hamparian.

The last call consumed more than thirty minutes and was placed just two days prior to the retired policeman's death.

The prosecutor said nothing of this to his superiors, confident it was only the beginning of an avalanche of discovery. He could not yet prove that Charles Carver had made an appointment with the victim, as Janice Price had insisted. And he was further still from confirming her belief that Carver was the killer. Nonetheless, Jack finally had tangible evidence that he was on the right track and Charles Carver was entangled in more than warranty fraud. The logjam was broken.

Milham Detective Tom Concannon arrived without an appointment, taking a seat before Jack Meehan could say a word. "I'm Concannon." He loosened his tie and then his shoelaces, leaned back, and groaned with fatigue. "You know me," he declared. "I was your witness in a big drug case once. What was the guy's name? Schumaker. Leon Schumaker. Remember him? You remember that case? He's dead now, you know."

Jack nodded, though he knew Concannon largely by his reputation as "Mr. Plainclothes." When Columbo gets a new raincoat, they joked, he gives the old one to Concannon. Even dressed for court, the detective looked unkempt in ill-fitting suits.

"I'm due in court just now myself." Jack looked at his watch.

"Only take a minute." Concannon was unwrapping a cigar, pulling the waste bucket close for an ashtray. "You've been asking questions." The ruddy-faced policeman struck a match and lit his cigar. "About Parkside. The auto dealership. Charlie Carver's dealership. You've been all over asking questions." He puffed on the cigar. "Do I lie?"

"What? No. That's true."

163

"But you haven't been to see me. I wonder why that is, Mr. Meehan. Because I know that place. I've had dealings with those people. I know them, I know them all."

"I'm prosecuting in the murder of the Parkside bookkeeper, James Goodfellow."

"I don't know him," Concannon said. "He wasn't Carver's employee. Was he?"

"An independent contractor."

"I thought so. Because I know all the people there. Right now, I'm working a case. A warranty fraud. Well, you know all about it. I hear you been looking into it yourself. And I wondered if maybe we could share information."

"Where did you get my name, Detective? Who sent you here?" And why, the prosecutor might have added, for he feared an effort to protect Charles Carver.

"Nobody sent me. I just got your name somewhere. And I came because maybe I can help you. If you've got an interest in these people. Well, I know them. I know them personally. I've bought cars from Charlie Carver. I go in there all the time. Parkside VW is a pretty important business in Milham."

Jack watched the rumpled detective carefully. He seemed too anxious to tell his story, as though he'd rehearsed it. Or was the prosecutor being too distrustful?

Jack ventured, "There's one name I'm very curious about. Paul Barrasso."

"Gone. Disappeared. Which isn't like him. I've known Paul since he was a kid stealing bicycles. I was in uniform back then. He was always a scummy little prick. The whole family, they're like that. Even his grandmother. She was up the station a few days ago. She's going to sue us because we didn't return Paul's tape deck. She says we stole it, somebody, some officer stole it. Well, how do we know he even owned this tape deck? All the inventory says is stereo system."

Again, Jack glanced at his watch.

"My point is, Counselor. I know Paul Barrasso. I've known him for years. So, if you've got any questions about him. Who better to ask?"

"Paul Barrasso told me. Among other things. He strongly

164

implied that Charles Carver killed the VW investigator, Hamparian. And maybe others before him. He was terrified of Carver."

"Terrified?" Concannon chewed on his cigar. "No."

"I've got it on tape."

"If Barrasso said that, he had to be lying. I'd go back and talk to him again."

"Now why didn't I think of that?" Jack snickered.

"Because I know Charlie Carver pretty good. And I know lots of people think he's an arrogant asshole. But nobody's afraid of him, physically afraid of him. Now, you want to talk about that other character in the shop there. Ripler. He plays at 'Mr. Charm.' But nobody who really knows him crosses Ripler. I give the icy son of a bitch a wide berth myself. Carver, he's so scared of the guy. It's like Ripler's taken over the dealership."

Jack's eyes narrowed. "I talked to Paul Barrasso. Ripler he never mentioned. He said he was scared of Charles Carver. And he said he wasn't the only guy who was."

"Yeah. Well. All I can tell you is this, Counselor. Barrasso complained to me once. Not officially. But recently, within the past year. And I thought he was half serious at the time. But he complained to me that Richard Ripler had threatened his life."

"That's really out of left field, Detective. You've got some record, some evidence of this?"

"The evidence is," Concannon said, "I'm telling you it happened. That's the evidence." Concannon flicked ashes into the wastebasket. His teeth were stained yellow. He blew a dense cloud of smoke across the room.

"I thought you'd know this guy, Tony. I thought you knew everybody in town."

"Yeah. Well, that's what I wanted to talk to you about." Reaching across the table for salt, Harwood Police Sergeant Tony Silva pulled the wax paper from his meatball sub. "Okay. I'm asking around. Does anybody know a guy named Richard Ripler? And somebody says. 'Oh, yeah. The Little League guy.'

And that's when it clicks. I *do* know him. When my youngest boy was in the Little League. This Ripler was his coach. They all called him 'Mr. Rip.' New to the town then. Very intense fella during the games. He's still involved in the Pony League and the Youth Ice Hockey, I hear."

"Tony, you're going to be chief someday. Tell me more."

"Well, what can you say about a guy, he's always working with kids? He's . . . a nice guy, I guess. I remember he smiled a lot around the parents. Sort of a politician."

"A guy I talked to called him icy," Jack said. "How'd your kid like him?"

"He didn't."

"Oh?" Jack raised his eyebrows slightly.

" 'Mr. Rip' took the game seriously. Liked to win. He was hard on the kids sometimes. Especially his own kid. My Manny, he called the guy a phony. And maybe he is. Maybe he smiles on the top and the ice is underneath. That's the sort of thing a kid will see when an adult won't."

Jack shrugged. "Somebody gave me this guy's name. And I figured I should go back and take another look at him. But so far, the worst I've found out is that your kid didn't like him. I called Greenfield police. Out west. Where he used to live. But he's got no police record and the officer I talked to. He didn't know the name."

"Maybe it's an alias."

"I thought of that. I thought of that, Tony. And I checked the registry. Apparently, Richard Ripler has held the same driver's license continuously for over twenty years. I sent along a picture of him to Greenfield. They're going to ask around about him."

"So." Tony washed down a bite of his sub with Coca-Cola. "You can cross him off your list."

"Well, maybe not. After listening to you. One thing I've got to ask myself. About Ripler. When he's out coaching all these baseball teams and hockey teams. When he's involved in all that. Town activities. Does he cross paths with Georgine Goodfellow?"

Driving home, Jack remembered the beefy little fellow in the white shirt sporting the VW logo. Up to now, when Jack imagined Georgine's sordid rendezvous, the man was Charles Carver, with his Yankee self-assurance and his perfectly capped teeth. You could understand a lonely woman touched by all that salesman's charm, seduced by the bulge in his pockets, the promise of unlimited possibilities.

But Ripler?

Oh, Georgine. Why this, this nonentity? This glorified mechanic dressed like a bank vice-president.

Of course, it couldn't be true. It was Carver, not Ripler, involved in murder. And the Barrasso tape proved it.

With Rose at night school, the kids in bed, Jack shut himself in his office and played that tape again. He'd not heard it, couldn't bear to listen to it, since the housebreak. On tape, Paul Barrasso spoke like a voice from the dead, the sound insubstantial and tinny as if it emanated from the bottom of a trash can.

"Look. You didn't get any of this from me. But. Even before. There were stories. Rumors. About him killing people. Someone. Something from years ago. I heard he even had clippings, newspaper stories about it. Which, I thought that was bullshit. Until he showed them to me. Like he was proud, you know? He does these things. Then, he's got to tell somebody. Because he's so proud of himself. Strange. But I'll tell you. He's got people in there scared shitless. . . . You know Carver."

Jack had answered, "Carver?"

"Carver's fucking unreal. He's got so goddamn much money. And there's no ripoff he won't try."

A chill ran across the prosecutor's shoulders. "Holy shit!" he whispered. Why hadn't he realized before? He hurriedly reversed the tape, replaying the crucial exchange.

"He's got people in there scared shitless. . . ." Then, a pause, as if he takes a breath or looks away momentarily. Finally, he says, "You know Carver."

Does he mean Carver is scaring people? Or does he mean that Carver is one of the people scared? Had Barrasso, like Georgine Goodfellow, been too afraid to even mention the murderer's name? Had he spoken of Carver to abruptly change the topic?

Judging by his inflection, either interpretation could be correct. Words mean what they say. And when you're careful, as any good lawyer should know, they don't say anything. Had Barrasso been deliberately obscure?

This discovery might have depressed the prosecutor, another key assumption proved questionable. Instead, he saw again that facing the truth opened up new possibilities. He'd jumped to the conclusion that Barrasso had fingered Charles Carver.

Well, suppose he hadn't.

Jack Meehan hadn't wanted to make the trip, his fourth this week through city traffic to the airport. Flight attendant Lori McKenzie was no more enthusiastic, not even bothering to sit down. Wrapped in a wool coat, hefting a large travel bag, she hovered over the desk, anxious to leave for home.

"It was a cold day," Jack explained. "Freezing."

"I remember the flight."

"You do?"

"I remember it because I'd worked twelve days straight. We're not supposed to do that. But we'd had such a bad winter, so many people out sick. I volunteered. I worked twelve days. And after that flight. I took a week off. So I remember it because I counted the hours."

"This passenger. You might remember him because he could have been very, very nervous. Irritable maybe. He was in a hurry. Under a lot of pressure. And he might have shown that."

"I remember the flight, sure. But the chances of remembering an individual passenger . . ." Glancing at Carver's photo she was momentarily quizzical. Then, picking it up, she gave it her complete attention. She dropped slowly to a chair. "Yeah . . . yeah . . ." She looked up. "What do you want this guy for?"

* * *

"How much was it?" Jack winced as Rose placed a huge package on the kitchen table.

"Wait'll you see what it is," she said.

Jack tore back the wrapping. "A what? A video recorder?"

"And camera." Rose was smiling the sort of smile, Jack decided, that only comes from spending money. Having shown thrifty restraint for all their married life, Rose seemed to have succumbed totally to this pleasure.

"Don't you think you could have asked me first?"

"I wanted to surprise you," she said. "You always talked of getting one of these to take pictures of the kids. And now that we can afford one. Jack, they're so much better than the old home movies. They gave me a demonstration at the store. . . ."

She went on about the machine, taking parts from the box, explaining the features, expecting her husband to be as happy and excited as she was. Instead, Jack's face had gone off-color with worry. He wondered about the price tag these good things always carry, and wondered about the new job that was supposed to pay for them. Clearly, he was caught in a trap that would punish him no matter which way he turned.

"What's wrong?" Rose finally asked.

"What?"

"Something's bothering you. What is it?"

"No." Jack touched one of the boxes.

"The job. It's the job, isn't it, Jack. Oh, God, what's happened. Did you lose the new job?"

"No, no. In fact, I'm seeing the guy from the arena authority. The chief counsel. I'm having breakfast with him in the morning."

"Jack, there's something you're not telling me."

"No. Well. There is one thing. It's nothing really. I'm going to ask him for more time. More time to finish up my work at the district attorney's office. I'm sure they'll give it to me. Once I explain how important —"

"But what if they don't?" Rose demanded.

"If they don't." He shrugged. "If . . . well. I'll just have to honor their wishes. I wouldn't want to lose this job. I've worked too hard. We both have. I couldn't disappoint you like that."

Carefully, she put the video camera back in the box. "Why is it so important that you have more time? You've been on this case for months."

The prosecutor went to the sink, turned on the tap, filled a glass with water. His mouth was very dry and he took a long swallow.

"It's important." He looked down at the glass. "Because I'm so close. Because I now know why Goodfellow and the others were murdered. And I think I know who killed them."

Rose stood. "Well . . . who?"

"I don't want to say." Jack turned. "Until I'm sure. Until I've proved it. And for that I need more time."

"I see. But. You can tell them. Whoever takes your place. You can tell them everything you've found out."

"It won't work, Rose. They see this thing all different from the way I do. Mullins and Flaherty. They want Georgine Goodfellow in prison. So they can close the book. Once they lock up Georgine. They can write off Walter Hamparian as a mugging victim. All of which gets their friend Charles Carver off the hook."

"Carver? But why should they care about Carver?"

"They're protecting Carver. Have been all along. Because he's politically connected through his attorney, Biddle. They've both got access to lots of money. And Rich Flaherty is going to need money to run for Congress. That's a big job. Congress. A guy might do things he wouldn't ordinarily do with that kind of temptation. An important job like that and all he has to do is look the other way for a minute."

"You mean Carver's bribed the district attorney?" Rose was shocked.

"He doesn't have to bribe anyone. Because he's one of them. You see? They don't think for a minute that Charles Carver would be a part of murder. They see his money. His background. The clubs he belongs to. The people he knows. Skip Biddle says Carver's all right. Well, he must be all right then. It's easy to believe that if you want to believe it bad enough.

And what they're doing now. They're trying to keep his name clean. Keep Charles Carver as far from any ugly accusations as possible. It's a favor. Because someday soon, Carver or Biddle will do a favor for them."

For a long time, Rose looked sadly at the pile of equipment on the table. "Maybe," she said, "maybe they'll give you the extra time to get your work done. After all, they've been pretty good to you up to now."

Jack was struck by this last remark. Yes, they had been good to him. Why were they so good to him?

23

At one time, Bull Feeney enjoyed the downtown Runway Lounge. Sitting at the rear, watching Edna's act, his excitement increased wickedly as the crowd grew louder.

Edna always got them shouting too. Pale and sweet-faced, she seemed shy, even afraid, stepping out there. But as her clothes came off, she began to smile, to move with wild pleasure. At the end, her milk-white body was so loose, her eyes so frank and hungry, it seemed that any man who dared to mount the stage could have her right there.

"I love to watch them," Edna would say. "Even the creeps who try to put me down. Because I'm shaking it under their fucking noses. I let them see everything. And they'd die to have a taste. To have a touch even. And they're screaming. Katie! Katie! Because they don't even know my real fucking name. And they're never going to get more than a look."

"Yeah." Bull would be grinning by now.

"But you, baby. You can look when you want. You can have me whenever you want. I'll do what you fucking tell me to do. When I'm out there, that's our secret. Always in my mind. How what they're screaming for, you own. You fucking own me, Bull."

Well, it wasn't quite true.

Lately, he didn't like coming in here. He particularly didn't like the way they watched him, the other girls, the bouncers, bartenders, and the manager. He didn't like their false smiles. As if Edna was one of the girls taking customers out back. (She swore on her mother's picture that she wasn't.) As if Bull didn't support himself very well doing jobs for his uncle. (Right now, for example, he was storing some items in the apartment.)

Face it, Edna's "occupation" hadn't bothered him in the beginning because he hadn't expected to be living with her six months later. But when he'd begun hinting that she quit, Edna resisted. Why the hell should she sacrifice her career just because Bull said to?

"Money," she hollered. "Where else do we get this kind of fucking money?"

In the late afternoon, a handful of men watched a dark-haired, dead-eyed teenager sleepily take her clothes off to the frantic beat of "Maniac." Edna sat with Bull at a table far from the stage.

"You always say I don't make enough," Bull was saying. "Well, with this job I'm going to make plenty."

"It sounds fishy to me," Edna replied. "What does your uncle say?"

"You think I got to ask my uncle every time I fart? This is *mine*. Got that? Tomorrow, I see this guy again. We got an appointment. He's paying five thousand for three shit handguns. Five thousand dollars! And that's just the start. This guy wants me to be his supplier. Whenever he needs something."

"And did you finally find out this fucking guy's name?" Edna asked.

"John." Bull nodded. "He says his name is John something."

"What? John Doe? You fucking don't even know who the Christ you're dealing with. What does he want these guns for? Where'd he get your name?"

Bull scratched his eyebrow. "He . . . he heard of me around. What of it? A lot of guys know about me."

"Sure, you're fucking famous."

"And he wants these pieces for protection. He's a businessman. You can tell that's the truth by looking at the guy. He wears nice clothes. And the way he acts and talks, so polite. Like he's your pal. You can tell he's a businessman or something. Respectable, wimpy sort of guy."

"For all you know he wants these guns to blow away the president. You'll have the fucking FBI at our door in the morning."

Suddenly, Bull backed away from the table, his chair scraping the floor. "You think I'm stupid. Is that it? I'm stupid. I'll tell you how stupid I am. This guy is paying five thousand dollars for three pieces my uncle give me for free. And I'm fixing it so he pays for them twice."

"Twice?"

"When he comes to see me tomorrow for the guns. He don't know it. But he's going to see Wachman and Matteo first. In the alley. Okay. So, he wants the pieces he's going to have to go back and get more cash."

Edna watched Bull from the corner of her eye. A woman who lived by illusions, she hadn't any concerning her hulking, live-in lover.

"Well," Bull demanded triumphantly, "what do you say now?"

"I say you oughta be fucking locked up for your own fucking protection."

Bull didn't stay for Edna's evening performance. Instead, he walked four blocks and over the bridge to their apartment, where he planned to watch the hockey game.

In the shadowy hallway, as he unlocked the door, a voice from behind said, "I hope you won't mind, Bull. I couldn't wait until tomorrow."

He turned, amazed and uneasy at the sight of the stranger, the man who'd agreed to pay so much for a trio of Saturday night specials.

"Uh, John."

"I've brought your money, Bull. Can we go in?" He all but pushed the big man inside.

"How'd you find out where I live?"

"I asked around." He lied. In fact, "John" avoided asking questions, being seen, calling attention to himself in any way. He'd simply followed Bull home one afternoon. He'd spotted the girlfriend that same evening, and on subsequent visits learned of her remarkable profession with its demanding hours. He'd taken a lot of time and gone to a lot of trouble, but it was crucial to his plan that he obtain these weapons without leaving a trace of having done so.

Inside, the battered apartment looked like a warehouse. Stacked about the kitchen and living room were televisions, microwave ovens, radios, clocks, and other goods, still in their cartons.

"Well." Bull was confused. "You brought the money?"

The "businessman" patted his coat pocket. "I hope I haven't upset your plans somehow. I assumed you had the items here."

"Uh."

"Show them to me."

Hesitantly, Bull led him into the bedroom with its pink spread and matching curtains. Mirrors were everywhere, even on the ceiling over the bed. Bull stepped over a discarded pair of panties and opened the closet door. He'd been wondering how he could stall John until tomorrow.

Yet, the unexpected visitor seemed so sure of himself — so sure of everything. You didn't want to make a mistake and queer a five-thousand-dollar deal with the possibility of more to come.

Bull reached into a hole in the back wall of the closet and slowly withdrew a string. Like fish on the line, the weapons followed: one, two, three. Small, cheap, twenty-two-caliber pistols.

"These are guaranteed clean from the factory," Bull said. "No serial numbers."

"That's what I'm paying for." The man took the guns, snapped each from the string, and quickly examined them. Noticing they were unloaded, he tested the firing mechanisms. Finally, he began pushing each one into a separate inside pocket of his knee-length coat.

"The money." Bull held out his hand.

"We're going to be doing a lot of business together, Bull."

The stranger placed the third weapon in a deep inner pocket near his waist. Withdrawing his knife, he stabbed Bull where the big man's jacket hung open, right in the center of his stomach. The steel moved in and out so fast Bull never even saw it. He was caught exhaling. Round-eyed, sweating, motionless.

"John" helped move the wounded man back to the bed, where he collapsed with a pitiable groan. Looking up from the edge of the pillow, he fixed disbelieving eyes on his attacker.

"It's not as bad as you think, Bull. Stomach wounds can be a lot of trouble. Very painful. But it doesn't have to be fatal if you get prompt medical attention." He held a restraining hand over Bull. "Try not to move. The worst thing you can do is move around. Now, I plan to make a phone call to the police when I leave. Tell them to come get you. But I want you to prove your good faith first. Cooperate with me."

The attacker felt a tremendous exhilaration. He was cool and in control, the way he'd been the night he killed Grover Durham. For some time now, he'd been afraid he'd lost his nerve. Obviously, he hadn't.

Bull clutched at his gray corduroy shirt, but he could not stem the incredible gush of blood that poured warm through his fingers. And when he closed his fingers, it rushed from beneath his palms, flowed down his sides, and collected in puddles at his back, staining the pink spread black-red. The numbing pain increased if he moved at all.

"These pistols have no shells. Twenty-two ammunition. Now, I can't be seen buying any. You're supposed to have some shells for me. Where?"

Mouth dry, Bull could not speak. His feet and hands began to tingle. He felt dizzy and afraid, completely at the mercy of this madman.

"Are the shells in this room?"

Bull managed a weak nod.

The attacker went to the closet to empty it. Methodically he threw the contents behind him: coats, dresses, jeans, shoes, a hair dryer, several vibrators, lacy costumes, and blankets. All landed in a heap at the center of the room.

"Our appointment tomorrow, Bull. Started to worry me. You were so concerned about how I was getting there. Was I driving or walking? You must think I'm pretty dense, Bull. I wouldn't catch on. Anyway, let it be a good lesson to you about doing the deal straight."

He stood over the bed and sniffed the air. "Somebody's cooking Italian downstairs. Don't try to talk. I'll find the shells." Big Bull's chest heaved. Where his shirt was not wet with blood, it was saturated with sweat. There was no sweat on his face, however. Clammy white, he was two brown eyes trying to read his attacker's mind. God, don't let me die.

"I'm not afraid to kill, Bull. One thing I figured out a long time ago. If you cheat on your taxes. You'll get caught. Because it's all down there on the record. If you waste somebody. And you keep your wits. Well, they can't find you. Or if they do find you. Hell, they can't prove it because the best witness against you is dead."

The attacker remembered Gallo, the first man he'd killed. Like Bull, Gallo had tried to play him for a fool. Gallo with his plaid pants and white belt, his fat jowls and cigar. Smiling, he'd puff smoke in your face while he picked your damn pocket.

So he killed him. He slammed the wrench into the back of Gallo's skull. Before the blow landed, he knew Gallo would die. The thieving bastard slumped to the cement floor while his cigar, still smoking, rolled off to one side. Remarkable. Gallo was dead, but his cigar was alive. And that was frustrating because you couldn't make him pay, couldn't hurt him anymore.

"I'm not going to kill you, Bull. So stop worrying." He pulled out drawers, moved tables. "The way you tried to rip me off. You deserve it. If I just stood here and watched you bleed to death. You deserve that. But I won't let you die. I won't because you can't identify me. And you're young. I feel sorry for you."

Still wielding the knife, he swung his arm as he spoke, casually cutting the phone line. He was enjoying this rare opportunity to speak candidly.

"Do you realize what an advantage it is, Bull? If you're willing to kill in your own best interests? If you're able to do it coolly, competently. Most guys would get emotional. They'd give themselves away. I remember. The first man I ever killed. And this was years ago. I finished him with one blow." He pantomimed. *"Bam!* And after. I kept waiting for the lightning bolts. You know. To see ghosts. Or hear voices. To feel something. Because if you kill somebody. Take a life. Things, the world has got to be a little different after that."

He moved close to Bull, who groaned and gurgled.

"I found out how it is, Bull. Something they don't want anybody to know. The truth. That you can kill somebody. And the world doesn't change at all. If you keep the right attitude. Like, I killed this guy. But I acted like it didn't have anything to do with me. That's how I acted, and pretty soon, it didn't have anything to do with me."

Reaching under the bed, he found another gun and a small box of shells pushed against the wall. Already, blood had leaked through the mattress and box spring and was dripping on the rug. Bull moaned softly, breathing with difficulty. His pupils had lost that urgent sparkle, his eyes no longer seemed focused.

"The law isn't equipped to deal with me, Bull. I'm smart and I'm willing to kill anyone who threatens me or mine. That's why I need these guns. For my plan. I have a way out. Just, so audacious. A certain assistant district attorney won't know what hit him."

Bull was no longer watching the killer and was probably not even listening. Mouth open, lips blue, skin chalky, he looked up, horrified, watching the mirror on the ceiling, watching himself die.

In the morning, the newspapers reported the murder of Carl ("Bull") Feeney, whose body was discovered by his girlfriend, Edna Miller, who danced professionally under the name Katie Miller. While giving no motive, police noted that the victim had been part of a scheme to sell stolen merchandise.

It was still dark the next morning when the killer bought his paper at a small convenience store. He read the account of Feeney's death with pride. His confidence grew.

24

Much later that morning, Georgine Goodfellow and Betsy Levin drove through a steady drizzle to the back entrance of the district attorney's office. Jack Meehan was waiting, holding the door.

"Sorry we're late." Betsy urged Georgine inside. At once, her client moved away from the glass door.

"Good to see you both." Jack straightened his tie. "Well . . . Beginning to look like winter will never end."

"We had to drive all the way in town." Betsy yanked off her rain cap. "Georgine thought someone might be behind us. What was it, dear?"

"Uh . . . an old Volkswagen."

"So, we went all the way in town. And once we got through the tunnel, we came back. Doubled back."

"No old Volkswagen out there." Jack peered through the freezing rain.

Upstairs in the hallway, when a secretary passed by, followed by another assistant district attorney, Georgine blanched and retreated partway down the stairwell. Head bowed, she pulled her hood nearly to her eyes. "You promised no one would see me."

"All these people work for the district attorney's office," Jack said softly. "The only people you're going to see here are law-enforcement personnel. You're perfectly safe."

Georgine would not look up.

"I'm going to scout ahead," Jack said. "It's only a few steps to the library. But I'm going to scout ahead and make sure no one, no one sees you go in there. Understand, it wouldn't matter if they did see you. These people here are all professionals. But just for your peace of mind. I'll make sure no one sees you."

"I don't . . ."

"What?"

"I don't want to be left." She took hold of his wrist and looked him in the eye, pleading. Jack couldn't move or speak. He stared, forgetting to breathe, forgetting to think.

It hadn't occurred to him that she would reach out and touch him, or that his response would be so extraordinary. He wanted very much to embrace her.

"Mr. Meehan will be right back." Betsy gave Jack a queer look as she stepped between them. Georgine let him go.

Jack went to each door, asking coworkers to please stay inside. "I've got a very nervous witness coming by." He even warned the receptionist not to turn her head as they passed.

In the library, they found Phil Ahlquist, the polygraph expert, presiding over his cache of gauges and wires. Georgine again held back.

Jack made the introductions. Ahlquist, a veteran polygraph examiner, was remarkably personable, even friendly. He patiently explained each piece of equipment to Georgine. Meanwhile, Betsy Levin perused the carefully preselected questions.

"I'll ask everything twice," Phil told Georgine. "First time just for practice. So you'll know what's coming. What to expect. The second time, you'll be connected to the machine. Which doesn't hurt a bit. I promise."

But like the friendliest dentist, Ahlquist could never completely ease anxieties. Silent and watchful, holding her arms close to her side, Georgine sat without removing her coat.

"I can see you're nervous, Mrs. Goodfellow," Phil said. "Now a lot of people worry. When a question makes them nervous. They worry that it might — because of nervousness — it might register as a lie. But I want to relax you on that point. The polygraph simply doesn't work that way."

"This machine." Her voice was barely audible. "It'll tell if I'm guilty?"

"Well." Phil clasped his hands. "It's not quite that simple."

"What if I'm not guilty. Okay? But it says I am?"

"I don't think you have to worry if —"

"What if it doesn't work right?" She turned to her attorney. "It's going to say I'm lying. I know it is."

"We've been over this," Betsy said.

"If . . . I mean, God, why should I trust my life to a machine, to that machine? Why should I trust —"

"Georgine!" Betsy spoke sharply, then bent close, whispering. "I told you. We have nothing to lose by taking the test. Nothing to lose."

Georgine couldn't take her eyes off the strange box. Her foot tapped incessantly. She wouldn't look up at anyone.

For Jack, all this was a rude surprise. After the intensity of their last meeting, she did not trust him at all. Rather, she acted as if she'd blundered into a trap. My whole life has been a trap, her eyes seemed to say. So why should this be any different?

"Why don't you let me take your coat?" Jack said. He might have been speaking a foreign language, she gave him such an odd look. He'd tried to sound friendly, supportive, but it had come out nervous and clipped. He kept his distance too, afraid she would touch him again.

In fact, it didn't matter how he sounded, or if she was at ease, or if she trusted him. The important thing was, she was here. And the polygraph would prove her innocent of murder.

"Give Mr. Meehan your coat," Betsy instructed.

Georgine stood.

At that moment, Frank Mullins blundered in. Betsy Levin glared. Jack was speechless.

"Uh . . . yeah." Frank's eyes locked on Georgine, examining her from head to toe, studying her to the point of being rude.

"We're busy here, Frank."

"Could, could I see you outside, Jack?"

"I really wish you hadn't done that." In the corridor, Jack muttered fiercely. "You're going to scare her right out the door."

"So what?" Frank replied.

"So what?"

"It's just like Mr. Flaherty said when he got wind of all this. What the hell is Jack Meehan doing fucking around with polygraphs? What is the point?" Mumbling, Frank turned away. "Don't look now, but here comes 'Butch the Wonder Dog.' "

"What's the delay here?" The ample Betsy Levin suddenly stood between them. "Are we going to get on with this, Mr. Meehan? My client is under a lot of strain."

"I'll be with you in a minute," Jack replied. "Promise."

Mullins smiled. "This is a private conversation, Counselor."

"Just what are you people trying to pull here?" Betsy demanded.

"What? Nothing," Jack insisted.

"Why is he here?"

"I work here," Frank smirked.

"The first assistant had to be informed of our arrangement. That's routine." Jack tried to keep between these two.

Betsy eyed Frank with bald contempt.

"I give you my word," Jack declared, "I am dealing with your client in good faith."

"If she doesn't trust us," Frank said. "To hell with her. Let her take her chances with the jury."

"Just." Jack wheeled. "Stay out of this, Frank. Will you please."

"I don't like this one bit," Betsy said.

"Please." Jack turned again. "Please, Ms. Levin. I promise. Everything will be okay." He was already urging the first assistant up the hall. "Just, please, wait in the library until I've spoken with Mr. Mullins."

"Yeah," Frank called over Jack's shoulder, "go take a load off your feet."

"Are you trying to sabotage me? Is that the idea?" Jack paced before the first assistant's desk.

"I'll tell you, Jack. I'll tell you exactly what I'm trying to do. Which is to wake you up. Because I'm your friend. And because I've been hearing things around here. Whispers. About the way you're leaving, leaving the office in three days. But instead of winding it up, you call this woman in here. She's already confessed to murder. More than once. But you get her

181

in here. You bend over backwards to get her in here. And for what? To take a damn polygraph. On a case somebody else is going to have to prosecute. Let me tell you, my friend. People are starting to have second thoughts about you. They're starting to ask, What's with that guy? He doesn't have all four wheels on the road, that guy."

"Who says these things?"

"Lots of people."

"Like Frank Mullins?"

"I'll tell you what I say. I say whether Georgine Goodfellow takes a polygraph or not is irrelevant. Even if she flunks totally. You can't use it in court."

"I don't want to use it in court," Jack said. "I just want to be reasonably certain the person prosecuted for murder is actually guilty of murder."

"That's not your business, my friend. I say again. Because you seem to have forgotten. By the time Goodfellow comes to trial you'll be gone. To the arena authority. Where your big worry will be how to spend all your money."

"No."

"I should think when you leave —" For a moment, Frank seemed confused. "What . . . what did you say?"

"I said I'm not leaving," Jack admitted. "The job. I called them this morning. Turned it down."

"Well . . . that was dumb."

"Yeah. I guess sometimes I'm dumb."

"I went to a lot of trouble, finding you that job."

"I haven't forgotten who found me the job," Jack said.

"What are you going to tell your family? Your wife?"

"That's my worry." Jack grimaced.

"I can fix this." Frank grabbed for the phone. "It's not too late. I'll just tell them you changed your mind."

Jack watched, spellbound, as the first assistant dialed. Of course, Frank was right. You don't throw away good jobs. A man's first obligation is to his own family.

Yet, without Jack Meehan, Georgine Goodfellow had no chance at all. She was waiting now, expecting another injustice and half believing she deserved it. The prosecutor wanted to be able to walk in that library and look her in the eye without feeling ashamed.

"Put the phone down, Frank."

The first assistant slowly shook his head. "You aren't that crazy. You mean you can't use a one-hundred-percent raise?"

"You know I can use it. You know how bad I want it, need it. You were counting on that."

"I'm not with you, Jacko."

"Maybe I'm way off base, Frank. But I think you saw this coming way back when we met with Biddle at Flaherty's fundraiser. You saw I might be a problem. And you found a neat, painless way to get rid of me, to buy me off."

"I got you a top job. Awful me." Frank replaced the receiver. "What are you going to do once Flaherty goes to Washington? Have you thought about that? Because you'll be on your own, sport. And just getting started in private practice? Getting an office and getting started will cost thousands. Can you afford that? Starting up again. From scratch. With word getting all over town that you're a troublemaker."

Jack took a deep breath. "I'm involved in this Goodfellow case. I'm going to see it through. And if there's any interference. Are you listening, Frank? If there's any interference. Your candidate is going to see what trouble really is. And I mean fucking front-page trouble."

"Is that right?"

"I wouldn't expect you to understand how I feel about this, Frank."

"Oh, but you're wrong. I do understand. I understand fine. I mean, I just had a good look at the lady and I understand perfectly." The first assistant gave a vulgar smile.

"You better watch your mouth."

"All I'm saying —"

"I won't take that shit!" Jack snapped. "Friend or no friend."

Prudently, the first assistant sat. "You don't know who your friends are. That's your problem."

Jack hurried toward the law library. In a few days, he might kick himself for throwing away the big job, damaging his career, disappointing his deserving wife. He couldn't think of any of that now, however. There was only anger for these people who thought they could run him.

Because Jack had played the game with Flaherty and Mullins, they assumed he could be bought the way they'd been bought. Just find a job big enough and he'll plop into the tank.

The assholes, he thought. They don't know the first thing about me. After all these years.

In the library, Phil Ahlquist was alone, packing his equipment.

"Where are they?" Jack looked about.

"Long gone." Phil nodded to the door. "The minute you people went out the hall there? Mrs. Goodfellow took off. Out the back way. If you ask my opinion." He slammed shut his case. "She doesn't want to take this test."

Jack chased down the back stairs, certain he'd find Georgine in the stairwell, huddled with her lawyer, Betsy coaxing her back. But the stairwell was empty and when he ran out to the parking lot, Levin's car was gone.

Driving in the rain, Jack believed he would find Georgine and quickly get matters back on track. He'd staked a lot on the polygraph test, needing something concrete to at last corroborate Georgine's story.

Face to face, he would finally make it clear that he had her best interests at heart. He would speak to her in a low, soft voice. *I only want to help, to spare you more pain.*

But time is running out. Powerful people are working against you. I alone believe in you. And if I seemed cool and impersonal before. Well, that was a mistake. A performance meant to disguise the fact that I care. I care too much.

Damn! None of this would matter if she'd just taken the test.

Bursting into Betsy Levin's office, Jack brushed past the protesting secretary and pushed through the inner office door. He was disappointed to find the rotund attorney alone, sprawled on the couch with a wet towel over her forehead.

"Don't knock or anything." She rose slightly.

"Where's Georgine?"

"Gone."

"Where?"

"I don't know." Propped up on her elbow, she snatched off the cloth. "I drove her back here. To pick up her car. Which she insisted on. I told her, begged her, to go back and take the test. I said over and over. We have nothing to lose if you take the test. But. You know, she was convinced the thing wouldn't work right. That she'd answer honestly. And the thing would say she was lying."

Looking confused and sad, Betsy sat up, leaned back, and squeezed the damp cloth in her hand. "You give a person your best. You show them you care. And still they disregard your advice." She looked up at Jack. "Now why is that?"

Jack spent the afternoon in search of Georgine. Driving past her house, her friends' homes, even Charles Carver's estate, he looked for the big green station wagon. She could be anywhere. Maybe at a movie. Maybe driving around the way he was. Or, she could have run away.

On a given afternoon, Jack Meehan is unable to locate Georgine Goodfellow. No cause for alarm, certainly. Yet, nagging at the prosecutor was the feeling that he'd missed his best chance — perhaps his last chance — to save this woman's life.

25

THE rain had turned to snow. The stuff came fast in the windless, dead air, making everything in the half-filled parking lot quiet and oddly warmer. The district attorney's office was nearly empty at this late hour.

As Jack Meehan left his car, he heard a toot from a nearby parked car. Of course, it was Georgine! And didn't it figure?

Just as he'd been looking for her, she'd been looking for him. Jack glanced up, smiling.

"Hey, Meehan. John Meehan." But this was a man's voice.

Jack moved cautiously into the parking lot.

"Don't you know who I am?" He'd rolled down his window. Hair combed carefully, he looked boyish, healthy.

"Charles Carver." Jack knew the black Porsche, license CAC1, better than the face. "You're Charles Carver."

"I need to talk to you, Meehan. Talk. And I thought maybe you'd like to talk to me."

Jack maintained a safe distance. Snow fell steadily between them. "I'm all ears, Mr. Carver."

"Yeah, but we can't talk like this. Not here. We should sit down someplace. I've got a lot to say. Because. Honest to God. On some things. Are you ever turned around wrong, Mr. Meehan."

"All right. Let's go inside."

"Inside there? Inside your office?" He laughed. "No. No thanks. I'd prefer more neutral ground."

"You're making conversation difficult, Mr. Carver."

As Jack moved closer, Carver suddenly hurried from his car. He approached with an outstretched hand, which Jack ignored. He looked fit, strong enough to have killed Walter Hamparian. However, the prosecutor did not feel threatened. For months he'd wanted to talk with this man.

"One block down." Carver pointed toward the square. "There's a bar called Ye Olde Village Pub. Very dark place."

"I know it."

"Let's take a walk. I'll buy you a drink."

The famous car dealer wore his full-length leather coat, collar up. As they entered the bar, people stared, but he kept his head down, furtively looking about before spotting a rear table. Seated, Carver scarcely spoke until the waitress had taken their order, served their beers, and left.

"You probably think I'm ridiculous. Sneaking around like this. But I'll tell you frankly. I'm afraid for my life. Right now I'm trying to sell my business, then scoot. To someplace safe."

He winced, as if on cue. "Stomach. I've had bleeding. Coughing up blood. All the tension. Always looking over my shoulder."

Both men looked over Carver's shoulder. The dimly lit bar was relatively busy. Now that he was seated, no one paid them the least attention.

"I'm not blameless," Carver admitted.

Jack gulped his beer. "You're not?"

"When I started out. You couldn't give Japanese cars away. So. I thought. Volkswagen. Germans. Efficient. Car of the future. Only, along came those goddamn Rabbits. Then recession. And it was back to the bunker with those guys." He shook his head. "If a guy's going to survive, he's got to take the shortcuts. And maybe he doesn't think about down the road and all the shit he's going to get into. Like with me. I didn't start thinking of that until it was too late."

"Which isn't exactly to the point, Mr. Carver."

The man's eyes grew small. He was unprepared for Jack's tone. His hand went to a bag of beer nuts, which he plucked up, then dropped, then picked up again. "Okay. I'll tell you this much. This should be enough. You're after me. I know you are. You're wasting time on me. Investigating me. I'm the wrong guy. All I ever did was rip off a few auto parts. Do you think I'd kill someone over that?"

"I did," Jack admitted. "I did for the longest time. Because at least three people were dead, all connected in one way or another to your dealership. And it seemed obvious. Each was killed to cover up your warranty scam."

"No."

"Well, it seemed to make sense. Until. I got into it deeper. And there was more information, lots of information. But instead of the motive becoming clearer, more obvious. Well, it didn't. It never quite added up that people would be killed over some white-collar crime."

Grim-faced, Carver followed Jack's explanation intently.

"The cover-up figures in," Jack said. "But it's not the motive. It's only the excuse. An excuse to kill. Because what it was, it was murder for its own sake."

Carver began to nod. "You think he's crazy and you don't know how right you are."

"I think this is someone who kills either for pleasure or out of compulsion. Whether that's crazy or not I'll leave to the shrinks. I'm guessing. If he is crazy. It's not like you see in the movies. Frothing at the mouth. Attacking teenagers with axes. The person I have in mind, I'm guessing, is very competent. People who know him casually, they'd be astonished to learn what he's really like. I understand he was involved in this sort of thing before. Homicide. And since he got away with it then, he has the idea he can kill as he pleases. That the law doesn't apply to him. Does this ring any bells, Mr. Carver?"

Carver lowered his voice. "Look, Mr. Meehan. I'm with you on this. The guy should be gotten off the streets. No argument. He's certifiable and he should be put away. For everyone's sake. In fact, I want to help do it."

"But there's something stopping you."

He smiled sheepishly. "You got to understand, Mr. Meehan. I come from a long line of Yankee traders. I don't cooperate. I don't take that kind of risk and get back nothing in return." He leaned close. "I will not go to prison. I'm decided on that."

Jack should have been surprised just to have Charles Carver sitting across from him. But the car dealer had tried every other strategy to shake the threat of prison, so it made sense. In desperation, he was relying on his salesman's skills, the personal touch.

"I'm not the guilty party in this," he insisted. "If that's what you're thinking. No. You're simply wrong. I might be a thief, a kind of thief. But I'm no murderer."

"Where were you when Walter Hamparian was killed?"

"Chicago," Carver said eagerly.

Jack stared stonily until the beginnings of a helpless, guilty smile came to Carver's mouth.

"On the day before Hamparian died," Jack began, "you took the evening plane home. You used an alias. You sat in the next to last row. And whenever you wanted something from the stewardess. You snapped your fingers." Jack snapped his. "I talked to her myself and she remembered you, Mr. Carver. It should teach you a lesson about being rude to people. I mean, did your mother bring you up that way?"

He smiled, then shrugged.

"You arrived home in the early evening. Several hours before Walter Hamparian was killed."

"Look. You're on the wrong track here, Meehan. This is exactly what I warned you about. I mean, ask yourself. Would I kill Hamparian? Why should I? Where's the advantage?"

"Where's the advantage in breaking off a business trip and flying home from Chicago under an assumed name?"

"All right. I did that. I came home. But it wasn't to kill anyone. I was trying to prevent a killing. To save this fellow's life. Because I knew we had someone here capable of murder. Someone who'd been calling me. About Hamparian, getting rid of him. And I realized I better get home in a hurry. And calm things down. I even telephoned Hamparian before I left Chicago. We made an appointment to talk. So I could explain how he might be in some danger. But by the time we were supposed to meet. By that time Hamparian was already dead."

"Why didn't you tell him over the phone about the danger?" Jack demanded.

"I did. Sort of. But I had to win his confidence before I could explain everything. See, I didn't want him turning around later and making trouble for me with VW. I wanted his word on that."

"How is it you never went to the police? Even after the man was killed?"

"At first, I stayed away from the police because I was afraid to get involved. Afraid I was culpable. In the fraud. And then in murder. Only later I started to understand that I had bigger worries than the police. Because once I went to the police and cooperated, he'd still be free. Maybe on bail, but free. With the best excuse in the world for killing me."

Jack leaned away. "Why come forward now?"

"Well, because now I have no choice. I can see the way things are going. I can see the day when I become the scapegoat. Because I've got a little money, it'll be open season on me. You don't know how vindictive people can be when they

189

think you've got money. Croak the rich. Blame me for murder. Even though I'm more or less completely innocent. Completely innocent where murder is concerned."

Jack was silent, staring at Carver, who fidgeted nervously, then blurted, "Well, what do you say? Can we deal?"

Jack toyed with his glass. "Mr. Carver, I have to know first how deeply you're involved. You have to tell me everything. So I can begin to assess whether or not you're telling the truth. And so I can be sure. You didn't kill. Or order anyone to be killed."

Charles Carver seemed offended by Jack's blunt skepticism. For the remainder of the interview his answers were cryptic, even snappish.

The name Grover Durham drew a complete blank. "Sounds like a cartoon character," he muttered. And though the disappearance of parts driver Paul Barrasso had shaken him, Carver could offer no fresh information on that mystery.

"Barrasso? What do I know about him? A parts driver. I don't deal very much with people like that."

He was unmoved by a reference to Georgine Goodfellow. Yes, he'd met her. Maybe once. Briefly. "I remember her vaguely. Dark hair. Attractive. Of course, I saw her picture in the papers. After her husband's death."

"You don't know her any better than that?"

"No."

"You don't know where she is right now?"

"Why? Should I?" Carver asked.

"That Porsche you drive. Am I to believe that's a company car?"

"For tax purposes," Carver replied.

"And any of your employees can drive it?"

"God, no. But some do. My management people."

Jack nodded. "It was seen in the Goodfellows' neighborhood all last summer."

"If it was. Well, I wasn't the driver."

"Who was the driver?"

"I'm sure you can figure it out," Carver insisted. "After all, who was the only man in the shop to even meet Walter

Hamparian? Who goes around bragging about what a dangerous fellow he is? Who, Christ, he lives in Harwood. That's where Goodfellow lived."

"Maybe you'd like to expound on this theory to the grand jury."

"The trouble with you, Meehan. You want something for nothing." The car dealer took a deep, calming breath, then bent to the table. "Now. If I wanted something from you. I'd make sure to offer you something in return. For example, it's worth a great deal of money to me. Staying out of prison. Now, don't dismiss what I'm saying until you've thought it over carefully. I'm a very wealthy man and you won't get an offer like this for the rest of your life. Let's talk figures. One hundred thousand dollars. I could put a good, top-flight attorney on retainer. A man like yourself. One hundred thousand dollars over several years wouldn't be a high price to pay for that sort of legal help."

Jack took a swallow of beer. "One hundred thousand?"

"Figures can be worked out." Carver reached into his coat, the leather squeaking. "Just to show I'm serious." He extracted a thick pile of bills, all hundreds and thousands.

Jack was disturbed by his own reaction. He should have been indignant, refusing it bluntly. Instead, he stared at the cash and could not speak.

"This is just walking-around money for me," Carver said.

Perhaps Jack should have expected the offer. In fact, he'd never faced such a situation before and was knocked completely off balance now. One hundred thousand dollars. And all he had to do was reach out and take it.

"They say money can't buy happiness," the car salesman smiled. "Well. With this much money. Take my word. They make an exception."

Jack gave a low, involuntary laugh. He was still staring at the cash in Carver's hand.

"Here." Carver glanced over his shoulder while extending the bills. "Touch it."

"I . . . I don't know."

"Listen, John. This goes on all the time."

"I'm sure it does."

"People, you'd be amazed at the people who've taken money in this world. Good people too. If you're still playing strictly by the rules. Let me tell you, you're the last one."

"I'm sure." Jack forced himself to look away. One hundred thousand. It couldn't be real. The figure was too large. Carver would find a way to cheat him out of it. And he remembered the man's indifference at the mention of Georgine's name. Some people can buy their way out of anything, Janice Price had said.

"Well?" Carver was more insistent.

"Can't."

"What? Why not? Why? Why not?"

"Lots of reasons. I couldn't say for sure which one counts the most. I like to think it's because I have too much respect for the law and the people who depend on it, who depend on me. But, I have to admit, I'm also scared. Too scared to even consider it."

"John. There's nothing to be scared of. I swear."

"Yeah? Well, I think there is, looking at the way you sweat."

"Come on, John, you —"

"I don't want your money. And if you don't get it out of my face I'll shove it right down your goddamn throat! Now, is that plain enough?"

Angrily, Carver stuffed the greenbacks into his wallet. "Remember this." His teeth clenched. "I will never go to prison. You think of me as some big, rich prize you're going to land. Well, coming after me is the mistake of your life. You think anyone cares if you turn down a hundred thousand dollars? They're going to give you a medal or something? Like hell. If they find out, they won't care. Except to wonder why you don't have your fucking head examined. Asshole. And I'll tell you something else. The joke's on you. I gave you the chance to step out of the way. And you didn't take it. Which is too fucking bad. Because I've got the clout to run you right over."

Jack waited until the purple in Carver's face receded.

"I'll give you my card, Mr. Carver. When you've made a decision," he slid the card over, "you can call me. Remember, if you decide to cooperate and make a full statement. I promise you'll get every consideration. That might not seem like much of an offer. But it's a lot better deal than Walter Hamparian got."

Jack Meehan left Ye Olde Village Pub several minutes after Charles Carver had stormed out. He decided to return to his office, to call Rose. And to try to call Georgine. The snow was falling faster, beginning to mount.

Coming up the alley, Jack saw Charles Carver in the nearly empty parking lot, scraping snow off his Porsche. Straightening up, the man eyed Jack through swirls of white, then, flipped the scraper into his car and climbed in after it.

Trudging through wet snow, Jack watched Carver roll toward the exit, his lights off. After a few yards, he stopped, as if pausing to consider his next move. The black Porsche hummed.

Crunching snow, the front wheels turned to point directly at Jack Meehan. When Carver cranked down the window, Jack assumed he wanted to talk. Maybe he had decided to cooperate. Or would he offer more money? Now Carver drove slowly toward him. Jack almost smiled. The car dealer was near to cracking, he thought. The end was in sight.

The Porsche accelerated; in a matter of feet it was rocketing, spitting snow to the rear. Jack was confused, then horrified as the black car came at him. In the narrow alley, Jack could not turn. Could not run.

At the last instant, he leaped, hoping to hurdle the little vehicle. He sprung up and rolled like an old-fashioned high jumper. Amazed, he watched as time seemed to stop and the car passed beneath him.

Then, his hip collided with something. Maybe the roof or the trunk. Impact so hard he couldn't breathe. His flesh felt shaken loose of bone. He smelled blood. It poured from his nose.

Jack was bounced, hurtling, cartwheeling, out of control.

Break the fall! Save yourself!

But how? Going too fast. His limbs could not coordinate. The earth and sky ran together. His head swirled.

The wet pavement caught his shoulder. He slid, skidding. His shoulder burned.

Briefly, he lost consciousness. Blood streamed down his face. Jack could hear the malevolent hum of the Porsche. Hazily. The sinister black snout slithered toward him. To finish the job.

Get away, Jack.

But where? How? His head lolled. Nothing seemed to work. He decided to scream. Help! But he didn't hear anything.

Likewise, he decided to run to the office. Pound on the door for the janitor. He made the decision to get up and run, but it didn't happen. Legs, arms, nothing responded — as if he was paralyzed, or drifting in and out of consciousness. Like in a nightmare, the most prodigious effort could not move him any nearer to safety.

My God. I can't move. I can't do anything. Something grabbed inside his throat. Every inch of him felt panic. God, I can't crawl. I'm helpless.

The car came at him. Tires popping. The choking odor of exhaust and the heat of the engine on his back.

But, it stopped! A reprieve. Jack wanted to laugh with joy. Except . . . except the killer would come out now, the blade catching the glow of far-off streetlights. Hamparian had been stabbed sixteen times. Butchered like meat.

When he comes out I can fight. You can't fight a car. But a man, you can suddenly reach up and seize the knife, turn the knife away. But Jack could barely raise his arms. Oh, Jesus. Tears came. God help me. He didn't want this. If only he could fight.

Come on! Jack finally raised himself a few feet off the ground. Dizzy. His head seemed to swell. The brain engorged by blood. His face dropped back to the snow. He was startled by the smell of his own vomit.

Can't . . . fight.

He heard the car door open.

Run. Try to get up and run.

He managed, instead, to crawl. Toward the office. God, wasn't there someone passing by or looking out a window? Someone who would see him?

Every move brought pain. He was close to passing out.

He rolled over, collapsing on his back. The last thing he would see was the snowfall.

Jack studied it through half-opened eyes. Great, clinging clouds of the stuff, spinning and floating beneath the streetlamp, collected on his face and hair. A wonderful snowfall.

He imagined that he was with Karen and John and Rose. Squatting between the children, an arm over each, he pointed up at the snow. The glorious snow.

26

THE minute the car headlights hit the window the dog was on his feet, barking like mad. "Shhh!" Georgine leapt up, switched off the television, and stood frozen with fear. The car's headlights went out and its door shut loudly. Only then, she went slowly to the window.

Peering into the night, she couldn't quite see . . . but it seemed to be . . . it looked like Charles Carver's Porsche, now parked in the driveway beside her wagon. She heard the garage door opening.

"Oh, God," Georgine whispered, closing her eyes. "Oh, God, be with me."

She hustled the dog into the basement, turned and faced the breezeway door, her heart racing. For the longest time no one came, as if her visitor had gotten lost in the garage or something. A blaze in the fireplace, the only light, made hypnotic, dancing shadows on the walls. "What's taking you," she muttered.

The key scratched inside the lock. In the beginning, her lover had insisted on owning her house key, regarding it as a sort of prize. Ironically, this was the first time he'd ever used it.

The door swung open.

"You're up."

"I . . ." She could barely speak. "I sleep in the day a lot now. My, my schedule . . ."

The killer went straight to the couch and the fire. "Oh is it good to get inside. To sit down and rest."

For nearly a minute, she stood silently, watching over him. "What . . . ?"

"I came to see you." He smiled up at her. "I miss you. What else?"

Still, Georgine did not move.

"We're in love. Lovers should be together." He turned back to the fire. "There is one thing. A favor you could do for me. Little favor. If I could leave something in your garage."

"Leave . . . what?"

"It won't be for long."

"If you mean the Porsche. It, my garage's got big windows, you know. If you're trying to hide it. Well, somebody would see it. They'd walk up to the window and see it."

"The fire's going out."

Georgine went to tend the fire.

"Great." He leaned back. "Get it going good. Warm things up in here."

As Georgine turned, her large, dark eyes caught the flames.

"God," he said, "you are beautiful. How could I have stayed away so long?"

She turned back to the fire. "I gave up on seeing you again. Ever."

"That's crazy, Georgine. You haven't been out of my mind for one minute. All this time. I thought of you. And no one else."

Very suddenly, she faced him. "Something's happened. Hasn't it? Maybe you should tell me. So I can know. What I'm up against."

"What you're up against?" He sat back, smiling again, unsnapping the smart leather coat. "I can tell you what I wish you were up against."

"They asked me about a policeman. Killed. In Welton. I didn't answer. I told myself it wasn't you. I hoped . . ."

He raised his hand and let it drop. "What can I tell you,

Georgine honey? We started this business. The first time. Maybe we didn't want to do it. But he left us no choice. And the next time. Well, it had to be done to cover up the first. And so on. Until, maybe, by the time we're through. We're just left wondering how it all got so fucked up."

At the fire, she bent to stoke the burning logs.

He sprang from the couch. Gripping her wrist, he pulled her up. "Don't think I like all this."

"No."

"What anyone else says. It doesn't matter. Only you. What you think is the only thing in the world that matters to me. That's how I keep going, Georgine. Through all this shit." He pulled her close. Georgine's eyes were huge, her mouth half-open.

"I've killed for you," he said. "And I don't regret it. If you were to die, then I would die."

He ran his hand down her flannel nightgown, groaning because she wore nothing beneath it. "Do you know how many times I've driven past this neighborhood?"

"How many?"

"Dozens of times."

"You never stopped," she said.

"I was afraid the police were watching."

"You never called."

"I was afraid the phone was tapped." He kissed her. "Don't think I didn't want to see you," he said fiercely. "Don't think I didn't want to call. I haven't once stopped wanting you." He clasped her shoulders. "Remember how you kissed me that day? Our first kiss? Kiss me again like that."

Feeling her tongue, his restraint failed. His powerful hands ripped the flannel gown from its modest V neck halfway to the floor. He kissed between her naked shoulder and neck. With a sigh, she arched her back and the gown fell away. He dropped slowly. Descending, cheek, lips, and tongue worked gently, exploring everywhere. Smooth, warm skin. Her scent energized him.

Frantically, his tongue pushed, until she closed her eyes. Until, forgetting herself, she lost her balance.

Laying her down on the thick sheepskin rug by the fire, he began, tenderly, with hands and fingers and lips, to work her muscles. Georgine went limp with dreamy pleasure.

"Forget," he whispered in her ear. "Forget it all. Just think how good this feels." Soon she had the first orgasm, crying out in a girlish voice.

"Beautiful, Georgine. That was beautiful." He spread her legs. A touch and she responded. "You just relax." He pushed inside carefully, his hands still playing on her hips and shoulders. With each push, her body shook.

Georgine felt the fire on her face. For a long time, she studied its reaching fingers.

"How is it?" he asked.

"Don't . . . stop."

She came again quickly. He followed. And, at once, he was ready again.

"No," she said.

"No?"

"Let me rest a minute. Let me think about what just happened. Linger on it."

Hesitantly, he said, "Okay."

"That was good."

"Was it? Did I fuck you good?"

"I'm still feeling it." She touched herself. "It's like you're still in there."

He grinned like a boy.

"Can I get you something?" Georgine asked.

"Just lie there. Let me look at you." He sat on the couch and studied her.

"I bet you'd like cocoa. I'll get some hot cocoa. Then, we can have more fun."

He thought about this. "Well. Maybe a sandwich too?"

At the kitchen door, she turned to say, "Just so I'll be prepared. See, I can't relax . . . unless. Can you tell me what's happened? Something went on tonight. And it makes me nervous, not knowing."

She watched him watching the fire. Strange, after all these

months alone, to see a naked, glowing, orange man on the living room couch.

"Nothing happened tonight," he said. "Nothing you need to know."

A log fell, raising a shower of sparks.

"Anyway," he concluded. "We have no worries. By morning. All our worries will be gone."

"I'll make the cocoa," Georgine said.

Jack Meehan no longer trusted Frank Mullins. He hadn't actually said this, but his attitude was clear. And about time, as Rose saw it. Even when her husband's law-school buddy was hailed as a sort of benefactor, she found the man coarse and insincere. She was not surprised to learn that the new job had strings attached.

And yet, it was nearly midnight. Who else could she call?

Each time she went to the window, the snow was falling harder. At eight, a neighborhood boy had shoveled the driveway. Now it looked as if it had never been touched. Where would Jack park the car?

Where was Jack?

Finally, Rose called Frank Mullins.

"Well." He came slowly out of sleep. "Jack left the office this morning and never came back. I can't imagine where he'd be at this hour."

"Jack is never late." She spoke softly. The children were asleep. "Whenever he's late, he calls. Calls and tells me. He's very considerate."

Funny, it had never occurred to Rose to be afraid for Jack. She tended to forget the odd times he came home from a crime scene, ashen faced, or returned from court to describe his prosecution of an animal-like felon. No one had promised that prosecutors were immune from the violence and horror. Yet even in this case she'd always assumed Jack was safe.

"I'm sure there's a simple explanation," Frank was saying. "I'm sure Jack is . . . Well, he's probably just stuck in the storm somewhere. Right?"

"I guess."

"Jack can take care of himself. And if there was any great problem. You know, I mean, anything bad. Well. You'd have heard by now."

Frank was encouraging, kindly. Rose was glad she'd called.

"I'll make some phone calls, Rose. So, all you've got to do is stay loose and don't worry. We'll track him down."

Rose watched the phone. At any minute, Jack would call. Or drive up. And this business with Frank Mullins would be an embarrassment. Just like Rose, they'd laugh. Jack is an hour late and she calls out the state police.

The snow was turning to sleet. Not a car came by the house. Nothing moved out there. Every so often she would hear a noise and run to the window. And she did not feel embarrassed, but sick with a tension and dread she would always remember.

In the driving rain, Charles Carver's Porsche was poised at the end of the pier.

"Wait a minute." The killer, in the passenger's seat of Georgine Goodfellow's station wagon, tried to remember something. "Wait," he said, holding up one hand. "Okay. I'll be right back."

Bent beneath the downpour, he ran to the little sports car and opened the door. Georgine watched him by headlights as he reached in to retrieve . . . a gun.

Dropping the weapon into his pants pocket, he felt momentary excitement as he reflected on his cleverness in bringing all this off. In one incredibly bold move, he had solved all his problems.

He removed the leather coat and threw it into the Porsche. Someone at the bar might connect John Meehan and Charles Carver through that distinctive coat.

"Aren't you cold?" Georgine asked, as he climbed back into the station wagon.

"Just drive into it. Push it."

Rain and wind had cleared the wooden dock of snow. Yet

traction was difficult, and the whole structure creaked and swayed beneath them.

"Are you sure this is a good idea?" Georgine's voice wavered. "I don't see the point."

"I've got to get rid of that car," he declared. "Now. Push it."

"But the water's not deep enough."

"The big yachts tie up here. It's dredged. Come on. Do what I tell you." He reached over and slapped the station wagon into drive. She jammed her foot on the brake; otherwise they might have hurtled off the pier. "Get going."

Slowly, she rolled forward until the two cars touched, bumper to bumper.

"Give it gas," he barked.

The back wheels spun, then caught. The empty Porsche lurched forward as the structure beneath them quaked.

"More gas."

"I'm afraid."

"More gas, I said." His foot displaced hers on the pedal. Recklessly, he pushed it to the floor. The cars jerked forward. Wheels spun and whined. The engine roared until they could smell the fumes. At the brink, the Porsche stalled before a single wooden plank. It protruded only inches above the dock's surface.

"There must be a better way," she pleaded, believing that the Porsche, like something alive, would drag them after it into the black, icy bay.

The sports car trembled, fighting that last lip of pier. "I'm afraid," Georgine cried, nearly hysterical.

Then he took her firmly by the shoulders and said, "Listen. This has to be done. Understand? For us to live together. And if it can't be done. And if we can't live together. Forever. Then I don't want to live at all. Do you?"

"Just . . . just I —"

"Do you?"

"I'm sorry I'm afraid," she cried. "I wouldn't — It would be easier if I knew — If you'd tell me —"

"Tell you what?"

"Why are we doing this? What's wrong with that car?"

"Nothing," he replied.

"Then why is it so important to get rid of it? What, what's in it?"

"You saw it. Did you see anything in it?"

"In the trunk?" Georgine's voice cracked. "I didn't see there."

"Georgine, Georgine . . ." He shook his head. "God, you disappoint me so. God. You break my heart."

"I'm sorry." She began to cry. "I'm sorry, but I'm just afraid." She opened the door and ran quickly through the cold rain to solid ground. She did not look back.

Sliding into the driver's seat, he gave the big wagon gas. The Porsche's front end hopped up and out, over the water. He jammed on the brake. As the smaller car's nose dropped, the back end levitated briefly to reveal its naked underside of snaking pipes. Then, with a tremendous crash, it slid into the void.

The pier shook violently, as if the car had crushed one of the pilings, and water splashed up at the station wagon. He braced himself and closed his eyes to the freezing seawater. But the wild motion calmed.

Walking to the edge of the pier, he saw the unsubmerged rear wheels. It was as if the Porsche was balancing on its nose in shallow water. He waited for it to tip and sink from sight. But it did not.

A steady rain washed the snow away. Frank Mullins was alarmed to find the D.A.'s office dark and locked up tight. Evidently, even the janitor had gone home early because of the storm. Jack Meehan's Chevette stood alone in the parking lot. Frank walked around it and peered inside.

"Shit." The car was empty.

Where was the prosecutor? Well, think about it. Who was ol' Jacko chasing when he lit out of here this morning?

Mullins raced back to his car. Before climbing in, he scanned the area, blinking back the downpour. He saw nothing unusual.

In his car, Frank smirked. He figured he'd heard Jack Meehan's lecture on ethics for the last time. Imagine a guy so straight he's a positive pain in the ass about it. Imagine him doing a thing like this.

27

SHOTGUN at the ready, state trooper William Euston moved cautiously. The spongelike meadow squished beneath his boots. Remarkably, morning temperatures in the sixties had followed the storm. Flanked by Jimmy Clogherty and Dan Richardi, Euston was sweating in his bulletproof vest and camouflage fatigues. The three men made quiet, careful progress, picking through a tangle of woods, thorns, and rocks.

When he sighted the Goodfellow home, trooper Euston crouched low and moved behind a boulder. At intervals, he peeked at the house, always popping up from behind the huge rock at a different spot. Above all, he was aware that the sniper might be looking back, patiently waiting to put a bullet through his skull. Though this was a remote possibility, it seemed more likely the more Euston thought about it. It did not, however, prevent him from making frequent observations of the oak-stained house.

Soon, support began arriving, Harwood officers in bulky, bullet-resistant jackets. Euston gestured emphatically. Stay back! If someone was seen, there would be hell to pay. The plan was to completely surround the place before the gunman knew what was happening.

The operation was more complicated on Wampanoag Road. Sergeant Tony Silva began telephoning each house, advising the inhabitants to collect their children and stay inside. Via backyards, state troopers were moving to each home, evacuating residents to adjacent streets where a church bus would be sent to take them to a temporary shelter.

On adjacent Acorn Lane, police cars began to pile up. They came from the state-police barracks, from Harwood, Pebbleton, Hanbury, and Standish. Even a SWAT team from the city had come to take part.

To keep this small army under control, no officer was allowed to leave the staging area without specific instructions about where to go and how to get there. Each man received photos of Charles Carver and Georgine Goodfellow, plus a mimeographed map of the area, drawn only an hour before by Sergeant Silva.

State Police Colonel Robert LeRoy lacked faith in small-town cops. Most had never used their weapons in the line of duty. Many had barely used them on the firing range. Thus, troopers and the city SWAT team went to forward positions, while locals filled the gaps farther back.

LeRoy feared that Carver would somehow slip through if he wasn't already long gone.

"For safety's sake," LeRoy announced. "We assume he is in there. We assume he is armed. After last night, we know he has no compunctions about killing law-enforcement personnel."

State Police Sergeant George Lewis, a Vietnam combat veteran, had established a backyard trail from Acorn Lane to the Garritt house. The two-story colonial was now a command post. Though on somewhat lower ground, and separated by a huge front yard and gravel road, this house offered the best view of the Goodfellow place some seventy yards away.

At a front window, Colonel LeRoy studied the scene. Mrs. Goodfellow's station wagon was in the driveway. A FOR SALE sign was planted on the lawn. All seemed ordinary, but for an unreal quiet and emptiness.

"Why can't we shoot the house?" A TV reporter complained.

"That's Colonel LeRoy's decision." District Attorney Rich Flaherty was desperate to escape the eager horde of media people, loudly demanding a place near the action.

"Suppose we sent a pool cameraman?"

"I'll certainly pass that suggestion along to the state police." Flaherty, walking backward, moved away.

"In that SLA shootout they had live pictures of the whole thing."

"That was California." Flaherty ducked beyond the police lines.

Grim-faced, the district attorney did not have a handle on this situation, which his own people seemed to have botched badly. He'd even heard mutterings about unethical conduct. The attorney general himself had called, asking, "What the hell kind of circus are you running down there, Rich?"

He didn't need this kind of trouble in an election year.

"I got here around two." Frank Mullins cleared his throat, tried to look alert, awake. He hadn't had much sleep. He sat at the kitchen table of the command house, waiting for the kettle to boil. "What I say? Two? Between three and two. Three. Closer to three. I checked the Chinese restaurant on Washington Street first. Then I came here."

"What did you expect to find?" asked a state-police detective, one of a team surrounding the table.

"I don't know what I expected to find. Well, it was Jack. Jack Meehan."

"At three in the morning?" The detectives exchanged looks.

"Well. You see, Jack was hot to talk Mrs. Goodfellow into taking this polygraph test. I figured, maybe he'd come here and maybe I'd see him leaving. I don't know."

"At three in the morning he does this?"

"Well," Frank shrugged.

"All right. You got here. What happened next?"

"I was parked across the street, right? I'd only been there a few minutes. When along comes a car. Station wagon. Mrs. Goodfellow."

"You recognized her?"

"Well," Frank explained. "It was a woman. A woman and a man, actually. And they pulled into her driveway. So, I just assumed the woman was Georgine Goodfellow."

"And the man?"

205

"At the time, I thought it was Jack." Frank shrugged. "It was dark, you know. Foggy. And I was ducked down. So they wouldn't see me."

"Did you make yourself known to these people?" a detective asked.

"No." Frank accepted a cup of coffee. "Thanks. No. I just watched while they went inside. I could see. The way they acted. I could see they didn't want to be bothered."

"Explain what you mean."

"I mean they were all over each other. For a while I thought they were going to . . . you know. Right there in the driveway. Anyway, when they went inside. I decided to wait. Wait for Jack to come out so I could ask him what in hell he was doing. You know, for one thing, his wife was worried about him. Not to mention. You could get into a lot of legal trouble for that sort of thing. What he was doing."

"Did you see anything while you were waiting?"

"Nothing for about half an hour. In fact, I was going to go home. When I heard. Now, I'm across the street. And I hear the stereo go on. Music. Then lights. Different lights in the house start going off and on. For a long time they were even in the garage. I got the idea," Frank grinned, "whatever they were doing. They were doing it in every room."

"At what point did the man come out?"

"When it finally started to get light. He came out the front door. And, you know, first thing. He looked right at me. Like he knew my car. So, I rolled down the window. And I called. I said something like, 'It's lucky I found you first.' "

"And?"

"And then he took a shot at me. I coulda shit. I scrambled out the passenger-side door. I was afraid he'd come after me. I came here. To this house. Pounded on the door until they let me in. Then I called the police. A cruiser got here in a few minutes and they were fired on too."

"From inside the house?"

"Right. He'd gone back inside. And he opened up on them before they got halfway down the street."

"Can you identify the man who fired at you?"

"Well, it wasn't Jack Meehan. I realized that after he took

a shot at me. He wasn't tall enough, for one thing. It wasn't Jack. It was Charles Carver. You found his car in the bay, didn't you? He's the one who ran down Jack Meehan.''

"We seem to be ready." Colonel LeRoy turned to State Police Detective Lyle Sullivan. "I gather Carver won't answer the phone in there."

"Right," Sullivan replied. "He's just letting it ring."

"And you're sure about the children?"

"They're, all three of them, are safe and sound with their grandparents."

Colonel LeRoy tried to think of what might remain to be done. "Well, everyone's in place. The neighborhood is completely evacuated." All around him was the clatter of heavily armed men. The colonel knew that few were trained for this situation. And some were scarcely trained for anything at all.

"Okay, gentlemen. Let's get on with it."

Hugging the side of the Garritt home, a state-police trooper spoke through an electric bullhorn. "You, in there. Inside number fifty-six. This is the state police. You are completely surrounded. Come out the front door. Hands on top of your head."

When this got no response, he repeated his instructions, only louder, the sound echoing off houses and trees, stray words carrying for miles.

Inside the Garritt house, an officer at an upstairs window put his binoculars down. "I saw a curtain move. Maybe a face. I think."

That observation was relayed downstairs to Colonel LeRoy, who nonetheless muttered, half to himself, "I don't think Carver's in there. I've got a gut feeling that house is empty."

Once the police presence was revealed, Wampanoag Road changed dramatically. Officers could be seen here and there, running among the pines. Men shouted and radios squawked.

Nearly one hundred police officers were involved, with half of these taking positions in sight of the Goodfellow home. They crouched in the woods at the end of the road. They lay behind rocks bordering Georgine's spacious backyard. While some peered from within neighboring homes, others found cover behind brick porches or garages, or in sunken driveways, lying flat.

"Make damn sure of one thing," they had been warned, "that no fellow officer is in your field of fire."

But the minutes passed and they began to relax. In the Goodfellow house nothing moved, and the only sound was the muffled yelping of Georgine's dog.

"I think we'll try the tear gas next." Colonel LeRoy rocked back on his heels. "We want to play it safe."

Soon, a trooper scurried into view on the front lawn of the command house. Dropping to one knee, behind Frank Mullins's abandoned car, he aimed an odd-shaped rifle and fired a tear-gas canister. It hurtled across the street and through Georgine's living room window.

Dull pops announced the launchings of gas bombs to the rear and side of the one-story home. These efforts were less successful. Most missed their targets and bounced ineffectively to the ground.

A breeze soon took up the swirling gas, driving it toward the woods at the end of the street, temporarily routing the men positioned there.

But, after nearly an hour, no one had emerged from the house. "Could be they're waiting it out in the basement," someone suggested.

More and more, it seemed the situation would come to what Bob LeRoy feared most — one officer making across open ground, forcing the door, and searching the place.

LeRoy had to face the possibility that Carver was watching and waiting. The fugitive hadn't shown himself for one simple reason. He liked to kill and, in particular, wanted to score a few cops. He would bide his time until the target presented itself.

"How are you, John?"

"Grateful to be among the living." Jack Meehan playfully raised one crutch, as if to fend off the media people surging toward him.

"How about last night?"

"Anyone get the number of that truck?" Jack retorted.

"Why did Charles Carver run you down?"

"Is it true you were about to indict him for murder?"

Jack turned away, but the pack converged, shouting questions, jostling, pushing microphones and cameras at the only news within reach. Finally, the prosecutor was pulled inside the police lines by a weary Frank Mullins. "You're safe now," he smiled. "This is the demilitarized zone. No reporters allowed." He gave the prosecutor a good look. "You're supposed to be in the hospital, my friend."

"I sent Rose to work, then I discharged myself." Jack groaned softly as he leaned against a patrol car and examined the white cast that imprisoned his throbbing ankle. "I've been out for hours. I even stopped over at the courthouse for an arrest warrant."

"I'm sure you're the only guy here who thought to bring an arrest warrant." Frank also leaned against the car. Through trees and shrubs they saw the back side of the Garritt house. For a long time neither man spoke.

"I heard you got Carver's car," Jack said.

"Yeah, pulled it out of the bay. That leather coat you described. Was in the car."

"You ought to check that car very carefully."

"Whatever you say, Counselor." The first assistant looked away, then gave a sort of laugh. "If you . . . if you want to gloat."

"I don't want to gloat, Frank."

"Or say I told you so. Well, I guess you — you're entitled. To say I told you so. I guess."

"I don't want to say anything."

"Look, we made a mistake," Frank admitted. "To put it mildly, Skip Biddle threw us a curve on this Carver. We should have listened to you. You knew the case best. We should have listened. Had more faith. Anyway, it's lucky we caught on before it was too late. We've got the son of a bitch now."

Moving his leg, Jack grimaced. "And you believe me now about Georgine?"

"Well . . . that's a different story."

"Different?"

"I saw them together, Jack. They went in that house together. They spent the night together. And they're still in there. Together."

"If she's under duress."

"I can imagine what she's under. And it's not duress. I'm telling you, she was enjoying herself when I watched them going inside. And I was watching real close. Because, you know, I came here looking for you."

Jack was suddenly dizzy, the horizon tilting. He wondered what medication they'd given him in the hospital. Frank was retelling his adventure, all he'd seen while parked in front of Georgine's house. Jack did not want to hear it.

Gear rattling, a squad of heavily armed police rushed past, like soldiers to the front.

"What happens now?"

"It's out of our hands," Frank replied. "A police matter. But. No one wants trouble. Carver and Georgine. They'll be stubborn for a few hours. And then, they'll probably just come out. Carver's not the type to go down shooting. He's probably got Biddle on the phone right now."

"Carver . . ." Jack momentarily closed his eyes. His head was pounding, a souvenir from last night. After a moment, the pain decreased. "Goodfellow. Durham. Hamparian. Killings to cover up killings. Killings for the hell of it. Well. It leaves one very good question."

"What's that?"

"How come, Frank? How come I'm not dead?"

"The janitor drove up and scared Carver off. That's what I heard."

"You think he can be scared off?" Jack could still hear the sound of the Porsche's door opening. Only it hadn't been the Porsche, but the janitor's car. Arriving for work, the man had found Jack lying dazed and helpless in the snow.

Leaning against a child's swing set, Sergeant George Lewis tightened his bulletproof jacket. He left the gas mask perched atop his head. The damn thing restricted his vision and hearing, and he'd only wear it as a last resort. First man in has enough problems.

Inside, the house would be dark, smoky, and unfamiliar. Carver had all the advantage, knowing the layout, where to sit and wait. Nor would he have to worry about shooting the wrong person.

All about were shotguns, high-powered rifles, and M16s. The squad wore camouflage fatigues. Puffing on a cigarette, George mused that in some ways this was not very different from the war. Except he was younger then, more confident of survival.

The split-level house adjacent to the Goodfellow place was just a little older, with larger trees and higher hedges.

"Move along the front of this house," one of the team advised.

"Right," Lewis said.

"Stay in among the hedges, Lew."

"Close to the foundation."

"He can't see you if you hug the foundation."

Lewis nodded.

"Between this house and the Goodfellow place there's about thirty yards of open ground."

"I've seen it."

"And a rail fence you'll have to get over."

Lewis felt the familiar weight of his M16, an old friend returned.

"You'll be covered from across the street."

"And from behind."

"And from the backyard and inside of this house."

"Yeah. Just make sure everybody's real careful. Okay? I don't wanna get popped by one of these damned local yokels." In fact, much of Sergeant Lewis's extraordinary courage stemmed from trust in his state-police backup.

Lying in the shrubs, George Lewis studied the broken front window where gas still curled out. Once, he caught a strong whiff of the stuff and had to turn away.

What if the woman is in there? Of course, I'll fire on anyone who makes an aggressive move. I'd be crazy not to.

"Looks empty," whispered trooper Veche, the second man in.

Lewis silenced him with an abrupt motion. Maybe it looked empty, but don't think about it, don't count on it. Expect the worst. Let an empty house be a pleasant surprise.

He took three even breaths of rubber air, then flipped the mask back up. If the gunman was watching . . . Well, as long as he hasn't seen me, I'm okay. If he's waiting for me to come charging around this particular corner . . .

Lewis broke from the hedges. He ran hard, uphill, across muddy ground. Adrenaline sent him soaring over the three-and-a-half-foot fence, legs pulled high. Flying, he cradled the weapon in his arms like something delicate and precious.

Pop.

In the Garritt house, Colonel LeRoy groaned. "Shit, no!" Trooper Lewis cleared the fence, arms flailing, out of control, then landed in a heap. The M16 cartwheeled down the hill.

"Jesus."

With great popping and cracking, the police arsenal erupted in full force. Windows went first. Bright flashes marked ricocheting rounds off brick and flagstone.

"He's up!"

The fallen trooper was suddenly scrambling, hurdling the fence and diving back to safety.

"He's okay."

A cheer went up.

Though men in authority shouted for it to stop, the assault continued. The FOR SALE sign on the lawn was peppered. A bird feeder near the front door exploded with one round. The porch light followed. Meanwhile, the station-wagon tires were flattened, the windshield shattered, the body pinged with hits. Even Frank Mullins's LTD, across the street, sustained a few holes.

From every conceivable angle, they fired on the house. The racket wouldn't stop.

"Saw him. Past the window. Did you see him run past the window?"

Radios discharged earsplitting squawks.

"They're drawing fire in the woods," someone shouted.
"We've got a casualty, Colonel."

A hurricane of gunfire smashed against the Goodfellow home. Whole window frames splintered and the curtains behind them were torn.

"When do they call for artillery?" someone asked.

Clearly, Charles Carver was also busy, running from window to window, keeping police heads down while attracting fierce fire.

Word came that a state trooper named Euston was being rushed to the hospital, his ankle pulverized by a single shot. Frustrated, Colonel LeRoy barked orders. "I want it stopped. I want it stopped now."

At the first burst of gunfire, Jack Meehan had hopped over the stone wall that bordered the lots on Wampanoag Road. With two crutches and one good leg, he raced, spiderlike, across a soggy backyard toward Georgine's house.

"Whoa." A uniformed trooper, built like an offensive lineman, came running out to block Jack's progress. "Who the hell are you? And where do you think you're going?"

"What are they doing out there?" Jack strained to see over the big man's shoulder.

"I want you to turn yourself around, pal." The policeman put a restraining hand on Jack's chest.

"I've got to . . . I've —" Balancing on the crutches, Jack fumbled for his ID. Firing continued, crackling to the left and right, not very loud but frightening to Jack because any one of those shots could kill her. Only, dammit, from here she could be dead already and he wouldn't know.

"I'm the assistant district attorney." Jack handed over his ID. "There."

"Hmm. So you are. But I still don't see how you're authorized to be here, Mr. Meehan."

"This is my goddamn case. Get me? I have more right to be here than anyone."

The firing wound down to sporadic bursts. Did that mean it was over? Jesus, no. They didn't kill her. Did they?

Examining the ID as if searching for instructions, the trooper said, "Well. Maybe it's okay for you to be here. Maybe. But not in the open. Only armed officers are allowed in forward areas." He handed back the card. "You can go inside this house here. Colonel LeRoy has taken it over as his headquarters. Just don'— Hey! Don't go wandering around without authorization!"

Jack was already hopping up the stairs. Inside, he met more frustration as yet another trooper, this time a young woman, refused to allow him out of the kitchen, where, again, he could see nothing.

"I'm an assistant district attorney."

"I don't care who you are," she said. "You're not allowed up here."

Jack couldn't wait. The whole thing was being decided on the other side of the door.

"I've got a right to know what's going on." His voice rose, he found himself pushing the young officer.

"You can't go in." She pushed back.

Jack's anxiety turned to anger. He was on the brink of panic when Detective Lieutenant Sullivan appeared at the door, shouting, "Christ, let him in. He's on our side."

Jack found the front room thick with cigarette smoke and police. Unsteadily, he headed for a window, nearly stumbling over the furniture piled about. At last, he could see Georgine's battered house, gas still drifting from the broken picture window. Nothing moved, except torn drapes and curtains pushed by the breeze.

"Maybe they'll come out now," an officer was saying.

There remained hope that Georgine was still alive. But if she came out now . . . Jack could almost see her stumbling, terrified, into the yard. If someone fired. If the barrage began again. She could be cut down. It was a real possibility.

But no one appeared. Jack saw no life at all, heard no sound. Suppose she was killed already? The prosecutor winced.

"We must've hit something."

"That house took a hell of a lot of rounds."

All eyes turned to the colonel. "Let's," he began. "Let's invite him to quit again."

By loudspeaker, as before, Carver was asked to surrender.

Or to send out Mrs. Goodfellow. Or merely to talk. They waited for an answer, watching for movement, listening for a sound. Anything. Jack grew hopeful. Georgine is in there. She wants out. But with all the shooting she's afraid to lift her head.

"I know Georgine," he announced. "I've dealt with her. Would it help if I talked to her?"

LeRoy gave him a severe look and turned away. "Who is that guy?"

"Tear gas again, Colonel?"

"Give me a goddamn minute, will you?" The colonel was relying on common sense, instinct, and years of experience. In some respects, however, he was no better off than his untested force. He had never directed this type of siege before. Nor had he commanded so many police officers at any one time. First and foremost, he wanted to keep his people from further harm.

LeRoy quickly ruled out tear gas, which hadn't worked the first time, blowing back on his own men. Neither would he risk a frontal attack. Sitting with his back to everyone, the colonel flicked his chin with an upturned thumb. An idea was forming.

The top-ranked officers huddled together. "It's getting dark and it's getting cold," one reminded them. Then the colonel outlined his plan in a deep, sure voice.

"What?" a nearby trooper whispered. "What's he going to do?"

"An armored car. He wants an armored car."

At the window, Jack Meehan studied the house for some clue to what was happening inside. Oddly, his sense of urgency was fading.

Late afternoon, two box-shaped Brink's trucks came grinding down Wampanoag Road in low gear. Unfortunately, the borrowed vehicles moved so slowly and awkwardly, and made so much noise, the element of surprise was surely lost.

In front of Georgine's house, the tanklike vehicles engaged in some involved manuevers until, wheel hub to wheel hub, they faced the front lawn. Only then did they begin to move forward.

While nothing could be seen in the house, not a hint of resistance, the tension was considerable. No one moved, no one spoke. Every gun was ready, every eye was on the armored trucks.

The tires sunk deep into the soggy lawn. The vehicles tipped and bounced on the uneven surface. For a moment, one was trapped, wheels spinning, in the mud. But it was soon moving again. As if to peep in the windows, they slowly neared the house. Still they had not drawn fire.

What now? Jack wondered, expecting troopers to pour from the trucks, guns blasting.

"There!"

"Hear that?"

Somewhat muffled, a burst of automatic fire came and went.

"They're in!"

An officer waved his walkie-talkie in the air. "It's over."

A moment later, someone explained what had happened. The armored trucks had been a diversion. As they crossed the lawn, State Police Sergeant George Lewis and his team had forced the rear door, bursting in on Charles Carver. The battle was ended.

28

JACK MEEHAN kept his coat buttoned up against the wind that swept through Georgine Goodfellow's house. Long after, he would recall the peculiar crunch of glass underfoot.

Jack couldn't imagine anyone living here again. It was unrecognizable as a home, filled now with men who chattered rudely and treated the place without respect, as if it belonged to no one.

Gas rose from the carpets underfoot. Tears ran down faces. The coughing never stopped. From time to time, Jack went to a window and looked out at the flashing red and blue lights as he gulped the fresh wintry air.

Planting his crutches with care, the prosecutor passed the Alsatian at the bedroom door. All but decapitated, the dog was the only fatality in the assault on Wampanoag Road. Storming the house, Lewis's men had been unable to approach the bedroom. The snarling animal had forced them to shoot.

In the bedroom, Charles Carver lay face down on the floor. Jack guessed that he had rolled off the bed. But maybe not. Looking very dead, his body provided no obvious clue as to the cause of death. Several empty liquor bottles lay nearby.

Jack hobbled toward the back of the room, separating himself from the men collecting about the bed. Some came in and out on business. Others came to gawk.

Georgine was on the bed, eyes opened as if she'd been surprised by something on the ceiling. Naked, covered by a spread from the waist down, her face was turned slightly to the left. A small, dry trickle of dark blood ran from her nose to the corner of her lip. Behind her right ear, her beautiful dark hair was unnaturally black.

Georgine's odd pose caught Jack's attention. It was as if a wave had nudged her toward the door.

Detective Lieutenant Lyle Sullivan stood beside him.

"These people have been dead for hours," Jack said.

"Yeah." The detective coughed. "We've been fucking blasting at each other all day. I wonder who was the idiot who shot the trooper? For that matter, which asshole fired that first shot?"

"Some overanxious patrolman, no doubt."

Jack turned and was shocked by more than a dozen happy faces. Portraits of the Goodfellow children at various ages lined the top of a chest of drawers. Each youngster, in each picture, was dressed and groomed with care. Their mother's love and pride was apparent. Georgine had worked hard to protect her children, but adult tragedies are not played out in a vacuum. As this horror had overwhelmed the mother, now it would overwhelm these three blameless children.

A stretcher arrived, was unfolded. Brusque, businesslike attendants lifted Charles Carver's body.

"Imagine," a police officer said, "a guy with all that money. Winding up like this."

Jack saw now that Carver, like Georgine, had been shot in the temple. The gun, a cheap twenty-two, was found beneath him.

Bathed in light, the Goodfellow home looked stark and ravaged. District Attorney Rich Flaherty saw it as a marvelous backdrop for a televised press conference.

"We say how we broke the case," he told Frank Mullins. "And we separate ourselves from this screwup of LeRoy's. The whole goddamn day shooting at two suicides."

"If we do it right," Frank advised, "we'll lead the evening news."

"Get Meehan to brief us on the details. Didn't I see him around here?"

When the assistant district attorney could not be located, they decided to proceed without him.

Driving toward Milham, Jack tried to concentrate on everything he knew about this case and everything that had happened over the past twenty-four hours. He remembered Carver in the bar, scheming, battling for advantage. Then, he saw the Porsche, roaring at him.

Whatever they'd given Jack at the hospital made him sleepy. He opened the car window. Felt the cold. The more alert he became, the more his head hurt, but it was important tonight that his mind be clear.

Georgine. He'd done so much and it hadn't been enough. I worked my ass off for her. And she threw her life away.

Damn her!

Her children's faces had smiled at Jack from the dresser. Hadn't she seen them? Could she study their smiles, then nod in the direction of the pistol? "Go ahead. Let's do it."

One mistake. She'd let that man into her life. A more worldly woman would have seen him for trouble, would have steered clear. Jack tried to picture the final moments in the bedroom.

What sort of choices did he give her? Did he hide the gun until the last moment.

"Oh, no, don't," she might have said.

She would have straightened out. Jack was certain. And that was the tragedy. Sure, Georgine faced big trouble. But she would have come right, for the sake of her children.

"God," he moaned, not wanting to think of Georgine.

In the end, he decided to be angry, to nurse a potent, smoldering rage toward the man responsible.

29

BEHIND Milham Square, beyond the abandoned shoe factory, is an old, brown three-decker. Its once white trim is cracked and peeling, its porches sag. Jack Meehan made the hall stairs very slowly.

The two Milham patrolmen lost patience and went ahead to the shadowy top-floor landing. As he caught up with them, the prosecutor's shoulders and his good leg ached. "Okay." He leaned on the crutches. "Okay, let me catch my breath."

The gasping made it all come back. Last night. The awful feeling of being beyond help. The Porsche hit hard, though it hadn't been going very fast. Abrasions, contusions, torn cartilage. The knock on the head was the worst of it. Anyway, he'd be safe here with two strong, young police officers for escorts.

In the dim light, he could not see their faces. One held the arrest warrant. Neither seemed very enthusiastic and both were annoyed that the assistant district attorney had invited himself along.

"Shouldn't have any trouble," Jack said softly. "But be ready."

He knocked twice before calling out, "Hello!"

"Somebody's in there," one officer said. "I hear voices."

Slowly, carefully, Jack turned the knob. To his surprise, the door opened.

The apartment was dark, except for the bluish light of a television. A deep, forceful newsman's voice described the siege that day in Harwood. On a big chair before the tube, the old woman snored peacefully.

Jack rapped sharply on the doorframe. "Mrs. Ready?"

She did not stir, but from the nearby couch rose a large, dark figure, an apparition in unearthly blue light. Paul Barrasso, open-mouthed and round-eyed, had returned from the grave.

Unsteady on his feet, the parts driver looked drugged. The Milham patrolmen moved toward him.

"Hands against the wall."

"Paul Barrasso, we have a warrant for your arrest. You have the right to remain silent —"

"Nooo!" Barrasso lunged for the door. Both policemen reached to restrain him. With surprising strength, he shook them off. Sent them reeling, crashing into lamps and tables. Startled, Jack limped backward, out into the hall. At full steam, Barrasso bulled straight for him. A stiff arm to the prosecutor's face.

Jack toppled. Back. Sitting on the banister. *Crack!* He gasped. The railing sagged. Tilting over the stairwell, he waited to spin down, but the heavy cast anchored him. The railing held.

Sliding a few feet to the floor, Jack swung at Barrasso with his crutch, catching the fugitive's foot as he tried to skip off the landing.

Jack winced. Though Barrasso's body went down the stairs, his feet did not. The husky man belly flopped, "Ugh," then bumped to the lower landing.

Back in action, the two Milham officers pounced on the dazed parts driver, quickly cuffing one hand.

Barrasso began flopping violently, like a fish on the hook. The policemen wrestled for his free hand, but Barrasso jerked this way and that, always out of grasp.

Meanwhile, two backup patrolmen were racing up the stairs.

Tenants opened doors. "What's all the noise out here?"

Somewhere, Mrs. Ready was shouting, "Don't hurt him. Please. Don't hurt him."

Then, as Barrasso calmed down, every voice was drowned out by a prolonged, hideous howl of pain. The fugitive, grunting and drooling amid growing numbers of uniformed bodies, had clamped his teeth on someone's hand. He would not let go.

Though policemen punched him, pulled his hair, and stomped his ribs and groin, Barrasso held on until a nightstick to the side of his face made him shout with pain. An officer fell away, his mangled hand violently trembling. Blood gushed from deep impressions of Barrasso's teeth.

Barrasso was roughly pulled to his feet, then rammed face-first into the wall. "Don't move, you fat fuck."

Applying the cuffs, an officer made certain they pinched.

"Aaaaa!"

"Police brutality," Mrs. Ready cried from the landing. "You bastards!"

"Goddamn fucking cannibal," a patrolman shouted.

The suspect spit blood, some of it his own.

"Paul Barrasso." Jack called the name several times. He came down the stairs, hopping on his good leg. "You're under arrest, Paul Barrasso. Arrest. Conspiracy to commit murder. Obstruction of justice —"

"No, no." Barrasso's eyes, red blotches, opened wider. His moans gave Jack no little satisfaction.

"You okay, Mr. Meehan?"

Outside the Harwood police station, Jack Meehan looked up at the clear night sky and filled his lungs with frigid air. "I'm okay."

"I hear that was quite an arrest." Tony Silva smiled admiringly. "I can't figure out. How'd you know this guy Barrasso was there?"

"I didn't," the prosecutor admitted. "But I never trusted Granny. And when she tried to discourage us from looking for Barrasso. I started to figure maybe that's because she already knew where he was. Then, she comes around asking for his tape deck. Well, your average grandmother doesn't know what a tape deck is. Unless someone tells her."

"And it wasn't Carver who killed all those people?" Tony looked dubious.

"Charles Carver was a thief. He made the mistake of associating with a dangerous individual. And he got drafted into the murder business."

"And you can prove that?"

"That's the problem." Jack opened the car door. "Even knowing what happened. And who's responsible. It leaves one hell of a job, proving it. And if we're going to have a chance in court. We've got to get someone on the inside. Someone who might have heard or seen something. We've got to turn the screws on them. And get some cooperation."

"And you think now he'll cooperate?"

Jack eased his cast into the car. "I have to believe he will, Tony. He's the only one left."

With that, they were off to collect Richard Ripler.

The service manager cleared his throat. "Yeah. I was afraid of Barrasso. I'd heard stories."

Jack Meehan said, "Tell us about it, Mr. Ripler."

"Carver. He had a Mafia mentality. He was into so many rackets. Illegalities. He was open to blackmail. You know? And Barrasso. His purpose, I suppose, was to head off those kinds of ideas. Charles Carver used Paul Barrasso to intimidate troublemakers. Brass was the enforcer. And when people started getting killed, I decided. For the sake of my family. I decided not to get involved. I suppose that wasn't very courageous, but . . ."

Sergeant Silva said, "We appreciate your cooperation now, Mr. Ripler."

"Well, there's . . . no reason not to. . . . You've got Barrasso arrested. Carver . . ." Ripler shrugged. "He's gone."

The three men sat in the interrogation room at the Harwood police station. The floor was dirty, last year's calender was on the wall. Ill at ease, Ripler loosened his tie and toyed with his shirt cuffs.

"How's business?" Jack asked.

"Today?" Ripler shook his head. "Today was busy as hell. Not so much in the repair shop. But the showroom. It's hard to believe. The salesmen think all this, you know, the, uh, tragedy. Mr. Carver's suicide. They think that's what's drawing them in. What can I say? Salesmen think like that."

"Mr. Carver didn't commit suicide," Jack said quietly. "For one thing, he just wasn't the type."

"Excuse me?"

"Charles Carver was murdered."

Tony, who'd heard this theory before, still looked surprised.

Ripler replied uneasily. "The television said . . . The district attorney, he was on the television and said —"

"He was wrong," Jack declared. "Oh, it was a natural mistake. We were all set up to believe it was suicide. But it was a scheme. And a brilliant one, when you think about it. Lots of people were fooled. But I wasn't fooled."

"Set up?" Ripler was incredulous. "You say it was a setup? How was everyone set up?"

"When Carver arrived at the Goodfellow home last night. He was already dead."

"Arrived dead?" Ripler smiled.

"The person who murdered Carver. Also murdered Georgine. And set it up to look like a double suicide. The killer is the same person who came to my office last night. With Carver. Now, I didn't see him. But all the same. He had to be there. In the car. He wanted Carver to buy me off. Bribe me. Which Carver tried to do."

"Bribe you?"

"I turned him down, I'm afraid. And as soon as poor Charlie got back to the car with the bad news. His . . . what's the word you used? Enforcer? His enforcer. Decided to kill him. *Did* kill him. Shot him right there in the car, then put on his leather coat. Made sure I saw him. In all the snow, I couldn't see him very well. But I assumed it was Carver because of the leather coat. And when he ran me down. Well, no wonder I survived. I was supposed to survive. So I could tell the world that Charles Carver is the killer."

"Is this . . . what?" Ripler looked from the prosecutor to Sergeant Silva. "Guesswork?"

"The way it was set up," Jack continued. "The two nude bodies in the bedroom. We were supposed to assume a thing between Carver and Mrs. Goodfellow. I had to wonder about that. Georgine told me something about her boyfriend. How she got tired of screwing him in parked cars. And right when she said it. I'm thinking. That doesn't sound like Charles Carver. Sex in a Porsche? A guy with money? With a big, empty house twenty minutes away?"

"If he wasn't the boyfriend," Ripler asked, "how did he wind up in her bedroom?"

"The killer brought Carver's body to Georgine Goodfellow's house. He carried it from the Porsche and stashed it temporarily in the garage, I'm guessing. This is a strong guy we're talking about. Lifting deadweights is no problem."

"Barrasso," Ripler muttered darkly, "he's a big, big guy."

"The killer managed to coerce or persuade Georgine to help get rid of the car. Getting rid of the car was something Carver might do if he really had tried to kill me and then panicked. Except Carver wouldn't have pushed the car off the end of a swimming pier, where the water's not very deep, where it would almost certainly be found."

Jack's voice deepened. "So they ditched the car. And went back to her house. And they went into the bedroom. He turned on the stereo, to drown out the gunshot. She didn't realize what was happening. Until. The last second. And she tried to get away. Just a move. She didn't get very far. . . . Once she was dead, he dragged in Charles Carver's body. Stripped him. Exchanged any bloodied clothing for his own. And that was your double suicide."

"My God," Ripler exclaimed.

Jack grimaced. "Finally. The murderer had the idea of getting out fast. Only he found my pal Frank Mullins on the doorstep. No problem. A few shots chased off both him and a police cruiser. The killer then went back inside, only to go out the rear door. He went through the woods. And walked home."

"Well." Ripler cleared his throat. "You guys have figured that out. Great. But can you prove it?"

"The lab people," Jack replied, "they should prove some of it. If Carver was murdered in his Porsche. Well, there's bound to be some physical evidence. Blood in the car."

Ripler nodded. He tried to seem helpful, while saying as little as possible. In fact, the service manager was afraid. "Has Barrasso admitted to any of this?"

"No confession yet," Jack conceded. "I don't think he's going to confess. We're talking about multiple murders."

"Multiple murders." Ripler slowly shook his head.

"Barrasso and Carver were alike," Jack observed. "I mean, socially, they were miles apart. But they reacted to this in the same way. Carver was afraid he'd be held culpable for the murders his enforcer had committed. He wanted the investigation to go away. Used all the influence he could muster to have it stopped. And when he couldn't. Well, he was getting ready to skip town."

Jack bent closer. "Barrasso *did* run away. And before that. When Welton detectives came by to ask questions. I'm told Paul made a scene. Refused to cooperate. Locked himself inside a van. Likewise, when I visited the dealership to see Carver, Barrasso went out of his way to tell me. Very belligerent. Very loud. How he's not answering questions. Well, at the time, I figured he was trying to intimidate me. So when he called a few days later, saying he wanted to cooperate. I had to wonder. I had to wonder why he'd been so adamant before. Can you guess why, Richard?"

Ripler cocked his head quizzically. "Well, no."

"It's because what he said before. About not cooperating. All that was said for your benefit."

"I don't understand," Ripler said.

"He was signaling to you. He was telling you he wouldn't cooperate with us. He wanted you to know he wouldn't cooperate. So you wouldn't kill him. The way you killed Hamparian."

Ripler said nothing.

"Well?" Jack prodded.

Ripler studied the floor. "You expect me —"

"Nothing to say?"

"It's bullshit." Ripler looked up.

"Is it?"

"What? Do you just make this stuff up? You're just — just bullshitting. Right? To get my reaction. Right?"

Jack turned to Tony. "I got off the track at the beginning. Because I had the idea that the man we were hunting had been arrested for murder before. I heard that story from Barrasso. Then, when I heard it again from Georgine. A slightly different version. I knew there had to be something to it. But the problem was. No one who worked at Parkside. No one associated with these killings had that kind of criminal record. Our friend here doesn't. And I started to think maybe I had my hands on some misinformation. But."

Jack looked back at Ripler.

"Lots of times we get information. It's not quite right. Things get mangled in the translation. People lie a little. They exaggerate. And I started to wonder. If in this case. If the reason there was no record of this homicide was because there had been no conviction. Now, that made sense because, obviously, the guilty party's still walking around free. He may not even have been a suspect in this homicide. Just a bystander. Georgine said he had a newspaper clipping of this murder. With his picture included. But she didn't say any more than that. Which left open the possibility that he was an associate. Or a relative of the victim. Maybe he found the body. The newspaper interviewed him. And no one suspected that he'd killed the victim."

Jack sat back. "I took this supposition. And I found it was surprisingly useful for eliminating suspects. Because if it was true, the killer couldn't be Charles Carver. If Carver had ever been *near* a murder, we'd know. Record or no record. He's a prominent man. We'd know about it.

"The same goes for anyone who's lived all his life in this area. Like Paul Barrasso. If he'd been mixed up in murder.

Someone, some police officer or probation officer. They'd remember.

"No. Our boy has to be someone from outside the area."

Ripler's eyes narrowed. As if in a trance, as if he'd withdrawn from the room, he stared at a point on the table.

"I got back to the Greenfield police. I asked them to review their homicides — particularly unsolved homicides — over the past ten years. I asked them to look for the name Richard Ripler. In any connection. To any homicide. But you know what? They didn't have to look. They remembered you this time."

Jack bent closer. "Five years ago, Richard Ripler opened a foreign-car repair shop. He had a partner. A man named Michael Gallo. A year later, Gallo was found on the floor of the repair bay. *You* found him. His skull had been crushed by a wrench. Money and tools had been taken. There was evidence of forced entry. Gallo's empty wallet was found about a mile away. Just the way Walter Hamparian's was found. The police called that case a robbery too. The detectives who worked on the Gallo homicides still remember how helpful and cooperative Dick Ripler was. No one considered him a suspect because he had no reason to kill his partner. Besides, he was a friendly guy, a good citizen."

Ripler's solemn expression remained unchanged. Like ice, Jack thought. He pretends to be above us.

"I have a warrant for your arrest." Sergeant Silva began chanting the rights of the accused.

"I know my rights," Ripler said. "I would prefer not to answer questions. I would like to call my lawyer."

He seemed smug, confident that legal niceties would be observed.

Gripping the table, Jack Meehan nearly gagged on a sudden rush of hatred and rage. The urge to crush Ripler's skull with his crutch or, better yet, to choke the life out of him with his bare hands was as strong as anything he'd felt for Georgine. Georgine had been used up and thrown away. And the outrage was that Ripler sat there knowing he would never suffer as she had.

"I've got to get out of here." Groaning, the prosecutor pulled himself to his feet, crutches banging the chair. He waited for Ripler to speak. *Go ahead. Just one word. So I can give back a piece of what you deserve.*

The killer's face was impassive, motionless.

30

THE corridor was cool and quiet. Jack hobbled toward the front desk, as far from Ripler as he could get.

His hopes now rested on Paul Barrasso, of all people. In Milham, they were interviewing the frightened parts driver. Jack believed he knew plenty. In fact, Barrasso had implied as much on tape, revealing the killer's need to boast of his crimes. Richard Ripler might very well have bragged to Paul Barrasso.

Arresting Barrasso for murder was a means of obtaining leverage, making him more afraid of the authorities than he was of Ripler. If offered immunity, he might become useful to the prosecution.

At the front desk, a red-faced woman was angrily demanding the release of her son. As near as Jack could determine, the drunken boy had been arrested for vandalism.

The Harwood deskman was patiently explaining, "Lady, I couldn't let him go if he was my own son. He's been formally booked. Now, what you've got to do is run down the courthouse in the morning and post bail."

Collapsing on a bench, Jack watched the heated exchange through weary eyes, half listening. At any minute now, he might nod off. Questions remained. Had Georgine met Ripler while having her husband's car serviced, or at some town function? Why was Grover Durham killed? What was the extent of Charles Carver's involvement in the murders? Would more victims be found? Probably they would never have complete answers to these questions. And such gaps weakened a less than perfect case.

But the specter of mass murder would inspire District Attorney Flaherty. No expense would be spared. Ripler had surely made mistakes, and a small army of detectives would be assigned to find them. The best attorney in the office would prosecute. With television cameras in the courtroom, Flaherty would do the trial work.

Ironically, Jack Meehan would be gone by then. His position at the office had become impossible. He shuddered at the task of finding work. Knocking on doors. Calling old friends. It was the penalty for being right.

The red-faced woman was raising her voice now, warning that she was a close, personal friend of selectman so-and-so. The veteran sergeant behind the desk nodded, his eyes reflecting boredom. Jack turned away, surprised to see Rose at the door. She sat down beside him.

"You look terrible."

"Well, don't be fooled. I feel worse than I look."

"I could have killed you when I found out you'd left the hospital. What are you trying to do to yourself?"

Jack rubbed his forehead. He'd meant to give his wife all the bad news earlier in the day. Only she'd looked so worried and worn-out, pacing alongside his hospital bed.

"Ah. Rose? Something. I've got to tell you. You won't —"

She touched his hand. "Later."

"No. No, I've got to tell you now. Get it done. Explain. About the big job. My big new job. Well . . ." He looked up. "I think you should know. There is no job. I've turned it down. And, well, that's . . ."

"I knew you weren't going to take it," Rose declared.

"You knew?"

"I saw it coming. I already sent back the rug and the video recorder. I threw away all those travel brochures. You know, it's like my mother always told me. Some people just aren't meant to be rich." She managed a half-smile. "At least we're all together. All in one piece. And that's even more important, don't you think?"

Jack held his wife's hand. He thought to tell her more, explain his confusion over these past weeks, how he'd been pulled in so many directions. It would be a relief to have all that in the open, with Rose to swear that it didn't make a bit of difference. Yet he knew the best idea was to say nothing about Georgine. Not unless Rose asked. Not until Jack understood it better.

"I'm going to be out of a job altogether, pretty soon," the prosecutor said. "Maybe very soon."

"I suppose you'll expect me to support you."

"Things could be tough for a while."

"Like it's been easy up to now?" Rose bent to her husband's ear, whispering that it was time to go home.

He nodded, watching the woman at the desk abandon her campaign to have her son released. She muttered something insulting about police in general and desk sergeants in particular. And before the officer could respond in kind, she walked away to sit, exhausted, on a bench directly opposite Jack.

Catching her breath, she stared at the floor, eyes vacant and red. Oddly enough, she did not seem very angry. It was as if she'd always known the argument with the officer was one she couldn't win.

They took the Parkside service manager to a lockup in the police-station basement. At all times, an officer remained outside the cell, supposedly reading a newspaper. Ripler resolved to ignore him, not wanting to give them the satisfaction of a complaint. He removed his suit, carefully folding it atop a stool. They'd taken his tie.

At the sink, he washed his hands with hard, yellow soap. They'd also taken his nail clipper, so he had to endure traces of grease beneath his nails. For the longest time, he sat on the floor (imagining the bunk might be lousy), studying the fingers, worrying about how awful they looked.

No regrets, he thought. He'd acted boldly to protect himself. His scheme would pay off yet. They had what? Circumstantial evidence. Maybe they'd found Paul Barrasso under a rock somewhere. But what did that loser actually know of these murders?

And the killer had been careful not to leave behind physical evidence, weapons, or fingerprints. He had been careful about not being seen. And when there *were* witnesses, he had disposed of them.

He thought, unexpectedly, of Georgine. That hurt. He had been ready to give up everything for her, only to find her keeping appointments at the district attorney's office. It just went to prove, you can't trust anybody.

Georgine was a painful memory. He struggled to think of other things.

What did Barrasso know? You couldn't be sure with a sleazy snoop like that. Every time you turned around he was there. Talking to him was the big mistake. What had been said during those long conversations? He strained to remember. Had he told the parts driver facts that might incriminate him now?

"What the fuck are you looking at?"

The policeman turned back to his newspaper.

Don't let Barrasso spook you. A junkie drug-dealer. Easily discredited. A good lawyer could handle him. One of those crisp, efficient characters in glasses and flawless suits. Dick imagined the elegant H. Bateman Biddle. The Ripler family arrayed supportively behind the defense table. Then, in walks that greasy slob. Paul Barrasso. A funny picture.

Richard Ripler was tired. He leaned against the cold concrete wall.

He'd be free on bail in the morning. When he thought about that, he relaxed for the first time. Jail was close to unendurable, but he could survive this brief visit by keeping his body cool, his mind on other things. Pretend you don't hear that drunk retching a few cells away. Remember what it's like to be free, to walk a beach on a perfect summer night, to enjoy the smell of salt air and a light breeze on your face.

Just how much did he know? Goddamn Barrasso.

"Goddamn Barrasso."

It was a name that kept him awake much of the night.